ii   Dr. Constance Santego

Constance Santego

Faith of a Soul

Dr. Constance Santego has been practicing and teaching *The Nine Spiritual Gifts, Granted From Spirit,* for over twenty-five years. She lives in Calgary, Alberta, Canada, with her husband and family.

www.constancesantego.ca

Published by
Editor & Interior Layout: Dr. Constance Santego
Book Layout: ©2017 BookDesignTemplates.com
Cover Design: Jennifer Louie
Soft Cover ISBN: 978-1-990062-55-1
eBook ISBN: 978-1-990062-56-8

Created and published in Canada. Printed and bound in the United States of America
Ordering Information: csantego@gmail.com

ALSO BY DR. CONSTANCE SANTEGO

NOVELS
Illegitimate Grace

Okanagan Trilogy:
Beneath the Vineyards
Under the Okanagan Sun
Guardian of the Lake

The Nine Spiritual Gifts Series:
Journey of a Soul – (Vol 1 Michael)
Language of a Soul – (Vol 2 Gabriel)
Prophecy of a Soul – (Vol 3 Bath Kol)
Healing of a Soul – (Vol 4 Raphael)
Miracles of a Soul – (Vol 5 Hamied)
Knowledge of a Soul – (Vol 6 Raziel)
Wisdom of a Soul – (Vol 7 Uriel)

NONFICTION
The Intuitive Life, The Gift Of Prophecy, Third
Edition
Fairy Tales, Dreams And Reality… Where Are You On
Your Path? Second Edition
Your Persona… The Mask You Wear
Archangel Michael's Soul Retrieval Guide
Tesla And The Future Of Energy Medicine
Beyond Tesla: *Advancing The Science Of Energy Healing*
Tesla's Code: *Mastering Energy, Frequency, And Creative
Power*
Scaling Beyond 6 Figures: *Strategies for Health & Wellness
Professionals*

Beyond the Mind: *Harnessing the Power of Astral Projection for Creative Awakening*
Bend, Don't Break: *Finding Your Way Back to Abundance*
Ring Therapy: *A Guide to Healing and Balance*
Ring Therapy Pocket Guide
Floraopathy™: *The Art and Science of Vibrational Healing with Essential Oils*

REIKI WISDOM, SERIES:

The Reiki Master's Manual
Angelic Lifestyle, a Vibrant Lifestyle
Angelic Lifestyle 42-Day Energy Cleanse
Reiki and the Power of The Joint Points: *Unlocking Energy Pathways for Healing*

SECRETS OF A HEALER, SERIES:

Magic Of Aromatherapy (Vol I)
Magic Of Reflexology (Vol II)
Magic Of The Gifts (Vol III)
Magic Of Muscle Testing (Vol IV)
Magic Of Iridology (Vol V)
Magic Of Massage (Vol VI)
Magic Of Hypnotherapy (Vol VII)
Magic Of Reiki (Vol VIII)
Magic Of Advanced Aromatherapy (Vol IX)
Magic Of Esthetics (Vol X)

ADULT COLORING JOURNALS

SERIES-ZEN COLORING:
Quantum Energy and Mindful Living Journal (Vol 1)
Reiki Energy Journal (Vol 2)
Nine Spiritual Gifts Journal (Vol 3)
I Forgive Journal (Vol 4)

SERIES – COLORING PROSPERITY:
Genie-Inspired Mandalas and Wealth Journal (Vol 1)
Entrepreneurial Mindset Reboot (Vol 2)

SERIES – HARMONIC MIND CODE:
Harmonic Mind Code Coloring Journal (Vol 1)

FOR CHILDREN
I am Big Tonight. I Don't Need the Light

Cast of Characters

**Some of the Residents of New York City, USA,
and other places.**

Alexandra (Lexi) Elizabeth Constantine:
Fashion designer in Upper East Side Manhattan.
Daughter of beloved parents—Olivia and
Marcus Constantine (Italian). Was a Fiancée to
Reverend Edward Julien Hawthorne. Her boss
was Sebastian. Friends with co-worker Southern
belle, Sherie. Was going to be engaged to Neo,
but is in love with Redington.

Susannah Grace Constantine:
Lexi's belated sister and now guardian angel.
Lived in Dumbo (Down Under the Manhattan
Bridge Overpass). She was an antique collector
for Aryeh Jacob Kofman and dated Billy
Randazzo.

**Olivia Sarah Constantine (Maiden name,
Austin)**: Mother to Lexi and Susannah.
Widowed housewife. Parents were from
England. She lives in Dyker Heights, Brooklyn,
NY. Deceased.

Reverend Edward Julien Hawthorne: Was a mortician and minister of his family's funeral home in Brooklyn. Was a Fiancé to Alexandra (Lexi). Casandra was his secretary. He had an accident and forgot everything. Another soul took over his body at the time of his death and lived as a walk-in.

Sophea (Tamara Reeve): Past Psychic medium and teacher of many of the Spiritual Gifts. Was a Fiancée to Greg Masones. Still owns her grandmother's brownstone in Brooklyn Heights. Now lives in Katmandu, Naples—in a monastery and is a monk.

Detective Ferguson "Red" Redington: Was 1st-grade homicide investigator, Manhattan Bureau – Midtown South Precinct, Shield number 1323, NYPD. Lives in Far Rockaway Beach, Queens, on Long Island, NY. His family comes from England. Now is a FBI agent.

Greg Masones (AKA Julian D'Angelo): At large. Accountant for the Genovese crime family. Italian immigrant. Son of Serena D'Angelo. Was Tamara's fiancé.

Sebastian: Lexi's boss at the fashion house.
Sherie: Lexi's co-worker at the fashion house.
Isabella Jackson: Famous actress. She moved around to wherever her next movie was being filmed. Friends with Lexi, Edward, and

Redington. Girlfriend of belated Hans (now Erland, an Elf) and mother to her beloved son, Aias.

Hans Magnusson (Erland): Lawyer. He lived in Switzerland but was from Sweden. He inherited his family's fortune, and his grandfather was Olof. After he died, he became a walk-in soul to Erland in the Elemental Realm of Alfheim, and still communicates with Isabella.

Aias Jackson Olof Magnusson: Son of Isabella and Erland. He was a half-elf with many gifts, the main one being able to heal. Deceased. Became an angel.

Kesia Bango: Gypsy tarot card reader. Daughter of Florence. Ancestral Granddaughter of Tatiana Masones and Clementina (Tatiana's mother). Related to Greg, he is her uncle. Loved Aias.

Luna: Kesia's Wiccan friend from high school. She lives in Jersey Shore.

Doctor Neo Singh: Edward's Neurosurgeon at Brooklyn Neurocritical Care. His Greek mother is Naida, and his East Indian father is Paal. Sister to Evangeline and uncle to her son, Todd.

Evangeline Singh: Neo's sister. Massage Therapist. Her son is Todd, and her fiancé is Jeff.

Delish Chakladar: Acharya Shri Sharma's assistant and devotee at Aias's gurukala (spiritual school) in Puttaparthi India.

Lieutenant Jerome Kennard: New York City fireman. Saved Lexi from the cave and briefly dated her.

Camillo O'Malley: A vulgar-mouthed Scottish man who practices Neuro Linguistic Programming.

Winston Charles Redington: the 2nd, Earl of Wrightenton. Redington's father from England.

Countess of Wrightenton, Gabriela: Redington's belated Mother.

Lord Wrightenton, Grayson: Redington's belated older brother.

Lady Wrightenton, Janelle: Redington's belated older sister.

Main Angel of each Novel

Book 1 – Archangel Michael
"Warrior"
Companion Book – Archangel Michael's Soul Retrieval Guide.
Book 2 – Archangel Gabriel
"Messenger"
Companion Book – Your Persona… The Mask You Wear.
Book 3 – Bath Kol
"Daughter of the Voice," the Holy Ghost, and Gabriel
Companion Book – The Gift of Prophecy.
Book 4 – Archangel Raphael
"God Has Healed"
Companion Books – Secrets of a Healer Series.
Book 5 – Archangel Hamied
"Miracles"
Companion Book – Secrets of a Healer, Reiki,
Book 6 – Archangel Raziel
"The Keeper of Secrets and The Angel of Mysteries."
Book 7 – Archangel Uriel
"Light of God"
Book 8 – Archangel Pistis Sophia
"Faith" and "Wisdom"

Faith of a Soul
The Gift of Faith

A Novel
8th in the series, The Nine Spiritual Gifts
'The Gift of Faith'

Dr. Constance Santego

Vol 8

Faith

Dedicated

to my grandmother,
Anne!
Thank you for all your
spiritual teachings and faith.

Faith of a Soul

The Nine Spiritual Gifts

In the New Testament my favourite story is "The Gifts."
Corinthians 1, Chapter 12, Verse 4-11
(Maybe a little differently worded depending on which Bible you have).

The variety and the unity of gifts
There are many different gifts, but it is always the same Spirit; there are many different ways of serving, but it is always the same Lord. There are many different forms of activity, but in everybody it is the same God who is at work in them all. The particular manifestation of the Spirit granted to each one is to be used for the general good.
To one is given from the Spirit the gift of utterance expressing **wisdom**; to another the gift of utterance expressing **knowledge**; in accordance with the same spirit to another, **faith**, from the same Spirit; and to another, the gifts of **healing**, through the same Spirit; to another, the working of **miracles**; to another **prophecy**; to another, the power of **distinguishing spirits**; to one, the gift of **different tongues** and to another, the **interpretation of tongues**. But at work in all these is one and the same Spirit, distributing them at will to each individual.
The New Jerusalem Bible

Awaken to the spirit world, for there lie your gifts granted by Spirit.

Dr. Constance Santego

Fact:

All biblical references, science, legends, and myths are real *(slightly changed to fit the character.* This novel was written as a story inspired by Spirit to give you, the reader, a new perspective, a new way to learn, and a new opportunity to empower your life.

Many locations and all characters are fictional.

Prologue

In the infinite expanse of existence, beyond the confines of time and space, there exists a realm where creation unfolds like a grand tapestry. This is the domain of the Divine, where God, the Eternal Architect, watches over the unfolding of the universe with an understanding that transcends all comprehension. Here, in this boundless sphere, the universe is not just a creation—it is a game. A complex, multidimensional game, where the stakes are nothing less than the evolution of the soul.

God, the Game Master, gazes upon this vast cosmic board, where galaxies swirl and stars are born, where the delicate threads of fate intertwine and diverge, guiding the souls that populate the universe on their journeys. Each soul, a spark of the Divine, is a player in this cosmic game, navigating through the intricate web of existence, striving to learn, grow, and ultimately, to return to the Source from which it came.

The rules of the game are ancient, woven into the very fabric of the universe. They are the Universal Laws—immutable principles that govern all things, from the smallest particle to the mightiest star, from the first breath of life to the final exhalation. These laws are the framework within which the game is played, setting the boundaries of what is possible and guiding the souls as they make their way through the myriad challenges that life presents.

In this game, the stakes are high, for the goal is nothing less than enlightenment—nirvana, the ultimate state of being where the soul, having transcended the cycle of birth and death, reunites with the Divine in perfect harmony. But the path to nirvana is fraught with trials and tribulations. Each soul must navigate the dualities of existence—good and evil, light and darkness, virtue and sin. These are the forces that shape the soul's journey, testing its strength, its faith, and its wisdom.

God does not play alone. The Game Master has helpers—beings of immense power and influence who shape the course of the game in their own ways. Angels, the messengers of light, guide and protect the souls, offering wisdom and solace, helping them to stay true to the path of virtue. Demons, on the other hand, are the challengers, the tempters who introduce obstacles and temptations, forcing the soul to confront its deepest fears and desires. Together, these beings ensure that the game remains a dynamic and ever-changing journey of growth and transformation.

Each soul is unique, starting the game with a set of spiritual gifts—abilities bestowed upon them by the Divine to help them navigate the challenges they will face. Some souls are young, just beginning their journey, while others are ancient, having played the game through countless lifetimes. But all souls, regardless of their age or experience, share the same ultimate goal: to reach enlightenment, to return to the Divine.

As the Game Master watches, the souls move across the board, making choices that will shape their destinies. Some will stumble and fall, losing their way in the labyrinth of existence. Others will rise, mastering their gifts, learning from their mistakes, and moving ever closer to the light. The game is complex, and the outcome is never certain. But through it all, God watches with infinite patience and love, knowing that every soul, in its own time, will find its way home.

And so, the game continues, a dance of creation and destruction, of growth and decay, of joy and sorrow. It is a game that has no beginning, and no end, for the journey of the soul is eternal. But for those who reach the final level, who master the game and achieve enlightenment, there is a reward beyond all imagining—a return to the Divine, to the Source, to the ultimate peace that is nirvana.

In this game, there are no losers, only players at different stages of their journey. And as the souls continue their quest, guided by the Universal Laws, influenced by angels and demons, and driven by the desire to reunite with the Divine, the Game Master watches, knowing that in the end, all will be as it should be. The game, after all, is just a part of the greater design, a means for the souls to learn, to grow, and to fulfill their ultimate destiny.

Chapter 1

The first rays of dawn cast a golden hue over the ancient stones of the monastery, a place where time seemed to stand still, where souls could pause and reflect. But this morning, the air was thick with anticipation and a subtle undercurrent of unease. Lexi, Isabella, Kesia, and Redington stood together, their belongings packed, ready to leave the sanctuary that had become their refuge and training ground.

For each of them, the monastery had been more than just a retreat—it had been a crucible of transformation, a place where they had faced their inner demons and honed their spiritual gifts. They had come to understand that their time here was not an end but a preparation for the final level of their soul's journey.

Lexi, her heart heavy, took one last look at the flower-covered walls that had sheltered them.

The vines, with their persistent growth, seemed to mirror her own journey—one of relentless striving toward the light. The serenity of this place had brought her peace, but she knew that peace was meant to be carried within, a guiding light through the darkness that awaited them in the world beyond.

Redington, sensing Lexi's sorrow, placed a hand on her shoulder. "It's hard to leave," he said softly, his own reluctance evident in his voice. "But remember, this isn't the end. We carry the sanctuary within us, no matter where we go."

Kesia, usually the most composed, was unusually quiet. Her brow furrowed as she stared at her handheld device, which had just delivered the news she had been dreading—her mother's health was rapidly declining, and time was running out. The email was a stark reminder that their journey was about to take a turn into the unknown.

"My mother's condition has worsened," Kesia said, her voice steady but her eyes betraying her worry. "I need to get back to New York. I have to be there with her."

Isabella, always resourceful, quickly stepped in. "My jet is ready and waiting." Her words were met with nods of gratitude from the others, their concern for Kesia overshadowing their own trepidation.

As they gathered their belongings, Sophea, the monastery's elder and their spiritual mentor, approached them. Her eyes, filled with wisdom and understanding, conveyed what words could not. "You are always welcome here," she said, her voice carrying the weight of many lifetimes. "But remember, the sanctuary is not just a place—it is a state of being. Carry its peace with you, wherever you go."

With a final embrace, the group made their way to the waiting taxi. As they descended the mountain, the monastery slowly disappeared from view, shrouded in the morning mist. Lexi watched as the sacred place faded into the distance, feeling a mixture of sadness and resolve. The lessons learned here would be their guide, their spiritual compass, as they entered the final level of their soul's journey.

As the taxi wound its way down the mountain, Lexi felt the weight of what lay ahead. The game was far from over, and the challenges they would face in New York would test their faith, their spiritual gifts, and their very souls. But as they left the monastery behind, she knew that they were ready.

Chapter 2

As the private jet descended through layers of cloud and smog, the sprawling expanse of New York City gradually came into view. The sight was a jarring contrast to the quiet solitude of the monastery—skyscrapers reaching ambitiously toward the sky, rivers of traffic flowing endlessly, and the ceaseless murmur of urban life enveloping the air. Lexi pressed her face against the cool window, her eyes tracing the familiar landmarks that speckled the horizon. The skyline, though unchanged, felt different now—a reminder of the life they had left behind and the challenges that awaited them in this new chapter of their journey.

The plane touched down with a gentle thud, rolling smoothly toward the private hangar where Isabella's staff awaited their arrival. The doors opened, and a rush of city air filled the cabin, carrying the sounds and smells of the metropolis they had once called home. The contrast was immediate and overwhelming—the tranquility of the monastery was replaced by the vibrant, unrelenting energy of New York. As they disembarked, Redington looked around, his expression a mix of nostalgia and apprehension.

Isabella led the way with an air of purpose, her demeanor unchanged by the city's overwhelming presence. "My staff arranged everything. We'll head straight to Aias's condo —it's been kept ready for such occasions," she informed them, her voice cutting through the noise of the airport with practiced ease.

The ride from the airport to Aias's condo was a quiet one. Each of them was lost in their thoughts, the city's vibrant pulse slowly seeping into their consciousness, reminding them of the life they had paused. The familiar streets outside the window sparked memories of past experiences, both challenging and cherished, each one a reminder of how far they had come on their spiritual journey.

As the private limo neared Aias's condo, the luxury of the surroundings stood in stark contrast to the simplicity of the monastery. The doorman greeted them with a nod of recognition as they entered the building, a subtle acknowledgment that they were not newcomers to this world, even if it felt that way. The elevator ride was brief, and soon, they were stepping into the spacious condo, where the cityscape stretched out before them in a dazzling display of light and life.

The condo was a haven of culture and intellect amidst the city's chaos. The walls were adorned with Eastern art, and the shelves were stocked with books—a comforting embrace that reminded them of the sanctuary they had just left behind. As they moved through the space, it became clear that Aias's influence was everywhere, a testament to the life he had lived and the knowledge he had shared.

Isabella made her way to her belated son, Aias's bedroom, her steps slow and deliberate, while Kesia walked to the window, her gaze settling on the bustling streets below. "It feels like another world," she murmured, the city's energy starkly different from the meditative calm of the monastery.

Lexi joined her at the window, placing a supportive hand on her shoulder. "It is, in many ways. But remember what Sophea said—the sanctuary we carry within us. We can find peace even here," she reassured Kesia, her words echoing the wisdom they had absorbed during their time in the monastery.

Kesia's voice trembled slightly as she whispered, "Do you think she will be okay?"

Lexi looked toward the bedroom where Isabella had gone. "You mean because we are back in Aias's home?"

"Yes," Kesia nodded.

"I'll be here for her. She'll be okay," Lexi said softly, though her thoughts also turned to Kesia's own worries about her mother's illness. The burden of concern weighed heavily on all of them, each carrying their own fears and doubts.

Redington paced the condo, his movements restless as he adjusted to their new surroundings. "Well, we might as well make the most of it. Tomorrow brings a new day and with it, unknowns," he said, his voice cutting through the tension. With a swift motion, he retrieved a bottle of wine from the kitchen and brought it into the living room, along with four glasses. "Iss, I've got a glass with your name on it," he called out, his tone light but with an underlying current of camaraderie.

The rest of the evening was spent unpacking and settling in. Lexi, ever mindful of their spiritual needs, organized a small area for meditation and spiritual reading, transforming part of the living room into a makeshift sanctuary. "We'll need this," she declared, her efforts to maintain their spiritual routine a testament to their commitment to integrating their monastic learnings with urban life.

As night fell over the city, the lights outside mirrored the stars they had often watched from the monastery's grounds. At this moment, the vastness of the city seemed a little less daunting, its rhythms not so different from the natural cycles they had come to understand. The city was alive, pulsing with a different kind of energy, but it was energy all the same—a reminder that life, in all its forms, followed patterns and rhythms that transcended the physical world.

Lying back in her old bedroom that night, Lexi listened to the sounds of the city—the distant honking of cars, the murmur of nightwalkers, the subtle rustle of trees swaying in the breeze. It was a different kind of quiet, a different kind of chaos, but beneath it all, there was a rhythm, a heartbeat that pulsed with life, just as it did everywhere. With a deep breath, she closed her eyes, the city's vast energy a reminder of the infinite possibilities that awaited them.

Chapter 3

The morning was heavy with the weight of impending challenges, the sky overcast and a gentle mist rolling off the Atlantic as Lexi, Isabella, and Kesia made their way to Jersey Shore. The drive was marked by a deep, contemplative silence. Each woman lost in her thoughts, the cityscape gradually giving way to the more serene yet solemn coastlines of New Jersey. Lexi's hands gripped the steering wheel with a quiet intensity, her mind focused on the task ahead.

As they arrived at the hospital, the atmosphere shifted—the sterile smell of antiseptics, the muted conversations, and the clinical whiteness of the walls were stark reminders of why they were there. The reality of the situation hit them hard, the weight of Kesia's mother's condition pressing down on them like the fog outside.

They navigated the labyrinthine corridors in silence, the fluorescent lights above casting a cold, pale glow on their path.

When they reached the door to her mother's room, Kesia paused, her breath catching in her throat. She glanced back at Lexi and Isabella, drawing strength from their quiet presence. With a deep breath, she pushed the door open, stepping into the room that had become her mother's world.

Inside, her mother lay in the hospital bed, surrounded by the constant beeping of monitors and the hum of medical equipment. Her appearance was frail, almost fragile, a stark contrast to the vibrant, strong woman Kesia remembered. Yet, when her mother's eyes met hers, there was a flicker of recognition, a spark that spoke of the same warmth and strength that had always defined her.

"Kesia, my girl," her mother whispered, her voice raspy but filled with a deep sense of relief and love.

Kesia crossed the room in a few quick strides, her emotions threatening to overwhelm her as she took her mother's hand in hers. The warmth of her mother's skin, despite the frailty of her body, brought a surge of emotions Kesia had been holding back—fear, love, hope, and a desperate need for reassurance. "I'm here, Mama. I'm here," she managed to say, her voice trembling with both reassurance and an underlying desperation.

Lexi and Isabella stood quietly by the door, their presence a silent pillar of support in the otherwise sterile room. They watched the reunion with a sense of reverence, understanding that this moment was not just about physical healing but about something deeper—something spiritual.

The room, once filled with the impersonal sounds of medical machinery, seemed to soften with the warmth of their presence. Kesia's mother, despite her weakened state, began to speak with more strength than she had shown previously, recounting memories of better times and sharing stories from the neighborhood. Her words were a lifeline, pulling her closer to the world she had once been so fully a part of, and Kesia clung to each one as if they were precious jewels.

As the hours passed, the initial tension in the room began to dissipate, replaced by a sense of connection and comfort. The conversation shifted naturally from the mundane to the spiritual, as if mother and daughter both knew these moments were to be cherished. Kesia spoke of her time at the monastery, sharing the wisdom she had gained and the faith that had been her anchor in the storm of life. Her mother listened with pride, her eyes reflecting a mixture of awe and sorrow for the journey Kesia had been on.

"Life tests us, Kesia," her mother said quietly, her grip on her daughter's hand firm despite her frailty. "It's not just about enduring, but about finding meaning in the struggle. Your faith, the love you carry—it's your anchor. Never let go of it, no matter how hard it gets."

The words resonated deeply within Kesia, striking a chord that reverberated through her soul. She realized that this moment, this conversation, was more than just a reunion—it was a reaffirmation of her spiritual journey. The spiritual gift of healing wasn't just about performing miracles. It was about the strength to hold onto faith in the face of suffering and the love that could bring comfort even in the darkest of times.

As the visit drew to a close, the reality of her mother's condition weighed heavily on Kesia. She leaned down to kiss her mother's forehead, feeling the warmth of her skin against her lips. "I'll be here, Mama," she promised, her voice steady now, filled with quiet determination. "We'll get through this together."

Her mother smiled the same warm smile that had always comforted Kesia as a child. "I know we will, my girl. I know we will."

Lexi and Isabella, sensing that the visit was coming to an end, stepped forward, offering quiet words of encouragement and comfort before they all left the room together. Outside, the day had faded into early evening, the mist lifting to reveal the soft glow of the setting sun.

Instead of returning to the city, the three women made their way to Kesia's mother's house. The drive was short, the familiar streets guiding them toward the home that had been Kesia's sanctuary long before the monastery. The house stood as it always had, a modest yet welcoming place filled with the echoes of laughter, love, and life.

As they entered, Kesia was greeted by the comforting scent of home—the faint aroma of lavender, her mother's favorite, lingering in the air. The house was quiet, and the stillness was a sharp contrast to the bustling hospital they had just left. But here, in this space, there was also a sense of peace, a reminder of the life her mother had built and the love that had sustained them both through so many trials.

"We'll stay here tonight," Kesia said, her voice soft but resolute. "I need to be close to her. And this… this feels right."

Lexi nodded in agreement, understanding the need for Kesia to be surrounded by the familiar comforts of home. "We'll be here with you," she assured her, offering a comforting smile. "You don't have to go through this alone."

Isabella, ever practical, began to set up a space in the living room where they could meditate and maintain their spiritual practices. "We'll keep our routine," she said, her tone firm. "It will help us stay centered."

As the evening wore on, they settled into the house, each finding a place where they could reflect and recharge. Lexi found herself drawn to the small shrine in the corner of the living room, where Kesia's mother had kept candles and photographs of loved ones. Lighting a candle, Lexi offered a silent prayer, asking for strength and guidance for the days ahead.

The night deepened, and the house became a haven of quiet reflection. Kesia, her heart still heavy with concern for her mother, felt a new sense of resolve. She understood now that healing wasn't just about physical recovery—it was about love, faith, and the strength to face whatever challenges life presented.

As she lay in her childhood bed, Kesia listened to the sounds of the night—the distant hum of cars, the rustle of leaves in the breeze, the steady rhythm of her own heartbeat. It was a different kind of quiet, a different kind of peace, but beneath it all, there was a rhythm, a pulse of life that mirrored her own journey.

Chapter 4

Lexi and Isabella found themselves navigating the bustling streets of New York City, the vibrant energy around them a stark contrast to the serene calm of the Jersey Shore, where they had left Kesia with her mother. The city buzzed with life, its relentless pace a reminder of the world they had once been so intimately a part of. Each turn and corner brought back a flood of memories, a reminder of the lives they had momentarily stepped away from and the challenges that awaited them as they sought to reconcile their pasts with the present.

Their first stop was a quaint café they used to frequent, a place that had been a small refuge amidst the chaos of the city. The smell of freshly brewed coffee and the clatter of dishes provided a comforting backdrop as they settled into their favorite table by the window. The café had changed little over the years, its familiar warmth was both a comfort and a jolt for Lexi's senses. She felt the past rushing back, not just as memories, but as vivid, tangible emotions.

Isabella watched Lexi carefully, noticing the subtle shifts in her friend's demeanor. "It must be strange, being back like this," she said gently, her voice filled with understanding.

Lexi nodded, her gaze drifting toward the bustling street beyond the window. "It feels like everywhere I turn, I'm walking through shadows of the past," she said softly. "Memories tucked into every corner—some beautiful, some painful. It's like the city is haunted with pieces of what used to be." A flicker of sadness passed through her eyes as thoughts of Edward surfaced, mingling with the quiet ache of loss.

After finishing their coffee, they decided to take a walk through Central Park. The park was alive with the laughter of children, the distant bark of dogs, and the rustling of leaves in the gentle breeze. The greenery offered a welcome respite from the concrete jungle, a pocket of nature that seemed to hold its own against the city's relentless pace.

As they strolled through the park's winding paths, Lexi found herself reflecting not on memories of a past with Redington but on the possibilities that had never come to be. She spoke to Isabella about the moments they had shared as friends, the unspoken connection, and the conversations that had hinted at something more—a future that was imagined but never fully realized. The park, with its serene beauty, felt like a fitting place to acknowledge the dreams that had once flickered at the edge of her consciousness but had never taken shape.

They paused by the Bethesda Fountain, a place that held significance not for what had happened but for what might have been. Lexi ran her fingers along the cool stone, her thoughts drifting to a day when she had stood here alone, wondering if her life might have taken a different turn. "I used to imagine what it would be like if things had been different," she said softly, her voice carrying the weight of unfulfilled dreams. "If Redington and I had ever taken that step… but it was just a thought, never more than that."

Isabella reached out, gently squeezing Lexi's hand in a show of silent support. "Sometimes, the things that never happen can leave just as deep a mark as those that do," she said, her voice filled with understanding. "But those imagined futures—they're part of you, too. They've shaped who you are in their own way."

Feeling the warmth of her friend's touch and the truth in her words, Lexi managed a small, reflective smile. Her eyes glistened with the emotions she had carried for so long—feelings of what could have been mixed with the strength that comes from embracing reality. "I know. And in a way, I'm grateful for it. It's just…

sometimes it's hard to let go of the dreams that never had a chance to become real."

They continued their journey through the park, the imagined memories washing over Lexi in waves—thoughts of what might have been, of paths not taken, and the silent connection she had felt with Redington, one that never fully blossomed into something tangible. With each step, she felt the heaviness in her heart begin to lighten as if acknowledging these unspoken possibilities was a way of honoring them and finally finding peace.

As the afternoon wore on, they visited other places that had once been significant to Lexi— not because of shared moments with Redington, but because of the potential that had lingered in the air, possibilities that had shaped her thoughts and dreams. The familiar sights and sounds, once so tied to her imagined future, now felt like relics from another life—a life that had shaped her but did not define her.

As the sun began to set, casting long shadows over the city, Lexi and Isabella made their way back to their temporary home. The day had been an emotional journey, filled not with memories of what had been but with reflections on what could have been. But as they walked, Lexi felt a sense of closure beginning to take root, a gentle release from the grip of those unfulfilled dreams.

Back at the condo, Lexi stood at the window, taking in the city skyline bathed in the soft, golden light of the setting sun. The city that had once been the backdrop to her imagined life with Redington was now a canvas for new beginnings. With a deep breath, she turned away from the window, feeling a newfound strength within her—a readiness to face whatever the future held, fortified by the peace she had cultivated within herself.

Isabella joined her, sensing the shift in Lexi's energy. "You're ready, aren't you?" she asked softly.

Lexi nodded with a quiet resolve in her voice. "I am. The past will always be a part of me, but it doesn't define me. It's time to move forward."

And with that, they settled into the evening, the warmth of the condo offering comfort after a day of confronting old shadows. The journey through those unspoken dreams had been necessary, a way for Lexi to reconcile her feelings and find the strength to continue on her path to enlightenment.

Chapter 5

As Redington stepped through the sliding doors of the FBI's regional office, the noise hit him like a wall. The symphony of ringing phones, clicking keyboards, and hurried conversations pulled him back into the rhythm of federal law enforcement—a stark contrast to the contemplative silence of the monastery in Nepal. He paused for a moment in the entryway, letting the bustling atmosphere wash over him.

This is your world now, he thought. *Back to the grind, back to the game.*

But something about it felt... off. The urban jungle of crime and deceit welcomed him like an old rival, taunting him to play the game he had spent years mastering. Yet, the lessons from the monastery whispered something different.

"Is this what balance feels like?" he muttered under his breath, striding toward his office. His reflection caught in the glass doors—a man in a sharp suit, carrying the weight of justice on his shoulders. *You can take the man out of the monastery, but can you take the monastery out of the man?*

Redington had been assigned to lead a task force investigating a high-profile financial fraud ring. The operation was as complex as it was dangerous, targeting a criminal network that thrived in the shadows of the city's financial districts. Millions vanished with a keystroke, leaving devastation in their wake. The stakes were high, and he was at the center of it all.

Meditation doesn't stop keystrokes. Justice doesn't wait for inner peace, he reminded himself as he entered the war room. The space was cluttered with maps, surveillance images, and screens filled with endless streams of data. His team greeted him with updates, their voices a blend of determination and fatigue.

But even in the chaos, he noticed things differently now. His time at the monastery had sharpened something in him—a stillness, a patience. Small details, like a suspect's hurried gesture on a video or the pattern of their transactions, stood out with startling clarity. It was as if he'd tuned into a frequency he hadn't known existed before.

Patience, he told himself. *The world will unfold as it should. Or so they say.*

He leaned over the table, studying the tangled lines of the investigation. The suspects were calculated, meticulous, almost admirable in their precision. For every lead they uncovered, two more questions emerged. Redington's gut instinct, once his most trusted tool, now wrestled with a new perspective.

"Why do people choose this path?" he murmured, drawing a few curious looks from his team. He shook his head, dismissing their unspoken questions. But the thought lingered. *Are they products of a broken system, or do they simply lack the discipline to resist temptation?*

These musings were more than intellectual exercises. The monastery had instilled in him a different way of seeing the world. It wasn't just about good and evil, right and wrong. It was about understanding—the why behind the choices people made.

Still, that understanding didn't make the job easier.

"Don't overthink it," he whispered to himself as the team broke for the day. "They break the law; you enforce it. Simple."

But it wasn't simple, not anymore. As he watched surveillance footage late into the night, his thoughts wandered back to Nepal—the crisp mountain air, the quiet mornings of meditation, and Sophea's cryptic lessons.

"Justice without compassion is hollow," one of the monks had said once. Redington had dismissed it as a platitude back then, but now it clung to him like an unshakable truth.

Compassion? For criminals? he thought, running a hand through his hair. *They don't give a damn about compassion. They take what they want, no matter who gets hurt.*

But another part of him—the part shaped by long hours of reflection and silence—argued back. *Isn't that the point? Isn't it your job to see what they can't? To hold a mirror up to their choices?*

The internal conflict simmered as he drove home through the bustling streets of New York City. The lights of the skyscrapers glowed against the night sky, a testament to human ambition and ingenuity. Yet, beneath it all, shadows thrived.

"Do you even belong here anymore?" he asked himself quietly, stopping at the light of a busy intersection. The world around him was alive with noise and movement, but inside, he felt the pull of two opposing forces.

The monastery had shown him peace, the possibility of a life unburdened by conflict. But here, in the heart of the city, he was needed. His instincts, his training, his drive to protect and serve—it all mattered.

"You're here because you're supposed to be," he muttered as the light changed. "But how do you hold onto what you learned when the world keeps trying to tear it away?"

Back in his condo, he sat with his journal, a practice he had started in Nepal, and couldn't seem to give up. As he wrote, he realized that the answer wasn't about choosing one world over the other. It was about finding a way to live in both.

Justice isn't just about punishment. It's about understanding, about balance. Maybe that's the real game—figuring out how to bring peace into a world that thrives on chaos.

Redington closed the journal and looked out the window. The ocean stretched endlessly before him, full of challenges he was now better equipped to face. The monastery had given him a compass, and now it was up to him to navigate the terrain.

"Virtue and sin," he said aloud, the words feeling both familiar and foreign. "Justice and mercy. Maybe it's not about choosing sides. Maybe it's about finding the balance."

Chapter 6

The night outside was still, the darkness punctuated only by the occasional flicker of streetlights and the distant hum of the city that never slept. Inside the small, dimly lit hospital room, the atmosphere was heavy with the quiet sounds of medical machinery—steady beeps and rhythmic breaths that marked the passage of time. Kesia sat by her mother's bedside, the soft glow of the bedside lamp casting long shadows on the walls. The air was thick with the scent of antiseptic, and the sterile environment was a sharp contrast to the warmth and comfort of the home they had shared.

Her mother lay still, her once vibrant features now softened by illness, her skin pale under the harsh fluorescent lights. Kesia reached out and gently took her mother's hand, feeling the frailness of her touch, the coolness of her skin. It was a painful reminder of the physical reality that they were facing—a reality that no amount of spiritual knowledge could fully erase.

Kesia closed her eyes and took a deep breath, trying to center herself as she had been taught at the monastery. The teachings she had absorbed over the past months filled her mind, each one a beacon of light in the darkness that threatened to overwhelm her. She knew that this moment was as much a test of her spiritual resolve as it was a challenge to her emotional strength.

As the night deepened, Kesia began to meditate, drawing on the techniques she had learned to calm her mind and connect with the deeper aspects of her soul. She focused on her breathing, each inhale and exhale a deliberate act of grounding herself in the present. The hum of the machines faded into the background as she visualized a golden light surrounding both her and her mother, a protective aura of healing energy.

The teachings from the monastery flowed through her consciousness—lessons on the duality of existence, the balance between the physical and the spiritual, and the power of faith to transcend earthly suffering. Kesia knew that her spiritual gifts were not just tools for healing others, they were also meant to heal herself, and help her navigate the challenges that life presented.

But as she sat there, the duality of her situation became painfully clear. The spiritual peace she sought was constantly at odds with the physical reality of her mother's condition. Her mother's labored breathing, the faint rise and fall of her chest, was a stark reminder that life in the physical world was fragile, finite. Kesia felt the weight of this truth pressing down on her, threatening to suffocate the calm she had worked so hard to cultivate.

She opened her eyes and looked at her mother's face, searching for signs of the woman who had been her rock, her guide through the early years of her life. But the vibrant, strong-willed woman she remembered was now a shadow of herself, trapped in a body that was failing her. Kesia's heart ached with the unfairness of it all, the helplessness that threatened to consume her.

Tears welled up in her eyes, and she blinked them away, trying to hold onto the teachings that had brought her comfort in the past. But the struggle was real, and it was intense. How could she reconcile the spiritual knowledge she had gained with the harsh physical reality that lay before her? How could she maintain her faith in the face of such overwhelming sorrow?

Kesia's thoughts drifted back to the monastery, to the serene faces of the monks who had taught her, their calm presence a constant reminder that peace was possible, even in the midst of chaos. She remembered the lessons on acceptance, on the need to let go of attachment to outcomes and to trust in the greater plan that the universe had in store. But those teachings felt distant now, almost abstract, as she faced the tangible reality of her mother's suffering.

Desperate for comfort, Kesia silently prayed, not for a miracle, but for the strength to accept whatever was to come. She prayed for the wisdom to see beyond the pain, to understand that her mother's journey was her own, and that all she could do was offer love and support. The teachings of the monastery had taught her that healing wasn't always about curing—it was about bringing peace, about holding space for whatever needed to unfold.

As she sat there, the hours slipping away in the quiet darkness, Kesia felt a subtle shift within herself. The struggle between her spiritual beliefs and the physical reality of her mother's condition began to ease, replaced by a deep, profound acceptance. She realized that her role wasn't to change the outcome but to be present, to offer her mother the comfort of knowing she was not alone.

With this realization came a sense of calm, a softening of the tension that had gripped her heart. Kesia's breathing slowed, and she felt the golden light she had visualized earlier expand, filling the room with a warmth that wasn't just physical but spiritual. She wasn't just healing her mother. She was healing herself, allowing the light of her faith to shine through the darkness.

Kesia leaned closer, gently stroking her mother's hand, her voice soft as she whispered words of love and reassurance. "I'm here, Mama. I'm here with you." The words weren't just for her mother; they were for herself, a mantra to ground her in the present moment.

As the night wore on, Kesia continued to meditate, to hold space for both her mother's journey and her own. The teachings from the monastery were no longer distant concepts. They were living truths, guiding her through the most challenging night of her life. And in that quiet, sacred space, Kesia found the strength to face whatever would come next, knowing that the love she carried within her was the greatest gift she could offer.

The first light of dawn began to filter through the window, casting a soft glow over the room. Kesia's mother stirred slightly, her breathing still labored but steady. Kesia smiled gently, feeling a deep sense of peace settle over her. She had found her way through the darkness, and now, as the new day began, she knew that whatever lay ahead, she was ready to face it, anchored by the faith that had guided her through the night.

Chapter 7

The morning light filtered through the tall windows of Aias's condo, casting a soft, golden hue across the polished wooden floors. The city below was already buzzing with activity, its relentless pace a stark contrast to the serene atmosphere within the condo. Isabella sat at the kitchen table, a cup of untouched coffee in front of her, staring blankly at the screen of her phone. The message that had just arrived was as cold and impersonal as the world she had once dominated—a brief note informing her that her contract with the studio had been terminated.

She had seen it coming, of course. The calls had slowed, the offers had dried up, and the once-glamorous life she had led as a famous movie star seemed to be slipping through her fingers. But knowing it was coming didn't make the reality any easier to accept. Isabella felt a sinking sensation in her chest, a hollow emptiness that threatened to swallow her whole. The life she had built on the foundations of fame and success was crumbling, and she didn't know how to stop it.

Isabella had always prided herself on being strong and on facing the challenges of her career with grace and determination. But now, sitting alone in the condo that had once been filled with the vibrant presence of her son Aias, she felt lost. The material success she had achieved seemed meaningless in the face of the deeper spiritual truths she had begun to explore. The teachings from the monastery, the quiet wisdom she had absorbed during her time there, seemed to clash violently with the world she was being forced back into.

Lexi, still staying in the condo as well, noticed Isabella's distant expression as she walked into the kitchen. She had sensed something was off with her friend over the past few days, a growing tension that Isabella had tried to hide but could not completely mask.

"Isabella, are you okay?" Lexi asked gently, sitting down beside her.

Isabella looked up, her eyes filled with a mixture of sadness and frustration. "I just lost my job," she said flatly, her voice betraying none of the turmoil raging inside her.

Lexi reached out, placing a comforting hand on Isabella's arm. "I'm so sorry, Isabella.

That's… I know how much your career has meant to you."

Isabella nodded, her gaze drifting back to the phone screen. "It's strange, isn't it? I spent so many years building this career, defining myself by it. And now, it's gone, just like that." She paused, her voice trembling slightly. "But the worst part is… I'm not even sure I wanted it back."

Lexi frowned, confused. "What do you mean?"

Isabella sighed, setting her phone down and rubbing her temples. "I don't know how to reconcile the two parts of my life anymore, Lexi. The life I had before, the fame, the success—it was everything I thought I wanted. But now, after everything we've been through, after everything I've learned, it all feels… hollow."

Lexi nodded, understanding dawning on her. "You're struggling to find a balance between your spiritual values and the world you used to live in."

Isabella met her gaze, her eyes filled with uncertainty. "Exactly. The material success, the money, the fame—it all feels so superficial now. But it's the only life I've ever known. How do I live out my spiritual values in a world that seems driven by materialism? How do I find purpose in that?"

Lexi thought for a moment, choosing her words carefully. "Maybe it's not about going back to that world as it was. Maybe it's about finding a new way to live in it, a way that aligns with who you've become. You don't have to reject everything you were—you just need to redefine what success means to you now."

Isabella absorbed Lexi's words, the idea resonating with something deep within her. She had spent so long equating success with the roles she played on screen, the awards she won, and the adoration of her fans. But those things, as fulfilling as they had seemed at the time, were fleeting. They didn't bring her the peace or the sense of purpose she now craved.

"I just don't know where to start," Isabella admitted, her voice barely above a whisper. "I've been defined by this industry for so long. I don't know how to be anything else."

Lexi squeezed her arm gently. "You're more than what you've done in your career, Isabella. You're strong, compassionate, and wise. Those qualities aren't tied to your fame—they're part of who you are. Maybe this is an opportunity to use those qualities in a new way, to find a path that's more in line with your spiritual journey."

Isabella looked at her friend, a small spark of hope flickering in her eyes. "Maybe you're right. But it's hard, letting go of the identity I've held onto for so long."

"It is hard," Lexi agreed. "But you're not alone in this. You've got me, and you've got the teachings we've learned. You'll find your way, Isabella, just like we all are."

Isabella smiled weakly, but there was a warmth in her expression that hadn't been there before. "Thank you, Lexi. I needed to hear that."

The rest of the day passed in quiet reflection. Isabella spent much of it wandering through the condo, touching the photographs and mementos of her past life. Each item, once a symbol of her success, now felt like a relic of a different time, a different person. She realized that the fame and wealth she had once chased were not what defined her worth. The peace she had found in the monastery the spiritual insights she had gained, were far more valuable.

That evening, as the sun set over the city, casting a warm glow over the skyline, Isabella stood by the window, looking out at the world she had once ruled. The material trappings of her past still held a certain allure, but she knew now that they were not the source of true fulfillment. The challenge before her was not to reclaim her former glory but to find a new path, one that honored both her spiritual growth and her need to contribute to the world.

As she stood there, Isabella made a quiet vow to herself: she would find a way to live out her spiritual values, even in a world that seemed to celebrate the superficial. She would redefine success on her own terms, seeking not just material achievements but a deeper, more meaningful impact. The struggle between faith and materialism was real, but it was a struggle she was ready to face.

Chapter 8

The crisp evening air bit at Redington's skin as he navigated the bustling streets of downtown, his dark coat blending seamlessly with the shadows. Around him, the city pulsed with life—horns blaring, laughter spilling out from crowded bars, footsteps echoing off wet pavement. He adjusted his hood, pulling it lower as he approached the glowing facade of the nightclub.

You're here because this is where the game leads, he thought, his jaw tightening. *Not exactly the tranquility of Nepal, is it?*

Ahead, neon lights cast a surreal glow over the rain-slicked pavement. The thudding bass from the club vibrated through his chest as though the building itself had a heartbeat. This wasn't just any club—this was the nerve center of a sprawling criminal empire, a place where fortunes were laundered and lives were bartered over cocktails.

Pausing outside the door, Redington murmured to himself, "Bold moves, Redington. No second chances here."

He stepped inside, and the atmosphere hit him like a tidal wave. The mingled scents of perfume and sweat mixed with a faint trace of something sharper—illicit substances lingering in the air. Strobe lights fractured the dim room into disorienting flashes while laughter and shouted conversations rose above the relentless music.

Stay focused. Watch. Listen.

His eyes scanned the crowd, cataloging faces and movements with practiced precision. Near the back, ensconced in a VIP booth, sat his target—a mid-level operative whose knowledge could topple the entire network. The man lounged casually, flanked by hulking bodyguards, his eyes flicking across the room with the sharpness of someone who knew danger was never far.

Redington muttered under his breath, "There he is. Time to play your hand."

He moved with calculated ease through the throng of bodies, his expression unreadable. As he neared the booth, one of the bodyguards shifted, his bulk creating an intentional barrier. Redington stopped, his stance relaxed but his voice firm. "I need a word with your boss. Just the two of us."

The target raised an eyebrow, curiosity and caution warring in his expression. "Who the hell are you?"

Redington met his gaze evenly. "Someone you don't want to regret ignoring."

The man studied him for a moment, then gave a small nod to his guards. They moved back reluctantly, their presence still a palpable threat. Redington followed his mark to a quieter corner of the club, where the pulsing bass softened into a distant thrum.

"You've got two minutes," the man said, his tone edged with irritation.

Redington leaned in slightly, lowering his voice. "You know why I'm here. The walls are closing in. You can cooperate, or you can take your chances when this place comes down."

The man smirked, though his eyes betrayed a flicker of unease. "Big talk. What makes you think I'd sell out my people?"

Redington's gaze didn't waver. "Because you're not as untouchable as you think. I know about the offshore accounts, the shell companies, the laundering routes. It's only a matter of time before we trace it all back to you. Help me, and maybe you walk away with something left."

The man's confidence faltered, his fingers tapping nervously against his glass. Redington saw the shift—the subtle tilt in his posture, the flicker of doubt in his eyes.

"I just need names," Redington pressed, his tone even. "Dates. You give me that, and I can make this easier for you."

Before the man could respond, Redington caught movement in the mirrored wall behind them. One of the bodyguards was approaching, his hand dipping under his jacket.

"Damn it," Redington muttered. He turned sharply, grabbing the target and pulling him to the ground just as the bodyguard's gun cleared its holster. The crack of a gunshot sliced through the music, followed by screams as patrons scattered in panic.

Redington gritted his teeth as pain flared in his side where the bullet had grazed him. "Stay down," he hissed at the target, dragging him toward the exit as chaos erupted around them.

The nightclub turned into a frenzy of bodies and noise. Using the confusion to his advantage, Redington shoved his way through the crowd, keeping a firm grip on the man's collar. Another shot rang out, but it went wide, embedding itself in the wall.

They burst into the cool night air of the alley, Redington's breath coming in ragged gasps. The pain in his side was sharp, but he pushed it aside, his focus on getting the target to safety. Backup was already waiting, and agents were swarming in to secure the scene.

"Nice of you to show up," Redington muttered as two agents hauled the target into custody. He leaned against the brick wall, wincing as he pressed a hand to his injured side.

"You okay, Red?" one of the agents asked.

Redington waved him off. "I'll live. Get him processed. I want every word he said recorded."

As the adrenaline began to fade, Redington's mind replayed the events. The target had given him enough to connect several dots in the case. It was progress—a small victory in a much larger war.

Yet, as he watched the suspect being led away, a familiar unease crept in. *What drives someone to this life? Greed? Desperation? Or is it something deeper—something broken?*

He touched the spot where the bullet had grazed him, his fingers brushing against the fabric. "Close one," he muttered, shaking his head.

The alley was quiet now, the distant hum of the city replacing the chaos of the club. Redington tilted his head back, staring at the towering buildings overhead. Their lights flickered like stars against the night sky.

This life is chaos, he thought. But maybe that's where the lessons from the monastery come in—finding peace in the middle of it all.

Pushing off the wall, he straightened his coat and started walking. The pain in his side was a dull throb now, but he barely noticed. *It's not about the fight itself. It's about why you fight.*

Chapter 9

The days following Redington's close brush with death were heavy with contemplation and an acute awareness of life's fragility. Lexi and Isabella, their hearts still heavy with the lingering fear of nearly losing him, sought solace in the myriad distractions of New York City. Yet, amid the bustling urban chaos, they found themselves drawn to a lecture on spiritual resilience in urban settings, hoping to find guidance on how to navigate their spiritual paths in an environment so starkly different from the monastery's peace.

The lecture was held in a small, unassuming building tucked between towering skyscrapers, its façade a stark contrast to the glass and steel that surrounded it. Inside, the room was filled with individuals from all walks of life, each seeking understanding and tools to maintain their faith in a city that never sleeps. The atmosphere was hushed, reverent—a sharp contrast to the city's relentless noise outside.

The speaker, Dr. Elena Mirov, was a renowned spiritual counselor known for her insightful talks on integrating spiritual practices into daily urban life. Her presence was calming, and her voice carried a warmth that seemed to soften the harsh lines of the room.

"As we gather here today," Dr. Mirov began, "we recognize the challenges that our environment poses to our spiritual practices. The noise, the speed, the sheer density of life can seem overwhelming. Yet, it is within this very chaos that our faith can find its deepest expression."

Lexi listened intently, her thoughts occasionally drifting to Redington. He had walked these city streets, his own faith a quiet strength amidst the cacophony. Dr. Mirov's words slowly helped her focus, weaving through her lingering anxiety and offering a perspective that resonated deeply.

"Urban settings," Dr. Mirov continued, "though often perceived as obstacles to spiritual growth, can also be fertile grounds for faith. It is not the tranquility of our environment that determines the strength of our spiritual life, but the tranquility we cultivate within ourselves."

Isabella, taking notes, found herself deeply engaged. The concept of internal tranquility resonated with her, reminding her of their days at the monastery. "It's about carrying our sanctuary within us," she whispered to Lexi, who nodded in agreement.

As the lecture progressed, Dr. Mirov shifted the discussion toward deeper spiritual concepts—exploring the nature of the soul, the idea of soul contracts, and the concept of divine timing. "We are all part of a grand design," she said, her voice imbued with conviction. "Our souls have chosen this path, this life, for a reason. Each encounter, each challenge, is an opportunity for growth, guided by a higher plan."

Lexi felt a stirring within her, a deep resonance with the idea that their lives were guided by more than just chance. She had often wondered about the strange twists and turns her life had taken—meeting Redington, their time at the monastery, and the close call they had just experienced. Could it all be part of a greater plan, a divine game where each move was deliberate and purposeful?

Dr. Mirov's words began to unlock something within Lexi, a curiosity that had been simmering beneath the surface since their time at the monastery. The concept of soul contracts intrigued her—the idea that souls entered this life with agreements, roles to play, and lessons to learn. It explained so much of the pain, the joy, and the seemingly random events that had shaped her journey.

"Divine timing," Dr. Mirov explained, "is the universe's way of ensuring that everything happens exactly when it's meant to. We may not always understand it in the moment, but looking back, we often see the threads that connect each event, each decision, leading us exactly where we need to be."

Isabella glanced at Lexi, sensing the shift in her friend's demeanor. Lexi's eyes were alight with a new understanding, a sense of connection to something greater than herself. The fear and uncertainty that had clouded her mind since Redington's injury seemed to be lifting, replaced by a quiet acceptance of the path they were on.

As the lecture concluded, the attendees were invited to share their thoughts or ask questions. The room buzzed with conversations about personal struggles and triumphs in maintaining spirituality amid daily pressures. But Lexi remained silent, her mind turning inward, contemplating the new insights she had gained.

After the lecture, Lexi and Isabella stayed behind to thank Dr. Mirov. The spiritual counselor offered them both a compassionate smile. "Remember," she advised, "The soul's journey is one of learning and growth. Embrace each experience, knowing that it is part of a divine plan. Trust in the timing of your life, and let your faith guide you."

As they left the lecture, the city's sounds seemed a little less jarring, its pace a bit more bearable. Lexi and Isabella walked in silence for a while, each lost in their thoughts, processing the profound truths they had just encountered. The city, once overwhelming in its noise and chaos, now felt like a place where they could apply their spiritual teachings—a proving ground for their faith.

Back at the Aias's condo, Lexi retreated to a quiet corner, pulling out the spiritual texts she had been studying. The words on the pages took on new meaning, each passage a revelation that deepened her understanding of the soul's journey. She read about soul contracts, the agreements made before birth, and the roles that souls play in each other's lives. It was all part of a larger, intricate design, one that was both comforting and humbling in its complexity.

That night, as Lexi sat by her window watching the city lights twinkle like distant stars, she felt a profound sense of peace. The chaos of the world outside had not changed, but her perspective had. She understood now that each challenge, each twist of fate, was an opportunity for growth—a step forward on the path of her soul's journey. The near loss of Redington, once a source of deep fear, now felt like a part of that journey, a test of faith that had strengthened her resolve.

Inspired by the lecture and the insights she had gained, Lexi resolved to embrace her journey with trust and courage. She would honor the soul contracts she had made, live in alignment with divine timing, and allow her faith to guide her through the complexities of life. It was a new understanding, a deeper connection to the divine plan that governed her existence, and with it came a renewed sense of purpose.

Chapter 10

The bustle of the FBI office enveloped Redington as he strode in, the familiar loudness of ringing phones, hurried conversations, and clacking keyboards washing over him. Despite the energy, a subtle dissonance settled in his chest. The chaos was a stark contrast to the tranquil rhythms of the monastery, where he had learned to navigate his thoughts and emotions with deliberate calm. Here, the stakes were tangible, the adrenaline constant, but something had shifted in him—his purpose, his approach, and even his perception of justice.

He made his way to his desk, a cluttered battlefield of files and reports. One particular case demanded his attention—a series of arson attacks on community centers in struggling neighborhoods. The crimes had left many without vital resources, amplifying the community's fear and desperation. As he reviewed the details, Redington's focus wavered, his thoughts wandering to the monastery's teachings about fear as a root of human suffering.

"Redington," Special Agent Gray's voice broke through his reverie, pulling him back to the present. Gray, his supervisor and longtime colleague, stood by his desk with a quizzical look. "You good? You've been zoning out a lot lately."

Redington blinked and offered a quick nod. "I'm fine. Just... thinking."

Gray studied him for a moment, then handed over additional files related to the case. "Well, think fast. This one's heating up, and we need all hands on deck."

The day unfolded in a blur of fieldwork, interviews, and piecing together fragments of evidence. Redington found himself speaking with witnesses who described their community's devastation—the places they'd once relied on for safety and connection now reduced to ash. As he listened, he began to sense a deeper narrative emerging: this wasn't just about the fires. It was about the systemic neglect and desperation that had allowed such crimes to fester.

Later that evening, Redington returned to his condo, the muffled hum of the waves filtering through his windows. He set his badge and gun on the table and sank into a chair, the weight of the day pressing down on him. Closing his eyes, he sought refuge in meditation, focusing on the monastery's teachings about balancing action with intention. Justice wasn't merely about catching criminals—it was about restoring balance, addressing the roots of harm, and seeking a broader understanding of humanity's struggles.

The next morning, his renewed focus brought clarity. As he interrogated a young suspect connected to the fires, he noticed the boy's trembling hands and downcast eyes. Rather than pressing hard, Redington softened his tone. "You're scared. I would be, too," he began, leaning forward slightly. "But you don't have to carry this alone. Tell me what's going on."

The boy's walls began to crumble. In halting sentences, he revealed that he'd been coerced by a local gang into setting the fires. He had no other choice—his family's safety had been threatened. The confession led Redington to uncover a larger network exploiting vulnerable youth, a systemic problem that went beyond individual crimes.

Later that week, the operation was dismantled. Redington stood in the courtroom, advocating for leniency for the boy. "He made a mistake," he told the judge, "But it wasn't his choice alone. He was a pawn in a much larger game, one that preys on fear and desperation. He deserves a chance to rebuild, not be condemned."

The court's decision to pursue rehabilitation over punishment felt like a victory—not just for the boy but for the community that would see the cycle broken. Back at the FBI office, Gray clapped a hand on Redington's shoulder. "Good work. You saw what no one else did."

Redington gave a small smile, but pride wasn't what filled him. It was a quiet, steady sense of alignment between his profession and his evolving understanding of justice. His time at the monastery had left a mark, not as a distant memory but as a living guide for how to approach his work.

As the city's lights twinkled in the night, Redington walked the streets with a renewed sense of purpose. The challenges ahead would be many, but he was armed with something far more potent than tactics or strategy—he carried the balance of wisdom, compassion, and action. The game of shadows and light would continue, but Redington was no longer just playing—he was rewriting the rules.

Chapter 11

Isabella stood at the edge of the small community theater stage, watching a group of young actors rehearse a scene. Their movements were unpolished, their lines hesitant, but their energy was infectious. She found herself smiling at their earnestness, reminded of her own beginnings when the allure of the stage had first captured her heart.

"Okay, everyone, let's take five," she called out, clapping her hands. The actors shuffled offstage, laughing and chatting, their camaraderie a balm to the doubts that had plagued her since stepping away from the spotlight.

One of the younger actors, a shy teenager named Lily, lingered behind. She hesitated at the edge of the stage, clutching her script as if it might provide some invisible shield.

"Ms. Isabella," Lily said tentatively, "Can I ask you something?"

Isabella turned to her, her expression warm and encouraging. "Of course, Lily. What's on your mind?"

The girl fidgeted with the edge of her script. "How do you deal with stage fright? Every time I step out there, I feel like I'm going to mess everything up."

Isabella smiled, her mind flashing back to her own first performances, the way her heart would pound so loudly she thought the audience could hear it. "You're not alone in that feeling," she said gently. "Even the most experienced actors get stage fright. The secret is grounding yourself. Take a deep breath, feel the floor beneath your feet, and remind yourself why you're here."

Lily tilted her head. "Why I'm here?"

Isabella nodded. "You're here because you have something to share, a story to tell. Acting isn't about being perfect. It's about connecting with the audience making them feel something. And you can't do that if you're stuck in your own head."

Lily's eyes brightened. "I'll try that. Thank you."

"You'll be great," Isabella said with a smile, watching as Lily walked away with a little more confidence in her step.

Later that afternoon, Isabella sat in the small office tucked behind the stage, reviewing notes for her mentorship program. When she started this project, she wasn't sure if it would fill the void left by her acting career. But now, as she watched these young performers grow and flourish under her guidance, she felt a satisfaction that went beyond personal success.

Her program wasn't just about acting techniques or industry tips—it was about teaching these young people to find their voices to remain true to themselves in an industry that often demanded conformity. It was about giving them tools to navigate not just the stage but also the challenges of life.

"Your craft is your gift," Isabella had told them during their first session. "But how you share that gift with the world is what defines your legacy."

That evening, Isabella returned to her quiet condo, the buzz of rehearsal still humming in her thoughts. She poured herself a cup of tea and settled at the kitchen table, pulling out her journal. The pages were filled with reflections on her journey—her time at the monastery, the struggles of reconciling her spiritual growth with the demands of her old life, and the slow but steady process of rediscovering her purpose.

Tonight, she wrote: *It's not about fame or recognition anymore. It's about guiding others to see their worth and potential. This is my legacy.*

Closing the journal, Isabella leaned back in her chair, a soft smile on her lips. The world outside her window was still as loud and chaotic as ever, but inside, she felt a quiet peace. The path she had chosen wasn't easy, but it was meaningful, and for the first time in a long while, she felt truly fulfilled.

She glanced at the framed photo of Aias on the bookshelf across the room. "I hope you're proud of me," she whispered, the words carrying both love and resolve.

As the city lights sparkled against the night sky, Isabella felt a renewed sense of purpose. The stage she stood on now was different, but the spotlight still shone bright. She wasn't just guiding performances but helping shape lives and proving to herself and the world that success was about so much more than applause. It was about impact, connection, and the legacy of faith and resilience she was determined to leave behind.

Chapter 12

That night, as the city hummed quietly below
the condo window, Lexi found sleep elusive.
The events of the day, intertwined with the
profound insights from the lecture on spiritual
resilience and the new understanding she had
gained, spun gently in her mind. Her thoughts
circled around the idea of divine timing, soul
contracts, and the intricate dance between faith
and the material world. Finally, as the clock
ticked past midnight, her eyes closed, and she
drifted into a deep, enveloping sleep. It was here,
in the realm of dreams, that the boundaries of
reality softened, and the extraordinary began to
unfold.

Lexi found herself walking along a serene
beach, the sand soft and cool under her feet, the
moon casting a silvery glow over the ocean. The
rhythm of the waves brought a sense of peace
she hadn't felt in days, a calm that seemed to

wash away the lingering fears and doubts she had harbored since Redington's close call. As she walked, a figure appeared in the distance, ethereal and radiant, moving toward her with a grace that seemed to transcend the earthly plane.

As the figure drew closer, Lexi saw that it was a woman, her presence commanding yet profoundly comforting. She was cloaked in an aura of ethereal white and silver, her hair long and flowing like a cascade of shimmering light, her eyes deep violet, radiating wisdom and compassion.

"I am Archangel Pistis Sophia," the figure spoke, her voice like a melody, resonant and soothing. "I am here to guide you through the complexities of your faith and to help you understand the divine plan that weaves through your life."

Lexi, awestruck, felt an immediate sense of reverence and connection. "Why have you come to me?" she asked her voice a whisper against the sound of the waves.

Pistis Sophia reached out, her hand touching Lexi's forehead gently. "You seek understanding of the paths laid before you, the intertwining of love, loss, and faith. These are not just trials but are also illuminations, highlighting the divine essence within you and all around you."

The beach around them seemed to glow brighter, the stars above more vivid. Pistis Sophia gestured to the sky. "Just as the stars guide the sailor, so too does your faith guide your spirit. It is both your anchor and your compass."

Lexi felt a warmth spreading through her, a clarity that filled her with both comfort and a profound sense of purpose. "How can I hold onto my faith when everything feels so uncertain?" she asked, searching the celestial eyes of the archangel.

"Faith is not about certainty," Pistis Sophia explained, her gaze deep and unflinching. "It is about embracing the unknown, trusting that the darkness will break with the dawn, and understanding that every challenge is an opportunity to forge your soul in the crucible of divine truth."

The dream shifted, and they were no longer on the beach but standing high atop a mountain overlooking a vast landscape. "Look," Pistis Sophia instructed, and as Lexi looked, she saw paths winding through the terrain, some steep and rocky, others lush and green.

"Your path is one of many, intertwined with the destinies of others," the archangel continued. "Each step forward is a step toward greater enlightenment, not just for you but for all whose lives you touch. Your faith is a guiding light, not just for yourself, but for those around you."

As Lexi gazed out over the landscape, she saw familiar faces—Isabella, Kesia, Redington—all walking their own paths, sometimes converging with hers, sometimes diverging, but always connected in the grand tapestry of life. She realized that their journeys were all part of a larger design, one that was both intricate and beautiful in its complexity.

"Remember, Lexi," Pistis Sophia said, her voice softening, "Your journey is guided by divine timing. Trust in the plan, even when it is not clear. The challenges you face are not meant to break you, but to shape you, to help you grow into the person you are destined to become."

As the vision began to fade, Lexi felt the archangel's presence beginning to wane, but her words lingered, a gentle echo in the fading dream. "Carry your faith like a lantern in the night, Lexi. Let it illuminate your way, and trust that you are exactly where you need to be."

Lexi awoke just as the first light of dawn crept across her room. The dream was vivid in her mind, each detail etched with clarity. She felt renewed, her heart lighter, as if the weight of her uncertainties had been lifted. The fear and doubt that had clouded her mind were replaced with a deep, abiding trust in the journey ahead.

With a newfound resolve, she rose from her bed, ready to face the world with her faith not just intact but invigorated, a beacon within guiding her forward. The city outside was the same as it had been the night before, but to Lexi, it now seemed different—softer, more welcoming, as if the dream had woven itself into the fabric of reality, blending the physical and the spiritual in a way that was both profound and reassuring.

She knew now that her path, though challenging, was part of a greater design, one that she could trust even when the road ahead seemed uncertain. Pistis Sophia's words echoed in her mind: Faith is not about certainty. It is about trusting in the journey, embracing the unknown, and allowing the light of faith to guide you through the darkness.

As Lexi stood at the window, watching the city come to life with the dawn, she felt a deep sense of peace and purpose. She was ready to face whatever the day might bring, knowing that she was not alone, that her journey was part of a divine plan, and that her faith would always be her guiding light.

Chapter 13

The morning was crisp and clear as Lexi strolled through Central Park, her thoughts reflective, buoyed by the profound dream encounter with Pistis Sophia. The archangel's words had resonated deeply, filling her with a sense of purpose and clarity that she hadn't felt in a long time. As she wandered along the winding paths, her mind replayed the wisdom and encouragement she had received, feeling more connected to her spiritual journey than ever before. Yet, there was a part of her still anchored in the past, to memories of Redington and the future they had once dreamed of sharing.

As she approached the Bethesda Terrace, a familiar spot filled with personal memories, she noticed a figure standing by the fountain—a man who seemed oddly familiar yet out of context. As she drew closer, recognition dawned, it was

Ethan, one of Redington's colleagues from the FBI, someone she had met on several occasions at gatherings and brief visits to the bureau.

Ethan spotted her approaching and waved, a small smile breaking over his solemn expression. "Lexi," he greeted her warmly as she approached, though his eyes held a tinge of sadness that matched her own. "It's good to see you, though I wish it were under better circumstances."

"Likewise, Ethan," Lexi replied, managing a small smile. "What brings you here?"

"I was just thinking about Redington," Ethan said, his gaze drifting towards the waters of the fountain. "He loved this place, didn't he?"

"He did," Lexi agreed, her voice soft with nostalgia. They shared a moment of silent remembrance, the sound of the water a soothing backdrop. But as they stood there, something about Ethan's demeanor set off a quiet alarm in Lexi's mind. There was a weight in his words, a finality that didn't align with what she knew to be true.

Ethan then reached into his coat pocket, pulling out an envelope. "I found this when I was clearing out his desk at work," he explained, holding it out to her. "He wrote it a week before… before everything happened. It's addressed to you."

Lexi's heart skipped a beat as she took the envelope, her fingers trembling slightly. The realization that Redington had left something for her, words that were unspoken, reignited a flicker of confusion. But alongside the confusion, a spark of concern ignited. If Ethan was giving her this letter now, did he believe Redington was… dead?

"Thank you, Ethan," she said, her voice barely above a whisper. Ethan nodded, his expression serious, as he excused himself to give her some privacy, understanding the gravity of the moment for her. But as he walked away, Lexi's mind raced. She knew Redington was alive. They had been careful, keeping his survival a secret after the dangerous mission that nearly claimed his life. If Ethan thought him dead, then Redington must have had a very good reason to let him believe that.

Alone now, Lexi sat on a nearby bench and carefully opened the envelope. Inside was a letter, Redington's familiar handwriting sprawling across the page. As she began to read, his voice seemed to echo in her mind, bringing with it a wave of love and profound sorrow.

My dearest Lexi,

If you're reading this, it means I wasn't able to tell you all this in person, and for that, I'm deeply sorry. These past months with you have been the most meaningful of my life. You've opened my heart in ways I never thought possible, and every moment with you has been a gift.

My hopes for our future are simple yet profound. I dream of a life where we continue to explore this beautiful, challenging world together, facing whatever comes with love and courage. I see us growing old, learning from each other, and sharing in the joy of each discovery.

Know that no matter where I am, my love is with you, a beacon that will always shine brightly. Keep following your path, my love, for it is a great one.

Forever yours, Redington

Tears blurred Lexi's vision as she folded the letter, pressing it to her heart. The words were a bittersweet symphony, each sentence both a dagger and a soothing balm. Though the pain of his supposed loss was sharp, the love that emanated from his words enveloped her in warmth and comfort. But there was more at play here. If Redington had crafted this letter knowing that Ethan would eventually give it to her, it meant he was orchestrating something bigger, something that required secrecy—even from those closest to him.

Gathering her strength, Lexi rose from the bench, a renewed sense of purpose settling within her. Redington's love, though no longer present in the physical sense, continued to guide her, just as her faith and the wisdom of the archangels. She had to trust that whatever he was doing, it was for a reason, a reason he couldn't yet share with her.

With a deep breath, Lexi continued her walk, each step a testament to the resilience of love and the enduring power of the human spirit. She would play along, keeping up the facade of grief, knowing that Redington was out there, somewhere, working to ensure their safety—and perhaps the safety of many others.

As she walked through the park, the words of Pistis Sophia echoed in her mind, reminding her that faith was not about certainty but about trusting in the journey, even when the path was obscured. Redington's journey, his path, was now shrouded in mystery, but she had faith that it would bring them back together when the time was right. She would carry his love like a lantern in the night, guiding her through the uncertainties ahead.

Chapter 14

The soft hum of hospital machinery filled the air, punctuated occasionally by the distant sound of footsteps and the quiet murmur of nurses at their station. Kesia sat quietly by her mother's bedside, her gaze fixed on the gentle rise and fall of her mother's chest as she breathed, aided by the machines that surrounded her. The room was dimly lit, the only light emanating from a small lamp on a table nearby, casting a warm glow over the otherwise stark surroundings.

Kesia's mind was a whirlwind of emotions, each thought intertwined with memories of her time at the monastery—the peace of the gardens, the depth of the teachings, and the spiritual practices that had become a part of her daily routine. Now, back in the chaotic world, sitting in the sterile environment of a hospital, those lessons felt both distant and desperately needed.

She reached into her bag and pulled out a small, well-worn book of meditations that Sophea had given her before she left the monastery. Opening it to a bookmarked page, she read softly to herself, finding comfort in the familiar words that spoke of finding strength in silence and solace in the spirit. The teachings of the monastery had always emphasized the power of the mind and spirit, even in the face of physical suffering. Tonight, those teachings were her anchor.

As the night deepened, Kesia began her vigil in earnest. She closed the book and placed her hands gently over her mother's, feeling the frailty of her skin, a stark reminder of the fragility of life. Kesia closed her eyes and began to meditate, her breath syncing with the beeping of the heart monitor, finding a rhythm in the midst of the stillness.

In her meditation, Kesia visualized a place of peace, a lush garden filled with the sound of running water and the scent of blooming flowers, a sanctuary she had often visited in her mind during her time at the monastery. She imagined her mother walking beside her, healthy and smiling, free from pain. The imagery brought a sense of calm over her, a reassurance that beyond the physical suffering, there was a place of peace for everyone.

As she continued to meditate, Kesia reflected on the teachings of Peter, the wise monk who had often spoken of the nature of suffering and the transformative power of faith and acceptance. His words echoed in her mind, reminding her that suffering was not an end in itself but a path to deeper understanding and compassion. She prayed—prayed for strength for her mother, for the wisdom to handle whatever came next, and for the ability to accept the things she could not change.

As the hours passed, Kesia found herself grappling with the duality of her existence—the spiritual clarity she had gained at the monastery and the harsh realities of the world outside. The sterile hospital room was a far cry from the serene gardens where she had found peace, yet she realized that this was where her faith was truly tested. It was easy to be at peace in a tranquil environment, but true spiritual strength was found in the ability to maintain that peace in the midst of chaos.

By the time the first light of dawn began to seep through the blinds, casting soft stripes across the hospital room floor, Kesia felt a renewed sense of resolve. She understood that her spiritual journey at the monastery was not just about finding peace for herself but also about bringing that peace into the lives of others, especially in times of turmoil. The teachings she had embraced were not confined to the tranquil settings of a monastery but were meant to be lived out in the real world, in the rawest moments of human experience.

Her mother stirred slightly, showing signs of waking from her restless sleep. Kesia squeezed her hand, offering a smile filled with love and fortitude. "I'm here, Mom," she whispered, her voice steady and soothing. "You're not alone."

In that moment, Kesia realized that her vigil by her mother's bedside was more than just a night of waiting—it was a profound moment of spiritual clarity and commitment. She was living the teachings of the monastery in the most tangible way possible, applying the spiritual knowledge she had gained to bring comfort and peace to her mother in her time of need.

The soft glow of the morning light filled the room, and with it came a sense of hope. Kesia knew that the road ahead would not be easy, but she felt prepared to face it with the strength of her spirit and the wisdom of her heart. The night had been long, but it had also been transformative, reinforcing her belief that the power of faith and love could transcend even the most challenging circumstances.

As she sat by her mother's side, Kesia felt a deep sense of peace settle over her. She was exactly where she needed to be, doing exactly what she was meant to do. Her journey at the monastery had prepared her for this moment, and she knew that she would carry the lessons she had learned with her, guiding her through whatever came next.

Chapter 15

The bustling streets of New York, usually a source of inspiration and energy for Isabella, now seemed overwhelming and indifferent. Her recent losses cascaded through her mind like a relentless storm. First, the shocking and untimely death of her son, Aias, had shattered her world, leaving her grappling with profound grief. Then, there was an abrupt end to her acting career due to industry cutbacks, which stripped away a part of her identity and purpose.

Isabella walked aimlessly through Central Park, the stark contrast of her internal turmoil against the serene backdrop making her feel even more isolated. The crunch of leaves underfoot was a reminder of the passing of time, of changes she couldn't control. She found herself at the Bethesda Fountain, where she and Aias had spent many joyful afternoons.

Memories flooded back, each one a sharp jab to her already aching heart.

Feeling adrift, Isabella sat on a nearby bench, her eyes unfocused on the cascading water. She pondered the teachings from the monastery about maintaining faith amidst hardship. "How," she whispered to herself, "Can I maintain faith when everything I've loved has been ripped away?"

Her thoughts turned to the monastery's lessons on resilience and spiritual endurance. She recalled Sophea's words about faith being not just the belief in the divine but also the belief in oneself, in the ability to withstand and grow from life's fiercest challenges. Yet, applying these teachings in the harsh reality of her current world felt daunting.

As dusk began to settle, Isabella watched the shadows lengthen across the park, mirroring the darkness that seemed to grow within her. She felt a pull, a need to connect with something, anything, that could anchor her drifting spirit. Pulling out her phone, she scrolled through contacts, hesitating when her finger hovered over a spiritual hotline she had added months ago but never called.

With a deep breath, Isabella dialed the number. The line clicked, and a warm, gentle voice answered, "Hello, this is the Hope and Faith Line. How can I support you today?"

Tears welled up as Isabella responded, her voice cracking with emotion, "I—I've lost so much. My child, my career... I don't know how to keep going. I'm trying to hold onto my faith, but it feels like it's slipping through my fingers."

The counselor on the line listened patiently, offering words of comfort and understanding. "It's normal to feel lost during times like these," the counselor reassured her. "Holding onto your faith doesn't mean you won't feel pain or doubt. Sometimes, it's about sitting with those feelings, acknowledging them, and finding small steps to rebuild your strength."

Isabella felt a small shift inside her—a flicker of hope. The counselor suggested practical steps to reconnect with her spiritual beliefs, like journaling her feelings, joining a support group, or engaging in community service, which could provide a sense of purpose and connection.

As the conversation continued, Isabella found herself opening up, sharing her fears and her hopes. The counselor's compassionate responses helped her feel less alone, reminding her that even in her darkest moments, there was still a path forward, however unclear it might seem. The practical advice felt grounding, giving her something tangible to hold onto amidst the emotional storm.

By the end of the call, the sun had set, and the park was bathed in twilight. Isabella stood up, feeling slightly steadier. While her path forward was unclear, she recognized that her journey through grief and rebuilding her faith was just that—a journey. It would take time, perhaps a lot of time, but tonight, she had taken a small but crucial step toward healing.

As she walked back through the now quiet paths of Central Park, Isabella noticed the city lights beginning to flicker on, one by one, like small beacons in the night. The conversation reminded her that even in her deepest despair, there were threads of connection and support ready to help guide her back to a place of peace and purpose. She just needed to keep reaching out and keep walking forward, one day at a time.

When Isabella arrived back at Aias's condo, she found Lexi sitting quietly on the couch, a book of meditations open on her lap. Lexi looked up as Isabella entered, sensing the shift in her friend's energy. "How are you feeling?" Lexi asked softly.

Isabella managed a small smile. "A bit better. I called that hotline… it helped to talk things through with someone."

Lexi nodded, her eyes filled with understanding. "I'm glad you did. We're all going through so much right now. It's important to reach out when we need to."

Isabella sat down beside Lexi, the warmth of their friendship a comforting presence in the otherwise quiet condo. "I think I'm ready to go back to Kesia's mom's house. She's been on my mind all day, and I want to be there for her… for both of them."

Lexi smiled, relieved to hear Isabella's resolve. "I was just thinking the same thing. Let's go together. Kesia needs us, and it will be good for all of us to be together right now."

The two women exchanged a look of mutual support, both knowing that the road ahead would be challenging but also knowing that they didn't have to walk it alone. They gathered their things and headed out the door, leaving the quiet of the condo for the embrace of the night.

As they made their way through the city streets, the noise and energy of New York City seemed less daunting, less overwhelming. Together, they were stronger, each step forward a testament to their resilience and the power of their bond. The journey to Kesia's mother's house was filled with quiet conversation, shared memories, and the comfort of knowing that they were heading toward a place where they could continue to support each other, heal together, and find strength in their shared faith.

When they arrived at Kesia's mother's house, the familiar warmth of the home surrounded them. Kesia greeted them with a tired but grateful smile, the weight of her vigil evident in her eyes. Isabella and Lexi embraced her, their presence a silent promise of support.

As the night continued, the three women sat together, sharing stories, offering comfort, and finding solace in each other's company.

Chapter 16

Kesia wiped her hands on an apron as she prepared soup in her mother's modest kitchen. The comforting scent of onions and garlic wafted through the air, mingling with the faint aroma of sage from a bundle drying by the window. The familiar smells transported her back to simpler times, to family dinners filled with laughter and stories, before life had scattered them in different directions.

Her mother, visibly stronger than she had been in months, sat at the small wooden table peeling carrots. Though her illness had left her weaker, there was a spark in her eyes that Kesia hadn't seen in far too long. The recovery wasn't just physical—it was as if some deep, inner light had reignited within her mother, filling the space between them with warmth.

"Do you remember when you burned the rice during our first big family dinner?" her mother teased, her smile pulling Kesia from her thoughts.

Kesia laughed, the sound bubbling up from a place she hadn't touched in months. "I was so nervous! I thought everyone would disown me for ruining Nana's famous curry."

Her mother's laugh joined hers, soft but full of life. "You were so sure you could fix it with extra salt. The look on everyone's face when they tasted it!"

They laughed together, the moment filled with an easy joy that reminded Kesia of the importance of being present. But as the laughter faded, her mother's expression turned thoughtful.

"Kesia," she said, her voice quieter now. "I've been thinking a lot about what you've shared with me about the monastery, about faith, healing, and finding purpose. It's inspiring. I can see it in you—you've changed. There's a calmness in you now, a sense of strength."

Kesia set down the wooden spoon she'd been using to stir the soup and turned to face her mother. "The monastery gave me so much," she said. "But I think what it really did was remind me of what's already within us. It's like… we have these gifts, these pieces of ourselves that we forget because life gets too noisy."

Her mother reached across the table, placing a hand on Kesia's. "You've always had a gift for seeing the world differently. Even when you were little, you would make up stories about how the stars were our ancestors watching over us. You've always found beauty and meaning where others see nothing."

They sat in comfortable silence for a moment, the weight of their shared memories settling over them like a blanket. Then her mother spoke again, her tone more serious. "What are you going to do with everything you've learned? It's one thing to carry that wisdom with you, but it's another to share it."

Kesia hesitated, her thoughts swirling. "I've been thinking about that. I want to blend what I've learned with the traditions you and Nana taught me—our recipes, our stories, and even the old remedies. Those things are a part of who we are, and I think they can help people heal in ways they don't even realize they need."

Her mother smiled, her eyes glistening with pride. "What you're doing matters, Kesia. You're honoring your roots while creating something new. That's no small thing."

That evening, after dinner, Kesia sat at her small desk by the living room window. Her mother had fallen asleep on the couch, a soft blanket draped over her shoulders. The sight filled Kesia with gratitude—a quiet reminder of why she had returned home and why this moment mattered so much.

She opened her notebook and began sketching plans for a new workshop series, the ideas pouring out of her as if they had been waiting for this moment. She called it Healing the Soul, A Journey Through Faith and Family. In her mind, she envisioned weaving guided meditations with traditional remedies, creating a space where participants could reconnect with themselves and their heritage. Each session would be a blend of spiritual exploration and the earthy wisdom passed down through generations.

The first workshop, she decided, would include the comforting recipes she had cooked with her mother, paired with meditations inspired by her time at the monastery. "Healing starts with what nourishes us," she murmured to herself, jotting down ideas with growing excitement.

As the first stars appeared in the night sky, Kesia set down her pen and looked at her mother, still asleep. Her chest swelled with a quiet certainty. This was the path she was meant to walk. It wasn't just about sharing what she had learned—it was about creating something meaningful, something that would touch lives in ways that echoed far beyond her own.

For the first time in months, Kesia felt a profound sense of peace. The struggles and doubts that had weighed on her felt lighter, replaced by the knowledge that she was exactly where she needed to be. As she turned off the light and climbed into bed, her heart was filled with a quiet determination. The journey wasn't over, but she was ready for whatever came next, grounded in the love and wisdom that had brought her this far.

Chapter 17

This week's drive back to Jersey Shore was quiet, with the city slowly fading into the rearview mirror as Isabella and Lexi made their way down the highway. The early morning light painted the world in soft hues, the golden rays casting a serene glow over the landscape. The air was crisp, the sky clear—a perfect autumn morning, yet both women felt the weight of the past few days pressing down on them.

Lexi kept her eyes on the road, her thoughts drifting between the recent events and the conversation she knew they needed to have. The rhythm of the tires against the asphalt was almost hypnotic, a steady beat that seemed to mirror the pulsing of her thoughts. Beside her, Isabella sat in quiet contemplation, her gaze fixed on the horizon, lost in her own reflections.

They passed through small towns and stretches of open countryside, the scenery shifting from urban to rural as they approached the familiar shore. The drive, though silent, was not uncomfortable. It was a shared silence, filled with the understanding that they were both processing the recent upheavals in their lives—Aias's death, Redington's close call, the uncertainty of the future.

As they neared the Jersey Shore, the ocean came into view, the waves rolling gently against the sand. The sight brought a sense of peace, a reminder of the constancy of nature in the face of life's unpredictable challenges. Lexi turned the car onto a quiet road that led to Kesia's mother's house, the path lined with trees whose leaves were beginning to turn vibrant shades of red and gold.

When they arrived, the house greeted them with a warm, welcoming presence, its exterior softened by the morning light. They parked the car and sat for a moment, neither of them speaking as they absorbed the tranquility of the scene before them. Finally, Isabella broke the silence, her voice soft but steady. "I feel like everything is changing, Lexi. But I'm not sure what's next."

Lexi nodded, her hand resting on the steering wheel. "I know what you mean. It's like we're standing on the edge of something new, but we don't quite know what it is yet."

With a shared look of determination, they stepped out of the car and walked up to the front door, feeling a sense of purpose begin to take root within them. The day at Kesia's mother's house had been one of shared comfort and quiet reflection. The three women—Lexi, Isabella, and Kesia—found strength in each other's presence, their bond deepening as they faced the challenges of life together. But as the night approached, a subtle shift began to take place, a sense that something more was on the horizon, something that would guide them to the next phase of their journey.

It was Kesia who first mentioned it, her voice thoughtful as they sat together in the last of the evening's light, sipping tea in the cozy kitchen. "I've been thinking a lot about the teachings from the monastery," she said, her gaze distant. "About how faith isn't just something we hold inside but something that actively shapes our reality. It's like… we're being prepared for something more, something we're not fully aware of yet."

Lexi nodded, understanding the feeling all too well. The dream encounter with Pistis Sophia left her with a lingering sense of anticipation as if her path was leading toward a significant turning point. "I've felt that too," she admitted. "It's like we're being guided toward something—or someone—that will help us see more clearly how our faith can shape the world around us."

Isabella, who had been quietly listening, finally spoke up. "I think you're both right. Ever since I made that call the other night, I've felt this… pull, like there's someone out there we need to meet. Someone who can help us understand how to use what we've learned in a more profound way."

Kesia's mother, who had been resting in the next room, called out softly, bringing their conversation to a brief pause. Kesia quickly went to check on her, offering comfort and ensuring she was comfortable. When she returned, the contemplative atmosphere had deepened, as if the house itself was holding its breath, waiting for what would come next.

"Maybe it's time we actively seek out this guidance," Lexi suggested. "We've been through so much, and while we've learned a lot, there's still a sense that we're missing a piece of the puzzle."

"Like a final teacher," Isabella added, her voice steady with newfound resolve. "Someone who can challenge us to take what we know and turn it into something that can truly impact the world."

The idea settled over them like a warm blanket, comforting yet invigorating. They all felt it—that quiet certainty that they were on the brink of something significant. The thought of finding this final teacher filled them with a mix of anticipation and purpose. It was as if everything they had experienced up to this point—the trials, the losses, the lessons—had been preparing them for this moment.

"We've been guided by our faith so far," Kesia said, her voice strong. "It's what brought us together, what carried us through the hardest times. But now, I think it's time we take a more active role in seeking out the guidance we need. Whoever this teacher is, I believe we're meant to find them, and they're meant to help us face whatever comes next."

Isabella nodded the determination in her eyes mirroring the resolve she felt within. "Then let's do it. Let's find this teacher and see where our faith can truly take us."

Lexi smiled, a sense of peace settling over her. The dream, the encounters, the struggles— they all seemed to point toward this journey, toward finding the person who could help them unlock the true potential of their spiritual paths. "I'm with you both," she said. "Let's follow this path and see where it leads."

As they made plans to begin their search, the atmosphere in the house seemed to shift as if the very walls were responding to their decision. The challenges they had faced were not behind them, but they were no longer burdened by uncertainty. Instead, they were driven by the knowledge that they were not alone on this journey—that they were being guided and that their faith would lead them to the answers they sought.

Chapter 18

The decision to seek out a new teacher had energized the trio. They spent the next few days discussing how they might find this person, where they should look, and what they were hoping to learn. Kesia, Lexi, and Isabella each felt the pull of destiny, a quiet but insistent force guiding them toward the next phase of their journey.

One morning, after a particularly intense discussion over breakfast, Kesia mentioned a name that had been lingering in her mind ever since they decided to seek guidance. "There's a spiritual center I've heard of," she said, her voice thoughtful. "It's a place where people go when they're searching for something deeper. It's called The Sanctuary of Light."

Lexi and Isabella exchanged curious glances. "What do you know about it?" Isabella asked.

"Not much, really," Kesia admitted. "Just that it's a place where many spiritual seekers have found clarity and purpose. The teacher there is supposed to be... different. People say he's able to see things in ways others can't, and he has a way of challenging everything you think you know."

Lexi felt a twinge of excitement. "It sounds like exactly what we need."

Isabella nodded in agreement. "Let's go. If this teacher is as insightful as people say, then maybe he's the one who can help us unlock the full potential of our faith."

That afternoon, they set off for The Sanctuary of Light. The center was located a short drive inland from the Jersey Shore, nestled in a more secluded, wooded area. The drive there was serene, with the familiar sight of the coastline gradually giving way to pockets of dense trees and marshlands that added a different kind of tranquility to the journey. The salt air was mixed with the scent of pine and damp earth, creating a peaceful atmosphere that contrasted with the bustling energy of the nearby shore.

As they neared their destination, the road became narrower, winding through quiet residential areas and patches of undeveloped land that hinted at the area's natural beauty. The landscape was flatter, with small clusters of trees providing shade and a sense of seclusion. The sight of the Atlantic was still close enough to remind them of the shore, yet the center itself felt tucked away, a hidden gem amidst the familiar scenery.

The Sanctuary of Light was modest in appearance, a simple building that blended harmoniously with the surrounding environment. It was constructed from natural materials that echoed the colors of the land—weathered wood, soft grays, and muted greens. The grounds were peaceful, with small gardens and a path that led to a quiet meditation area overlooking a small pond.

As they approached the entrance, they were greeted by a man who radiated warmth and kindness. He was dressed in simple, loose-fitting clothes, his hair silver and long, his eyes sparkling with a wisdom that seemed to see straight through them.

"Welcome," he said, his voice gentle but resonant. "I am Dorian, the teacher here at the Sanctuary of Light. I've been expecting you."

The women exchanged surprised glances. "Expecting us?" Lexi asked, intrigued.

Dorian smiled, his expression serene. "When seekers are ready, the teacher always knows. Come, let us sit together and talk."

He led them to a quiet area in the garden, where they sat on cushions arranged in a circle. The air was fragrant with the scent of the nearby ocean mixed with blooming flowers, and the sound of the breeze rustling through the trees added to the sense of tranquility.

"I understand you've been on a journey," Dorian began, his eyes moving from one to the other. "A journey that has brought you here, searching for guidance."

Kesia nodded. "We've learned so much already, but we feel there's something more we need to understand—something about how our faith can shape the world around us, not just our inner lives."

Dorian considered her words for a moment before speaking. "Faith is indeed a powerful force, but it is not merely a shield against the world. It is an active, dynamic energy that can transform reality. The challenge lies in learning how to wield it with intention and wisdom."

Isabella leaned forward, her eyes intense. "How do we do that? How do we take what we've learned and use it to make a real difference?"

Dorian's gaze softened. "It begins with understanding that faith is not passive. It is not something you simply hold within you. Faith must be lived, breathed, and expressed in every action every thought. It is a force that flows through you and into the world. But to use it effectively, you must be clear in your intentions and aligned with your higher purpose."

Lexi felt a deep resonance with his words as if he was articulating something she had always known but had never fully understood. "So, our faith isn't just about enduring or surviving—it's about creating, influencing, and shaping the reality we live in?"

"Exactly," Dorian replied, his eyes bright with approval. "Faith is the foundation, but your actions are the tools. Together, they can shape the world around you in ways you may never have imagined."

The conversation continued for hours, Dorian guiding them through discussions on the nature of faith, the power of intention, and the importance of aligning their actions with their spiritual beliefs. He challenged their assumptions, pushing them to think beyond what they had previously understood.

"You've already done so much," Dorian said as the sun began to set, casting long shadows across the garden. "But there is more to do. The challenges you face are not just tests—they are opportunities to shape the world. Remember, your faith is a living force, one that can influence the reality around you. Use it wisely, and you will find that the world responds to the intentions you set."

As the day came to a close, the trio felt a deep sense of gratitude and purpose. They had found the teacher they were searching for, and he had the tools they needed to take their journey to the next level. The path ahead was still uncertain, but they now understood that their faith could be a powerful force for change—both in their own lives and in the world around them.

Chapter 19

Back in New York City, in the quiet of the condo, surrounded by books and notes, Lexi found herself drawn deeper into her spiritual studies than ever before. The recent events had stirred in her a profound need to understand the mechanisms of faith—not just as a comfort but as a fundamental element of her existence. Her interactions with Dorian and her dream encounter with Archangel Pistis Sophia had opened the door to a new realm of spiritual inquiry.

Lexi had always been an avid reader, but now her reading took on a new intensity. She surrounded herself with ancient texts and modern interpretations, especially those focusing on Gnostic beliefs, which resonated deeply with her current state of mind. Among these texts, the figure of Archangel Pistis Sophia, representing faith, and the writings about enduring through trials were particularly compelling.

One quiet evening, as rain tapped softly against the window panes, Lexi found herself engrossed in a passage about Pistis Sophia, a figure of great wisdom and challenge in Gnostic tradition. The text depicted her not just as a passive recipient of faith but as an active seeker, enduring great trials to achieve a profound understanding of the divine.

This idea struck a chord with Lexi. The concept that faith was not just to be maintained but actively struggled through challenges and doubts offered a new perspective on her own losses and the trials she had faced. It suggested that her grief and the upheaval of her life could be part of a larger, transformative process—a crucible in which her faith was being tested and refined.

Inspired by this, Lexi began to jot down her reflections in a journal, a practice she had intermittently abandoned but now returned to with renewed purpose. She wrote about Redington, about their time together, the lessons from the monastery, and her recent spiritual encounters. Each entry helped her weave her personal experiences with the broader spiritual concepts she was studying.

As the days passed, Lexi's exploration of these texts deepened her understanding of the spiritual gifts she had been cultivating. She realized that her journey was about more than just healing from her past mistakes—it was about integrating her experiences into a larger understanding of her life's purpose. This integration, she realized, was what the Gnostics referred to when they spoke of achieving gnosis—deep, transformative knowledge that connected the soul to the divine.

Lexi's focus began to shift toward understanding soul contracts—the agreements that souls make before entering a lifetime, guiding their experiences and interactions. The idea that her challenges, her relationships, and even her losses were part of a preordained plan resonated with her. It provided a sense of meaning that transcended the pain, transforming it into a crucial part of her spiritual evolution.

Motivated by this insight, Lexi decided to reach out to others who might be struggling with their faith. She decided she was going to start a small online group for those wishing to seek spiritual solace. The group would meet weekly, discussing various spiritual texts and sharing personal experiences. Lexi was excited and knew that these sessions were not only to help others but also to strengthen her own understanding and faith.

Through these explorations and discussions, Lexi knew she would slowly reconstruct her own worldview and find in her hidden pain a pathway to deeper wisdom. Her past was still a part of her, a shadow in her heart, but now it was accompanied by a light—a growing understanding that her spiritual journey was about embracing all facets of life, the joy and the sorrow, as essential parts of her soul's evolution.

Meanwhile, Isabella was also experiencing a profound shift. Inspired by her recent conversations with Dorian and the desire to make a meaningful impact, she began volunteering at a local community center. The center, located in a struggling neighborhood, offered services ranging from food distribution to educational programs. Isabella found herself drawn to the work, and her past as a public figure helped her connect with people who were often overlooked.

At first, Isabella struggled with the stark contrast between her previous life of glamour and the harsh realities faced by those she was now serving. But as she spent more time at the center, she began to see the importance of this work. It was a way to live her faith to apply the spiritual teachings she had learned in a tangible, impactful way.

Isabella knew her work at the center would become a form of spiritual practice, a way to deepen her understanding of compassion and service. She realized that her role wasn't just about giving but also about receiving—that she would be learning from the people she served, gaining insights into resilience, hope, and the strength of the human spirit. Her faith would become a living force, guiding her actions and shaping her reality.

Kesia, on the other hand, was immersed in the documentation of her mother's illness, a process that was both painful and cathartic. She began to see this documentation as more than just a record of her mother's journey—it was a testament to the power of love, faith, and endurance. Each entry, each observation, was a way to honor her mother's strength and the lessons she had imparted, both consciously and unconsciously.

Kesia's writing became a spiritual practice in itself, a way to process her grief and find meaning in the midst of suffering. She realized that her mother's illness was teaching her profound lessons about the nature of life, the inevitability of change, and the power of acceptance. Through this process, Kesia was not only preparing herself for the ultimate challenge—whatever form it might take—but also deepening her understanding of the spiritual gifts she had been cultivating.

As the trio continued their individual journeys, they found that their paths, though distinct, were intertwined. Each of them was unlocking the final gifts of their spiritual journeys, preparing for the ultimate test that they knew was on the horizon. The teachings of Dorian, the guidance of their faith, and the wisdom they were gaining from their experiences were shaping them into the people they needed to become.

Chapter 20

The city pulsed with a strange, restless energy that Lexi couldn't shake.

It had been weeks since the news of Redington's supposed death, yet something deep inside her refused to accept it.

The thought that he might truly be dead had been raw—suffocating, at first. But now, a whisper at the edge of her consciousness suggested that there was something more to his death.

Something unresolved.

Back in the quiet of Kesia's mother's house, the scent of sandalwood and sage lingered from their evening meditation, grounding her as she curled up on the living room floor with stacks of old case files that she grabbed from Redington's condo, were spread around her like puzzle pieces waiting to be placed. The flickering candlelight cast shifting shadows along the walls, but it was the movement within her own mind that unsettled her most.

The last few weeks had changed her.

The meditations, energy work, and study of Pistis Sophia had done more than deepen her understanding of the unseen. They had sharpened something in her, tuned her instincts to frequencies she hadn't fully understood before.

She had learned that knowledge wasn't just found in books or whispered in ancient texts—it was felt. It was an inner knowing beyond reason.

The Gnostics believed in truth hidden beyond the veil.

And what if this was her truth?

What if she wasn't mourning Redington but searching for him?

He's not gone. Not truly.

The thought was irrational. The FBI had reported his death during an undercover operation gone wrong. There had been witnesses. There had been evidence.

But Lexi knew Redington.

He was always three steps ahead.

And yet, something about the way it had all unfolded didn't sit right.

She reached for the stack of papers beside her, flipping through Redington's old notes. The official reports didn't add up, but the missing pieces nagged her most.

Footsteps approached.

Lexi looked up as Isabella leaned against the doorway, arms crossed.

"You're doing it again."

Lexi barely glanced up. "Doing what?"

"Chasing ghosts."

Lexi exhaled, rubbing her temples. "What if it's not a ghost? What if he's still alive?"

Isabella's expression faltered, but she didn't dismiss it outright. "Lexi… you don't think the FBI would cover something like that up, do you?"

Lexi hesitated, then shook her head. "I don't know. But something feels off. I feel off. It's like I'm being drawn toward something I can't see yet."

Isabella sighed and walked over, settling beside her. "Don't you think the FBI is going to be looking for those files?"

"I don't think that they knew that Redington always kept a second set."

"Then let's figure this out," Isabella said, sitting down beside her.

The words sent a small wave of relief through Lexi. Because she felt deep down that she wasn't chasing a ghost, she was chasing the truth.

Lexi shifted, stretching her stiff muscles, when a voice from the nearby TV caught her attention.

"In other news, self-proclaimed spiritual leader Evelyn Stone continues to gain followers across the country. Her movement, The New

Ascension, has been met with both fascination and controversy, as critics warn that her teachings blur the line between enlightenment and dangerous devotion…"

Lexi's brows knitted together. The name tugged at something familiar in the back of her mind, but before she could place it, the door creaked open.

Isabella leaned against the couch, arms crossed. "You're doing it again."

Meanwhile…

The neon lights of the city buzzed and flickered, reflecting off the wet pavement.

A shadow moved through the alleyways, unseen by the crowds moving through the streets just a few feet away.

A man in a hooded jacket kept his head down, his movements precise and calculated. He had been careful. He had been thorough.

But the weight of staying in the dark, of erasing himself from existence, was starting to take its toll.

Redington exhaled slowly, pressing himself into the shadows as a group of passersby wandered too close.

He had survived things that should have killed him. He had played his part and disappeared as planned.

But this wasn't just about survival anymore.

Lexi.

He knew her.

Knew that grief wouldn't be enough to stop her.

Knew that she wouldn't just accept what the FBI had told her.

And that meant she was already looking for answers.

It was only a matter of time before she found them.

Chapter 21

The ocean breeze carried the scent of salt and the rhythmic crash of waves, rolling onto the shore in an unending cycle. Lexi stood at the water's edge, her bare feet sinking into the cool, wet sand. The steady pulse of the sea usually calmed her, its vastness a reminder that some things were beyond control. But today, an unshakable tension coiled in her chest.

She wasn't the only one feeling it.

"Do you sense it, too?" Isabella's voice broke the silence, soft yet weighted. She stepped up beside Lexi, her gaze locked on the horizon as if searching for something unseen.

Lexi nodded, wrapping her arms around herself against the chill. "Something's shifting. I don't know what it is, but it feels… big."

"Big doesn't always mean bad," Isabella offered, though there was hesitation in her voice.

Behind them, Kesia knelt in the sand, arranging stones in a loose circle. The scent of burning sage curled into the air as she lit the bundle, her movements methodical. Their spiritual practices have become more intense in recent days—each of them pushing deeper and seeking clarity and transformation. But something had changed.

There was an undercurrent in their work—an unease they couldn't name.

Kesia glanced up, her brow furrowed. "You two aren't exactly subtle," she called, dusting the sand from her hands. "What's going on?"

Lexi hesitated. "It's just a feeling. Like we're on the edge of something we can't see yet."

Kesia tilted her head, considering this. "Maybe it's the growing pains of transformation," she mused. "We've been pushing ourselves hard. Sometimes that stirs things up—internally and externally."

Isabella let out a soft laugh. "Trust you to make it sound so poetic, Kesia."

Kesia smirked but didn't respond. She turned back to the meditation circle, adding the last of the stones.

Lexi watched her, a flicker of envy stirring beneath her skin. Kesia always seemed so sure of herself, so rooted, even when the world around them felt unsteady. Lexi, on the other hand, felt like she was being pulled in a dozen directions at once, never quite finding solid footing.

"You okay?" Isabella asked, watching her closely.

"Yeah," Lexi replied quickly. "Just… tired, I guess."

Isabella didn't push, though her eyes lingered on Lexi with quiet concern.

They joined Kesia in the circle, settling into the sand as the sun dipped lower in the sky, its golden light reflecting off the water. The sage smoke curled around them, mingling with the cool ocean air.

Kesia's voice was steady as she began the meditation. "Breathe in the energy of the earth. Feel it grounding you, anchoring you. Let go of anything that no longer serves you."

Lexi closed her eyes and tried to follow the guidance, but her thoughts kept drifting. The tension she felt wouldn't loosen. It gnawed at the edges of her awareness, whispering of something approaching—something unseen.

As she sank deeper into meditation, flickers of images danced through her mind. *Shadows moving through a neon-lit alley. A name she didn't recognize. Evelyn.*

A distant voice echoed in her thoughts. *Ascension is near.*

Her eyes snapped open.

Kesia was watching her, her expression concerned. "You okay?" she asked.

Lexi exhaled, rubbing her temples. "I just can't shake this feeling. It's like… something's coming for us."

Kesia's face darkened, and for a moment, Lexi swore she saw a flicker of fear in her young friend's eyes.

"Then we need to be ready," Kesia said quietly.

"Ready for what?" Isabella asked, her frustration creeping through. "We don't even know what we're up against."

"We don't need to know," Kesia replied. "We just need to trust that we'll handle it when it comes."

The words were meant to be reassuring, but they only deepened the tension coiling in Lexi's chest. She nodded, though her mind was far from at ease.

As they packed up and walked back toward Kesia's mom's house, the unease followed them, clinging like a shadow.

Lexi glanced back at the ocean one last time.

Somewhere, just beyond the horizon, something was waiting.

And she wasn't sure they were ready for it.

Chapter 22

New York City's pulse had begun to shift, a slow, almost imperceptible hum beneath the surface of everyday life. Lexi had spent the last few days poring over Redington's old files, trying to make sense of the gnawing feeling in her gut. The deeper she dug, the more questions she uncovered.

But answers? Those remained elusive.

Late one evening, as the rain drizzled against the windows of Aias's condo, Lexi sat curled up on the couch, her laptop open on her lap. Isabella was across from her, flipping absently through a book on ancient symbols, while Kesia stood by the window, arms folded, gazing into the darkened streets below.

"This isn't healthy, Lexi," Isabella said finally, her voice laced with concern. "You've barely slept since you got those files."

Lexi rubbed her temples, exhaling slowly. "I know. But I can't shake the feeling that I'm missing something." She gestured to the screen, where a map of New York City was littered with red stars, each one marking a location connected to Redington's last known investigation. "Look at this. These locations—safe houses, meeting spots, and storage facilities—form a pattern. He wasn't just tracking them… he was circling something."

Kesia turned from the window, her brow furrowing. "What do you think he was trying to find?"

Lexi hesitated, the weight of the unknown pressing down on her. "Or maybe… what was trying to find him."

The room fell into a thick silence, each of them caught in the gravity of that possibility.

Then, as Lexi scrolled through Redington's old reports, she frowned. Something wasn't right. She rechecked the index, flipping back through her physical copies.

"Wait a second…" She muttered, her fingers tracing over a document number.

"What is it?" Isabella asked, leaning in.

Lexi held up two reports. "This file…" She tapped a case number from Redington's last known investigation. "It's missing from the database."

Kesia moved closer. "Are you sure?"

"Positive. Look." Lexi angled the screen toward them. "The records show an entry for it, but the file itself is gone. It's been wiped. This case was active before he went off the grid. If someone erased it—"

"Then they don't want anyone finding it," Isabella finished grimly.

Lexi's stomach twisted. Something was deliberately being covered up.

Then, her fingers stilled on the keyboard as a line of text blinked back at her.

A single note in Redington's handwriting, buried within an old file from his investigation:

"E. Stone—watch for patterns. Codes repeat."

Lexi's stomach tightened. "Evelyn Stone," she murmured, reading the name aloud.

Isabella glanced up. "The spiritual guru? I thought she was just some New Age influencer."

Lexi shook her head. "No. Redington flagged her for a reason. Look at this—" She clicked through a series of files, bringing up a list of known associates. "These people? Half of them are missing. The others? Dead under suspicious circumstances."

Kesia moved closer, scanning the screen. "That's not a coincidence."

"No, it's not," Lexi agreed, her pulse quickening.

A sense of unease settled in the room, the weight of realization pressing down on all of them.

And then—

A sudden knock at the door shattered the moment.

Kesia's eyes flicked toward Isabella. No one was expecting visitors this late.

Lexi stood first, her body tensed. "Did anyone—"

Kesia shook her head, already moving toward the door. She hesitated, then cracked it open just enough to see outside.

A package sat on the doorstep, but there was no return address.

Lexi moved forward, exchanging a look with Isabella before carefully lifting it into the house. It was wrapped in plain brown paper, nothing to indicate who had sent it.

"This feels… weird," Isabella muttered, watching as Lexi peeled the wrapping away.

Inside was a small, black leather notebook.

Lexi's breath caught in her throat. She knew that notebook.

It was his.

Hands trembling, she flipped it open. Redington's handwriting covered the pages— notes, timestamps, half-written messages.

Then, near the back, something that made the room seem to tilt.

"Lexi, if you're reading this, it means they've found me."

A chill ran down her spine.

She scanned the rest of the page. Most of it was unreadable—water-stained, smudged. But one phrase stood out beneath the scribbled mess.

"Meet me where the ocean and the earth speak as one."

Lexi stared at the words, heart pounding.

"The ocean," she whispered.

"Lexi," Isabella murmured, leaning closer. "That could be—"

"The beach," Kesia finished, realization dawning.

Lexi swallowed hard. The same place they had planned to go tomorrow.

She closed the notebook, pressing it against her chest as her mind raced.

Redington was out there.

And he was still fighting.

Chapter 23

The weight of the notebook sat heavy in Lexi's hands, its meaning rippling through her like a silent storm. Redington had left this message for her. He was alive—or at least, he had been when he wrote it.

But how long ago?

Had she found it too late?

Kesia and Isabella watched her closely, waiting for her to speak. The air in the room was thick with unspoken urgency.

"We have to go," Lexi finally said, her voice steady despite the whirlwind inside her.

Kesia frowned. "Go where?"

"Where the ocean and the earth speak as one," Isabella answered softly, reading Lexi's mind. "The beach."

Lexi nodded. "He knew I'd find this. He left it for me for a reason. That means he's waiting. Or… was."

The possibility that she was too late lingered between them, unspoken but real.

Kesia folded her arms, her logical mind warring with her instincts. "And what if it's a trap? We don't know who delivered that package. It could be anyone."

Lexi exhaled sharply, gripping the notebook tighter. "And what if it's not? What if he's out there, waiting for help, and we're sitting here second-guessing?" She looked between them, pleading. "I can't ignore this."

A long silence stretched between them before Isabella sighed and grabbed her coat. "I'm with you."

Kesia hesitated only a moment longer before nodding. "Fine. But we do this carefully. If Redington faked his death, then we need to assume he has enemies. Which means we might have them too."

Lexi agreed without hesitation. Within minutes, they were in the car, heading toward the beach.

The drive to the Redington's condo felt longer than it should have. Night had settled in, the roads nearly empty, the world draped in quiet shadows. Lexi kept glancing at the notebook, running her fingers over Redington's handwriting, as if she could will more answers from the ink.

Beside her, Isabella stared out the window, lost in thought. Kesia, ever the cautious one, kept checking the rearview mirror, scanning for any signs they were being followed.

By the time they reached the seaside, it was well past midnight.

The sound of waves crashing against the shore greeted them first, a rhythmic pulse against the quiet night. The ocean stretched before them, dark and endless, merging with the horizon.

Lexi stepped out of the car first, the salty air filling her lungs. The sand felt soft beneath her feet, but a knot of unease remained in her stomach.

No signs of Redington.

No signs of anyone.

Kesia and Isabella joined her, both silent, waiting for Lexi to make the next move.

Lexi pulled the notebook from her bag and reread the line:

Meet me where the ocean and the earth speak as one.

She scanned the shoreline, searching for something—anything—that felt like the right place.

Then, she saw it.

A set of footprints in the sand led toward the rocky outcrop further down the shore.

"Over there," she whispered, already moving.

Isabella and Kesia exchanged a glance before following.

The wind picked up as they walked, each step crunching softly in the sand. Lexi's pulse quickened. She didn't know what she was expecting, but every instinct in her body told her she was getting closer to something important.

As they neared the rocks, a shadow shifted in the darkness.

Lexi froze.

Isabella sucked in a sharp breath. Kesia's hand went to her pocket, where she had a small knife—just in case.

Then, the figure stepped forward.

And Lexi's world tilted.

Even in the dim moonlight, she could see him.

Redington.

Alive.

His hood was pulled low, his stance cautious, but there was no mistaking him.

Lexi's breath hitched, a flood of emotions slamming into her all at once—relief, shock, anger, disbelief.

"Redington," she mouthed, almost afraid to believe it.

His eyes met hers, sharp and unreadable.

"You shouldn't have come."

His voice was low, edged with warning.

But Lexi ignored the caution.

Because, for the first time in weeks, she knew—without a doubt—that she had been right.

Redington was alive.
And whatever he had gotten himself into…
It wasn't over yet.

Chapter 24

The morning was unusually still as if the world was holding its breath.

Redington had made the girls drive back to Jersey Shore. It wasn't safe for them in the city.

Lexi sat curled up in the corner of Kesia's living room, a blanket draped around her shoulders, a cooling mug of tea forgotten in her hands. Isabella and Kesia sat nearby, the quiet rustling of pages the only sound between them. A rare moment of peace.

One they all knew wouldn't last.

Then—

The sharp trill of Lexi's phone shattered the calm.

She glanced at the screen, her stomach tightening when she saw the name,

Agent Parker.

"Why is Parker calling you?" Isabella asked, brow furrowing.

Lexi shook her head, already uneasy. "I don't know."

She swiped to answer, then pressed the speaker button. "Agent Parker? What's going on?"

The silence on the other end stretched just long enough to send a ripple of unease through her.

Then, Parker finally spoke.

"Lexi, I need you to listen carefully. You're not safe."

Her grip on the phone tightened. "What are you talking about?"

A sharp exhale. "It's about Redington."

Lexi sat rigid, her pulse hammering.

"The reports were wrong. He's alive."

Her breath caught, her gaze flickering toward Isabella and Kesia.

They already knew this.

But how did Parker?

"I know," she said cautiously.

A curse from Parker's end. "Then you don't understand what that means."

Lexi stilled.

"The people who thought he was dead? They know now, too. And they won't stop until he's gone for real."

A cold weight settled in her chest.

"Who are they, Parker?"

Silence.

Then—

"I can't say over the phone." His voice was lower now, more urgent. "But listen to me—Redington's not just running. He's being hunted. And if you're involved, then so are you."

Lexi closed her eyes for half a second, Parker's words sinking in like a stone dropped into deep water.

She had known finding Redington was dangerous.

She hadn't realized just how dangerous.

"He left me a message," she admitted, testing Parker's reaction. "A warning."

A pause.

Then Parker's voice dropped even lower. "Then he knows what's coming."

A chill slithered down Lexi's spine.

"And now, so do you."

Lexi's mind raced. If Redington was in deeper than they thought—if she was now a target—everything was moving faster than she had anticipated.

She inhaled sharply. "How do I find Redington?"

"You don't," Parker said flatly. "You get as far away from this as possible."

Lexi's jaw clenched. "Not happening."

A resigned sigh.

"Then, at least be careful." Parker's voice hardened. "Because if you go looking for Redington… someone else will be looking for you."

The line went dead.

Lexi sat frozen, Parker's warning ringing in her ears.

He's alive.

She exhaled the words as if saying them out loud made them more real.

Isabella and Kesia exchanged glances.

"We already knew that," Isabella said slowly. "But Parker calling about it? That's new."

Lexi swallowed hard. "Because now, other people know, too."

Kesia leaned forward, her voice quiet but firm. "So what do we do?"

Lexi exhaled, her mind already made up.

"We wait for another message from Redington."

The three of them sat silently, the weight of the decision pressing down on them.

The morning's peace was gone.

Replaced by something darker.

Something inevitable.

Chapter 25

The morning sun filtered through the windows of Kesia's mom's cozy kitchen, casting a soft glow over the worn wooden table where Lexi, Isabella, and Kesia sat silently. The smell of freshly brewed coffee filled the air, but none of them seemed eager to break the quiet. Lexi stared at the steam rising from her mug, her fingers tracing absent patterns on its surface.

It had been weeks since Redington's funeral, but the loss still hung heavy in the air. His absence was a weight that Lexi carried everywhere, pressing down on her chest with every breath.

"Do you think he knew?" Isabella's voice was barely above a whisper, her eyes fixed on the table.

"Knew what?" Kesia asked, glancing up from the notepad where she had been writing ideas for their next meditation.

"That it would end this way," Isabella replied, her voice trembling slightly. "That his work would… take him from us."

Lexi's hand tightened around her mug. "He didn't know," she said firmly, though her voice wavered. "He was careful. He always had a plan. This… this wasn't supposed to happen."

"But it did. We saw his body in the open casket," Kesia said gently. "We have no choice but to accept it."

Lexi shook her head, her throat tightening. "I can't. Not yet. It doesn't make sense."

The memory of Redington's on the beach played like a loop in her mind—the hurried goodbye, the way he had looked at her with an intensity she couldn't quite place. She had tried to convince herself that it was just her imagination, but deep down, she felt like there was something he hadn't told her.

"Do you want to talk about it?" Isabella asked, her concern evident.

Lexi hesitated, then shook her head. "Talking won't bring him back."

The words hung heavy in the air, silencing any further attempts at conversation.

Kesia reached across the table and placed a hand on Lexi's arm. "Grief is a process, Lexi. You don't have to figure it all out today. Let yourself feel what you need to feel."

Lexi nodded but didn't respond. She appreciated Kesia's steady presence, but no amount of reassurance could fill the void that Redington had left behind.

Later that day, the three of them gathered in Kesia's mom's living room to continue their spiritual work. It was meant to be a distraction, something to keep their minds busy, but for Lexi, it only highlighted the absence of the one person who had become her anchor.

"Close your eyes," Kesia instructed her voice calm and measured. "Focus on your breathing. Let the energy flow through you."

Lexi obeyed, her eyes fluttering shut as she tried to quiet her racing thoughts. The room was silent except for the faint hum of wind chimes outside, their gentle melody mingling with the soft rustle of leaves.

But as Lexi sank deeper into the meditation, an image surfaced in her mind—Redington's face, his piercing eyes locked onto hers. It wasn't the memory of a conversation or a fleeting moment. It felt like he was there, reaching out to her.

Her eyes snapped open, her breath coming in quick gasps.

"Lexi?" Isabella's voice was filled with concern.

"I can't do this," Lexi said, rising to her feet. She paced the room, her hands shaking. "Every time I close my eyes, I see him. It's like he's… trying to tell me something."

"Maybe he is," Kesia said quietly, her expression thoughtful.

Lexi stopped pacing and turned to her. "Don't do that. Don't give me hope when there's none to be had."

"It's not about hope," Kesia replied calmly. "It's about listening. If you feel like he's reaching out, maybe you need to pay attention."

Lexi shook her head, tears welling in her eyes. "He's gone, Kesia. I watched them lower his casket to the ground. He's not coming back."

Isabella stepped forward, placing a comforting hand on Lexi's shoulder. "Kesia's just saying that maybe there's more to this. Sometimes, the connections we have with people don't end just because they're gone."

Lexi looked between them, her heart aching with the weight of their words. She wanted to believe there was something beyond the finality of death, that Redington could still be with her in some way. But every time she entertained the thought, the crushing reality of his loss came crashing back down.

"I just… I need some air," Lexi said, grabbing her coat and heading for the door.

Outside, the cool breeze did little to soothe her racing mind. She walked aimlessly along the shore, the waves lapping at the sand in a rhythm that felt both comforting and mocking.

"I don't know what to do without you," she whispered, her voice breaking. "You were always the one with the answers."

The wind carried her words away, leaving her with nothing but the sound of the sea and the ache in her chest.

Chapter 26

The flickering glow of a single overhead light cast long shadows in the small, windowless room. Redington leaned back in a rickety chair. His hands steepled beneath his chin as he stared at the wall covered with photographs, maps, and scribbled notes. Strings of red yarn connected dots on the map, a tangled web of leads he was chasing. It was meticulous and chaotic, much like the situation he found himself in.

The cover of his supposed death had worked, but it had come at a cost. Lexi's face flashed in his mind, her grief-stricken expression when she'd last seen him. He had watched her from the shadows, unable to comfort her, knowing it was better this way. Safer this way, he reminded himself, though the thought provided little solace.

Agent Parker had orchestrated the entire plan with surgical precision. A wax duplicate of Redington's body had been crafted—identical down to the smallest detail. The coffin that everyone had seen lowered into the ground hadn't contained Redington at all. The funeral, the public mourning—it had all been staged to convince the cult leader that Redington was no longer a threat. Parker had insisted it was the only way to protect Lexi. If the cult believed Redington was dead, Lexi would be left alone. And it had worked, at least for a while.

Redington had agreed to it because there had been no other option. The cult leader had been closing in on Lexi, and Redington knew that as long as he was seen as a threat, Lexi would never be safe. Faking his death had been the ultimate gamble—a way to lure the cult leader into a false sense of security while also keeping Lexi off their radar. But the price had been steep. He had watched from a distance as Lexi mourned, breaking apart under the weight of losing him. Every instinct had screamed at him to go to her, to hold her, to tell her the truth. But he couldn't. Not until the cult was dismantled for good.

Redington exhaled sharply, running a hand through his disheveled hair. His world now was this—secluded safe houses, burner phones, and sleepless nights chasing an organization that operated as if it were untouchable. The cult wasn't just a spiritual movement. It was a sophisticated, dangerous machine, pulling strings in the highest echelons of society. And it was his job to stop it.

The burner phone on the table buzzed, its sudden noise breaking the silence. Redington grabbed it, his movements precise. "Yeah," he said, his voice low.

"It's me," Agent Parker's voice crackled on the other end. "The news is out. Everyone really thinks you're dead this time."

"Good," Redington replied curtly. "That's how it needs to stay."

Parker hesitated. "I talked to Lexi earlier. She's devastated."

The words hit harder than Redington expected. He closed his eyes, the memory of Lexi's voice echoing in his mind. You'll always come back to me, right? she had once said. He had promised her he would. Now, he was breaking that promise.

"She'll be safer believing I'm gone," he said, his tone colder than he felt. "They can't use her against me if she's not a target."

"You sure about that? Because I've been following the threads you gave me and this group… they've got reach. If she's even remotely tied to you, they'll find out."

Redington's jaw tightened. "It won't happen. Just keep your end of the deal—feed them what they want to hear. Keep them off my scent."

There was a pause. "You know this illusion of your death can only go so far. Sooner or later, they'll realize you're alive."

"That's why I need to get to them first," Redington said, his voice hardening. "Did you find anything else on Evelyn Stone?"

"She's slippery," Parker admitted. "Her public persona is airtight—philanthropist, spiritual leader, the whole act. But behind the scenes, there are whispers about her connections to disappearances, money laundering, and worse. You were right about the cult being her operation. She's the key to all of it."

Redington leaned forward, his mind already piecing together the next steps. "If we can get her, the whole thing falls apart. Keep digging. I'll make my move when the time's right."

"Be careful, Red," Parker warned. "You've already sacrificed enough."

Redington hung up without responding, the weight of Parker's words pressing down on him. He had sacrificed—his career, his identity, and the life he had started to build with Lexi. But it wasn't enough. Not yet.

He stood, pacing the room. His side still ached where the bullet grazed him during the staged raid, a grim reminder of how close he'd come to making his death real. But pain was a tool, a motivator. It kept him focused.

The notebook on the table caught his eye. He flipped through its pages, filled with notes about the cult's operations, coded messages, and connections he had painstakingly uncovered. One name was circled repeatedly, Evelyn Stone.

"Who are you, really?" he murmured to himself, staring at her photo. It was a carefully curated image—a poised, elegant woman with a serene smile. But Redington knew better. Behind that facade was a puppet master pulling strings in a game far darker than anyone could imagine.

His stomach growled, reminding him he hadn't eaten since morning. He grabbed a protein bar from his bag and tore it open, eating mechanically as his eyes scanned the wall of evidence. He couldn't afford distractions. Not when so much was at stake.

Still, his mind wandered back to Lexi. She had always been the one person who could steady him, who saw through his walls. He imagined her now, probably sitting with Kesia and Isabella, trying to make sense of his 'death.' He hated himself for putting her through that pain, but it was the only way to protect her.

The phone buzzed again, pulling him from his thoughts. He answered, his tone sharp. "What now?"

"There's movement," Parker said. "Stone's holding an event tomorrow night—a private gathering for her inner circle. It's invitation-only, but it's the best chance you'll get to observe her in action."

Redington's pulse quickened. "Location?"

Parker hesitated. "You're not going to like it. It's in Manhattan."

Redington froze, the weight of the revelation sinking in. Manhattan meant proximity to Lexi. It meant danger—for her and for him. But it was also the opportunity he'd been waiting for.

"Send me the details," he said, his voice steady despite the storm inside him.

"Red—"

"Just do it," Redington snapped. He ended the call, tossing the phone onto the table.

For a moment, he stood there, staring at the wall of evidence. The tangled threads of the cult's operations, the faces of its victims, and the image of Evelyn Stone all seemed to blur together. This was it—the moment he'd been preparing for.

But in the back of his mind, one thought refused to be silenced, if I go back to Manhattan, can I stay away from her?

He grabbed his coat, pulling it on with a grim determination. There was no room for doubt, no room for hesitation. The game was far from over, and Redington intended to win—even if it cost him everything.

Chapter 27

New York City had always thrived on secrets.

Lexi knew this better than anyone.

The city hummed with energy as she and Isabella navigated the crowded streets, their coats pulled tight against the crisp air. The weight of unanswered questions pressed against Lexi's chest, a relentless tension that had been growing since Redington's death.

She went over the last few weeks in her mind—dug through his reports for the millionth time—but it wasn't enough.

Redington death seemed too perfectly timed.

Lexi's grip tightened around the burner phone Redington had put in her pocket the night on the beach, her thoughts drifting back to the mysterious message she'd received the night before…

"If you want the truth, come alone. 11 PM. 208 Mercer Street. The alley behind the bookstore."

She had considered ignoring it. It could be a trap. But something about the wording—the urgency, the secrecy—felt different.

Was Redington alive? Could it be possible? Her mind raced to remember his body in the coffin.

Isabella nudged her lightly. "You sure about this?"

"No," Lexi admitted, exhaling a breath she didn't realize she was holding. "But I have to see if it is him."

The city lights flickered above them as they reached Mercer Street. The bookstore was closed for the night, its iron security grate locked tight. A dim streetlamp cast long shadows into the alleyway behind it.

No sign of movement.

No sign of anyone at all.

Lexi and Isabella exchanged a glance. Then, slowly, Lexi stepped forward.

A creak echoed from the darkness.

Lexi's heart pounded as a figure emerged from the shadows, hood pulled low, moving with a careful hesitation—someone who was used to being watched.

A woman.

She was young, maybe in her mid-twenties, her blonde hair tucked beneath her hood. Dark circles lined her eyes, her movements twitchy, like a cornered animal.

"You're Lexi," the woman whispered. "I wasn't sure you'd come."

Lexi stayed alert. "Depends on who's asking."

The woman glanced around, then stepped closer, lowering her hood.

"My name is Mara. I used to be one of them."

Lexi's stomach clenched. "One of whom?"

"One of Evelyn's cult members."

Lexi's spine shivered with the mention of that name.

Mara's eyes darted toward the street before she spoke again. "I don't have much time. They're watching me."

"Who?" Isabella asked her voice tight with suspicion.

Mara swallowed. "Evelyn's people. The ones she calls her 'hands.' They're everywhere."

Lexi studied her. "Then why are you talking to us?"

Mara's expression hardened. "Because Redington isn't the only one in danger."

Lexi stopped breathing. *It's because Redington isn't the only one in danger.*

A gust of wind rattled the metal security gate. Mara flinched. "Evelyn has a plan," she whispered. "She's not just collecting followers— she's building something. Controlling something."

Lexi stepped forward. "What do you mean?"

Mara hesitated, licking her lips. "She's been gathering objects of power. Ritualistic things—things tied to old traditions. Books, artifacts, symbols. She believes she can rewrite reality itself."

Lexi took a deep breath.

Isabella muttered, "That's insane."

Mara gave a humorless laugh. "Is it? Then why has she already started? Why do you think people around her disappear?"

Lexi clenched her jaw. "Where is she now?"

"I don't know." Mara's hands trembled. "But I know that Redington got too close. He infiltrated her inner circle. He learned too much. That's why he had to disappear."

Lexi's pulse quickened, *disappeared, not died*. "Why did you call me?"

Mara hesitated—then reached into her coat pocket.

She pulled out a small, leather-bound notebook and shoved it into Lexi's hands. "Redington kept notes. He gave me this in case something happened to him."

Lexi's breath caught.

She flipped it open. The pages were filled with symbols, coded messages, and addresses.

But before she could read further—

A loud noise cracked through the alley.

Mara gasped—and then jerked forward.

Lexi caught her before she hit the ground.

Blood.

Dark red spread across Mara's coat.

A gunshot.

Isabella spun around. "We have to move—now!"

Lexi gritted her teeth, gripping Mara's arm. "Hold on—stay with me."

Mara's fingers dug into Lexi's wrist.

Her voice was faint—barely a whisper.

"Find him."

Then—her body went still.

Lexi's heart pounded.

She looked up just in time to see a dark figure sprinting down the alley.

"We've got to go!" Isabella shouted.

Instead of following Isabella, Lexi took off running, her boots slamming against the wet pavement. The shooter was fast—darting through backstreets, weaving between dumpsters and fences.

The wild, impossible hope that Redington might still be alive drove her forward like a spark-catching fire, her heart pounding in perfect rhythm with the frantic beat of her footsteps.

She gained ground, her breath coming in sharp bursts.

The figure vaulted over a chain-link fence.

Lexi followed.

They landed in a desolate parking lot. The figure turned—

Lexi lunged.

She tackled him hard, slamming him to the ground.

The person gasped, struggling beneath her grip.

Lexi yanked back their hood—

And froze.

It was a kid.

No older than sixteen.

Wide-eyed. Terrified.

Lexi's mind raced. "Who sent you?"

The boy's lips trembled. "I… I can't."

Footsteps thundered behind them—Isabella catching up.

Lexi tightened her grip. "Who gave the order?"

The boy's voice cracked.

"She sees everything."

Lexi's breath stalled.

Evelyn.

The boy jerked free—faster than she expected.

A flash of silver—a blade.

Lexi barely dodged before the knife slashed the air where her throat had been.

Isabella lunged. "Lexi, move!"

The boy threw the knife aside and ran.

Lexi pushed herself up, her heart racing. They could chase him, but it wouldn't matter.

The real message had already been sent.

Mara was dead.

And Evelyn now knew they were involved.

Chapter 28

Redington adjusted the cuff of his tailored suit, his reflection staring back at him in the cracked bathroom mirror. The disguise was impeccable—slicked-back hair, a neatly trimmed beard, and the faintest hint of cologne that screamed wealth and status. It was a far cry from the man who had been living out of safe houses and surviving on protein bars. Tonight, he had to blend in with the elite, the very people Evelyn Stone had wrapped around her finger.

He pocketed the forged invitation, a small card embossed with Evelyn's cult logo, a serpent coiled around a golden key. The irony wasn't lost on him. A snake guarding secrets, he thought, his jaw tightening. How fitting.

The event was being held in a Manhattan high-rise, the kind of building that glittered against the night sky, flaunting its wealth to the city below. Redington arrived in a black sedan, stepping out with an air of confidence that belied the tension simmering beneath his calm exterior. As he strode toward the entrance, he took in the sight of security guards stationed discreetly but effectively. This wasn't just a party. It was a fortress.

"Name?" The guard at the door glanced at him with professional indifference.

Redington handed over the invitation. "Daniel Archer," he said smoothly, the alias slipping off his tongue like second nature.

The guard scanned the card, then nodded and stepped aside. "Enjoy your evening, Mr. Archer."

If only, Redington thought as he entered the grand lobby.

Inside, the atmosphere was luxurious and unnerving in equal measure. Crystal chandeliers bathed the room in soft light, and waiters in crisp uniforms moved through the crowd with trays of champagne. The air hummed with conversation—polite laughter and the occasional hushed whisper. But Redington's trained eye saw through the facade. Beneath the glamor, there was tension, a careful dance of power and influence.

He spotted Evelyn Stone almost immediately. She was standing near the center of the room, her presence commanding without effort. Dressed in a flowing black gown, she moved with the grace of someone who knew she owned the space. Her piercing eyes scanned the room, locking briefly on Redington before moving on. It was a calculated gaze, assessing every person in her orbit.

She's dangerous, he reminded himself, his pulse quickening. Stay sharp.

Redington made his way toward the bar, keeping her in his peripheral vision. He needed to get closer, to observe without drawing attention. As he ordered a drink, a man in his mid-forties approached him, his smile too wide to be genuine.

"You're new," the man said, extending a hand. "Donovan Chase. I don't think we've met."

"Daniel Archer," Redington replied, shaking his hand firmly. "I've heard good things about Miss Stone."

"Ah, Evelyn," Donovan said, his tone light but his eyes sharp. "She has a way of bringing the right people together, doesn't she?"

"Indeed," Redington said, taking a sip of his drink. "I hear tonight's gathering is… special."

Donovan's smile faltered for a fraction of a second, just long enough for Redington to catch it. "Every event with Evelyn is special," he said smoothly. "But tonight, she's unveiling something that's going to change everything."

Redington leaned in slightly, feigning interest. "Care to elaborate?"

Before Donovan could respond, the lights dimmed, and a spotlight illuminated a small stage at the far end of the room. Evelyn Stone stepped into the light, her presence silencing the crowd with ease.

"Ladies and gentlemen," she began, her voice warm and commanding, "Thank you for joining me tonight. Together, we are building something extraordinary—something that transcends the ordinary constraints of society."

The room erupted in polite applause, but Redington barely heard it. He focused on Evelyn's words and the calculated way she spoke, weaving an equally inspiring and sinister narrative.

"Our movement is not just about enlightenment," Evelyn continued, her gaze sweeping across the room. "It is about power. Real power. The kind of power that changes the world."

Redington felt a chill run down his spine. Her words were carefully chosen, designed to draw in those hungry for control and influence. She wasn't just leading a cult—she was building an empire.

As Evelyn spoke, Redington noticed a man standing near the edge of the crowd, his posture stiff and his eyes scanning the room. He wasn't dressed like the others—his suit was ill-fitting, and his movements were too deliberate. FBI? Another agent? Redington wondered, his mind racing.

The man's gaze landed on him, and for a moment, their eyes locked. Redington gave the faintest shake of his head, a silent warning. The man looked away, but his presence added a new layer of tension. If the FBI was already inside, it meant the operation was further along than Redington had anticipated—and potentially more dangerous.

As the speech ended and the crowd applauded again, Evelyn stepped down from the stage, immediately surrounded by a cluster of admirers. Redington knew this was his chance. He moved through the crowd with practiced ease, positioning himself near her without drawing attention.

"Evelyn," he said, his voice smooth and confident as he extended a hand. "Daniel Archer. It's an honor."

Evelyn's eyes met his, and for a moment, he thought he saw a flicker of recognition. But her smile remained composed as she took his hand. "Mr. Archer. A pleasure. What brings you to our gathering tonight?"

"I've been hearing about your work," Redington said, keeping his tone neutral. "I wanted to see it for myself."

Evelyn tilted her head, studying him with a curiosity that made his skin crawl. "And what do you think so far?"

"I think you're onto something remarkable," Redington replied, matching her gaze. "And I'd like to learn more."

Her smile widened, but it didn't reach her eyes. "Then perhaps we should talk further. Privately."

Redington's heart rate spiked, but he kept his expression calm. "I'd like that."

As Evelyn gestured for him to follow, Redington glanced back at the man he suspected was with the FBI. The agent's eyes met his again, and Redington gave a subtle nod. Whatever came next, he would need to tread carefully. Evelyn Stone was more than just a charismatic leader—she was a predator, and Redington was walking straight into her lair.

Chapter 29

The private room Evelyn led Redington into was a stark contrast to the opulence of the gathering outside. It was minimal, almost clinical, with soft lighting and a large table in the center surrounded by high-backed chairs. On the walls hung abstract paintings, their swirling patterns oddly hypnotic. Redington took it all in as Evelyn closed the door behind them, her heels clicking softly against the polished floor.

"Do you drink, Mr. Archer?" she asked, moving toward a small bar in the corner.

"Occasionally," Redington replied, his tone measured.

Evelyn poured two glasses of amber liquid, her movements deliberate. She handed one to him, her eyes studying his face as he accepted it. "You seem… familiar," she said, her voice lilting with curiosity. "Have we met before?"

Redington chuckled lightly, taking a small sip of the drink. "I doubt it, though I've followed your work for some time. Your reputation precedes you."

"Does it?" Evelyn's lips curved into a sly smile. "And what, exactly, have you heard?"

"That you're building something unprecedented," Redington said, choosing his words carefully. "A movement that's as much about influence as it is about enlightenment."

Evelyn raised an eyebrow, clearly pleased by the flattery. She gestured for him to sit, taking the seat across from him. "You're not wrong," she said. "But influence is only a tool. The real goal is transformation—on a global scale."

"And how do you achieve that?" Redington leaned forward slightly, feigning genuine interest. "What's the secret to transforming the world?"

Evelyn's eyes glittered with something dark, something dangerous. "The secret," she said softly, "Is understanding power. True power. Not the fleeting kind that comes from wealth or status, but the kind that reshapes reality itself."

Redington's pulse quickened. He kept his expression neutral, nodding as though he were captivated by her words. "And you've found this power?" he asked.

Evelyn leaned back in her chair, her smile widening. "I've harnessed it. The question is, Mr. Archer, do you have the vision to be part of it?"

Before Redington could respond, the door opened, and a man stepped inside. He was tall and broad-shouldered, his face shadowed by the low lighting. His presence was immediately intimidating, and Redington recognized him as one of Evelyn's enforcers—the kind of man who handled problems with brute force.

"Evelyn," the man said, his voice low and gravelly. "There's been an incident."

Evelyn's smile faltered for the first time. She stood, her expression sharp. "Excuse me for a moment, Mr. Archer. Enjoy your drink."

Redington watched as she left the room, her enforcer close behind. The door clicked shut, leaving him alone. He set the glass down and took the opportunity to scan the room more closely. His eyes landed on a bookshelf against the far wall, its contents neatly arranged. He crossed the room, his fingers trailing over the spines of the books until he noticed one that seemed out of place—a thick leather-bound volume with no title.

He pulled it from the shelf, his heartbeat steady but fast. Inside were handwritten notes, diagrams, and symbols that matched what he'd seen in his research about the cult. Phrases like *"The Ascension"* and *"Phase Two"* jumped out at him, but it was a name scrawled in the margin that stopped him cold, Lexi.

Redington's breath caught. He quickly scanned the pages, piecing together fragments of information. It was clear that Evelyn was aware of Lexi and saw her as a potential threat—or perhaps an opportunity. Either way, it was clear she wasn't safe.

The door handle turned, and Redington quickly slid the book back into place, returning to his seat just as Evelyn re-entered the room. She looked composed, but there was an edge to her demeanor now, a tension she was trying to mask.

"Where were we?" she asked, resuming her seat across from him.

"You were telling me about transformation," Redington said, his voice steady. He needed to keep her talking, to gather as much information as he could before making his next move.

Evelyn smiled, "Ah, yes. Transformation. You'll see soon enough, Mr. Archer. If you prove yourself worthy, you may even become part of it."

Redington nodded, his mind already racing ahead. The stakes were higher than he'd anticipated. Evelyn Stone wasn't just a threat to him—she was a threat to Lexi, and he couldn't allow her to remain in the crosshairs.

As the conversation continued, Redington maintained his facade, but his focus had shifted. The clock was ticking, and he needed to act before Evelyn's plans reached Lexi—or worse, before Lexi stumbled into danger trying to uncover the truth on her own.

When the meeting ended, Redington left the high-rise with more questions than answers, but one thing was certain, Evelyn Stone was far more dangerous than he had realized. And the path ahead was going to test him in ways he hadn't yet imagined.

Chapter 30

The days in Jersey Shore unfolded with a calm, steady rhythm as Lexi and Isabella spent time visiting Kesia. The three of them had fallen into an easy routine, their focus remaining on deepening their spiritual practices.

Each of them had been diligently working to master the spiritual gifts they had been cultivating. But lately, something had shifted.

Beneath the surface of their quiet purpose, an unspoken tension lingered—the inexplicable sense that something momentous was on the horizon.

Lexi felt it most acutely.

It wasn't just intuition.

It wasn't just the creeping unease that had been lingering since their last meditation.

It was something more tangible.

Something real.

At first, she ignored the strange messages.

They had started as cryptic lines of text appearing in her inbox with no sender's address. The first few had seemed like nothing more than spam—fragmented sentences, disjointed phrases—but as the days passed, the pattern became impossible to dismiss.

The words were pieces of past conversations with Redington.

Lexi had read them over and over, trying to rationalize their existence. But no explanation made sense.

They were too specific, too personal.

They referenced places they had been together, private jokes no one else would know, and phrases Redington used that had been uniquely his.

And then, the messages changed.

They know about you. Leave the city.

Lexi's breath hitched, the weight of those words sinking deep into her gut. A disquieting sensation washed over her.

That evening, Lexi sat at Kesia's kitchen table, her phone screen glowing in the dim light as Isabella and Kesia leaned over her shoulder.

"I know it sounds crazy," Lexi murmured, her voice unsteady, "But these messages… they feel like they're from Redington."

Isabella frowned, studying the screen. "But Redington… he's gone, Lexi. We were there. We saw everything."

"I know," Lexi replied, her mind swirling with doubt and possibility. "But what if… what if he isn't? What if he had a reason to disappear again, to make everyone think he was dead for real this time?"

Kesia, who had been quiet until now, exhaled sharply. "And if that's true, why you? Why bring you back into the chaos?"

Lexi shook her head, staring at the screen.

"I don't know. But I need to find out."

She scrolled to the most recent message, one that had arrived just an hour ago.

Time's running out. Trust no one.

A chill ran down her spine.

Isabella crossed her arms. "If these messages are from him, he's warning you. Not just reaching out. This is serious."

Lexi nodded, gripping the phone tighter.

Kesia said, "Last time, it was a girl reaching you on that burner phone—one who, by the way, was murdered right in front of you. Why do you think this isn't someone else like her? And tell me this—how did she get that number if Redington slipped it into your pocket?"

Lexi shook her head, "I don't know."

Over the next few days, the trio immersed themselves in the shadowy remnants of Redington's last known activities, chasing ghosts through the fractured pieces of his life. They retraced his steps, spoke to the people who had known him, and reopened leads that had long since gone cold.

But the deeper they dug, the more twisted the path became—clues unraveling into dark corners where answers felt just out of reach. Connections emerged where there shouldn't have been any, as though Redington had been threading through a hidden world beneath the surface.

And then, all the loose ends tightened around a single name.

Evelyn Stone.

The name had been buried in old reports, whispered in the vague accounts of ex-FBI agents, and written in notes scrawled in Redington's old case files.

It was Kesia who made the connection first.

They were in the car. Isabella was driving them back from another fruitless attempt at getting answers when Kesia pulled up an old news article on her phone.

"Lexi," Kesia said, turning the screen toward her. "This is Evelyn Stone."

Lexi took the phone and scanned the article.

Beneath the headline was a photograph of a woman with piercing, intelligent eyes and a smile that felt more calculated than warm.

A leader. A manipulator. A force hiding in plain sight.

"She's a cult leader," Kesia continued. "She's been recruiting people under the guise of spiritual enlightenment, but Redington must have found out something bigger—something worth faking his own death for."

Isabella's voice was quiet but firm. "If Redington's in trouble, it's because of her."

Lexi gripped the phone tighter.

Time's running out. Trust no one.

She had a sinking feeling that they were unraveling something far bigger—and far more dangerous—than they had ever imagined.

And whatever it was, it was already closing in on them.

Chapter 31

Lexi had spent weeks grappling with the uncertainty of a man she thought was lost forever, only to uncover hints that he might still be alive—entangled in the shadows of a dangerous game. The unsettling truth that Redington could still be on a secret mission had shaken her, Isabella, and Kesia to their core. But the pieces didn't quite fit. A girl had been murdered right in front of them, and the same name kept surfacing—Evelyn Stone. One thing was certain, they were running out of time.

Lexi had spent years learning to trust her instincts and her faith. But what if this was a test? What if she was seeing only what she wanted to see? Was she truly following the path laid before her, or was she chasing ghosts?

The three of them returned to New York City with urgency, but unease coiled within Lexi's chest like a serpent. The towering skyscrapers, the neon lights reflecting off wet pavement, the thrumming energy of the city—it was familiar, yet it carried an undercurrent of something dark, something waiting just beneath the surface.

If Redington was out there, then they weren't the only ones looking for him.

Evelyn Stone's world was built on illusion and manipulation. She called her followers "The Chosen," whispering of enlightenment while pulling strings of control behind closed doors. Redington had spent months carefully weaving himself into her inner circle, proving himself worthy of her trust.

But trust was an illusion, too.

Every interaction with Evelyn was a game. A well-placed question here, a feigned show of devotion there. If she even suspected who he really was, the consequences would be fatal.

Tonight, he stood in the candlelit sanctuary of one of Evelyn's safe houses, watching as a small group of initiates sat in a trance-like state. Their eyes were glassy, and their breathing synchronized. He had seen cult indoctrination before, but this was different—more precise. They were being stripped of themselves, molded into something else.

Evelyn stood in the center of the room, her voice a hypnotic melody.

"Fear is the enemy of truth. Doubt is the enemy of power. You have been chosen to rise above both."

Redington swallowed his revulsion, keeping his expression neutral. He had seen this before— the slow, methodical erosion of free will. But something else lurked beneath it. The energy in the room shifted, a sensation crawling over his skin like static before a storm.

Then— a whisper.

She's coming.

His breath hitched, but he didn't react outwardly. The voice had come from nowhere, yet it was inside him. A warning? A hallucination? Or something else entirely?

Lexi.

He had to reach her.

That night, when the others slept, he took the risk. His burner phone had been destroyed weeks ago, but he found another way. An old contact still owed him a favor—a secure line to deliver a single message.

They know about you. Leave the city.

The girl's first stop was a safe house Redington had used in previous operations. The apartment was tucked away in an unassuming neighborhood, a place meant to be forgotten. The moment Lexi stepped inside, she could feel his presence—faint but undeniable. Dust coated the furniture, and the air held the stale scent of abandonment, but something told her he had been here recently.

Lexi moved toward his old desk, her fingers grazing the surface before stopping at a small, locked drawer. She reached for a hairpin and worked at the lock, a skill Redington had taught her himself.

A click sounded, and the drawer slid open.

Inside, she found a worn notebook and a single key.

Lexi's breath caught in her throat as she carefully flipped through the pages. Redington's handwriting filled every inch, his familiar shorthand detailing a tangled web of connections. Isabella leaned over, scanning the pages with wide eyes.

"He was tracking something—or someone," Isabella murmured, pointing to a name that appeared again and again.

Evelyn Stone.

Kesia frowned. "Her again."

Lexi felt a flicker of recognition. The name kept coming up. A spiritual leader. A rising influence in elite circles. A woman who promised enlightenment.

She swallowed hard. "Redington must have been investigating her. And if he was willing to stage his own death to stay hidden… that means she's more dangerous than we thought."

Kesia's eyes snapped open, her pulse racing. "Lexi, I think—" She hesitated, the weight of the vision pressing down on her. "We're not seeing the whole picture. There's something beneath the surface… something dangerous."

Lexi's expression hardened. "Then we need to uncover it—before it finds us."

They gathered Redington's notes and left the safe house, heading straight for the public library—somewhere they could search without drawing attention. The deeper they dug into Evelyn Stone's history, the clearer the picture became.

She was no mere spiritual teacher. She was the orchestrator of a powerful cult, a woman who had built a following among the city's elite, her influence stretching far beyond what the public saw. Her name was connected to a string of disappearances and unexplained deaths, all dismissed as tragic accidents.

But Redington's notes suggested something far more sinister.

"He got too close," Lexi whispered. "And it may have cost him his life."

Isabella exhaled sharply, closing one of the research books. "Then we continue what he started. And we stop her."

Kesia nodded. "But first, we figure out where that key leads."

Lexi pulled it from her pocket, turning it over in her palm. It was small and unmarked, the kind that could fit a locker, a storage unit, or a safety deposit box.

"There's a bank down the street," she said. "It's a long shot, but let's try."

Minutes later, they arrived at the bank. After some quick thinking and a little strategic misdirection, they managed to convince the clerk to check the records. To their surprise, the key matched a safety deposit box registered under a name that didn't belong to any of them—but the clerk, perhaps sensing their urgency or mistaking their confidence for authority, didn't press the issue.

A knot of tension coiled in Lexi's stomach as she slid the key into the lock, twisting it until the mechanism released with a quiet click.

Inside the box was another notebook—one more meticulous than the first—and a burner phone with a single contact listed.

D.

Kesia's breath caught. "Dorian."

Lexi didn't hesitate. She dialed the number.

After a few rings, a familiar voice answered.

"I've been expecting your call," Dorian said, his voice calm but firm.

Lexi gripped the phone tighter. "We found Redington's notes. He may be alive, but if he is, then he is in trouble. We need your help."

There was a pause, followed by a slow exhale. "I know. Redington has been working undercover, but his time is running out. The cult is closing in on him—and now they know about you."

Lexi felt the blood drain from her face. "What do you mean you know?"

"That is not the point. Evelyn has eyes everywhere," Dorian warned. "She doesn't take kindly to interference."

Lexi exchanged a glance with Isabella and Kesia, their expressions mirroring her own unease.

Dorian's voice softened slightly. "Lexi, walk by faith, not by sight. You won't see the whole path yet but trust that you're meant to walk it. Redington needs you now more than ever."

Lexi swallowed hard, forcing herself to steady her breath. "He's alive?"

There was another brief silence before Dorian spoke again, his tone carrying an unshakable weight.

"Meet me at the Sanctuary."

Lexi's doubts still whispered at the edges of her mind. But she was willing to believe it to be true.

Chapter 32

The drive back to the Sanctuary of Light was heavy with silence. Lexi, Isabella, and Kesia sat in tense contemplation, the weight of their discovery pressing down on them. The revelation that Evelyn Stone knew about them had changed everything. They weren't just chasing Redington's leads anymore—they were being watched. And hunted.

"Are we doing the right thing?" Lexi finally asked, her voice barely above a whisper.

Kesia, who had been staring out the window, turned to look at her. "You're doubting Dorian?"

"I don't know," Lexi admitted. "We don't have all the answers. We're trusting a man who always speaks in riddles. What if he's leading us into something worse?"

"He's helped us before," Isabella pointed out, though her voice carried the same hesitation. "But I get it. This feels… rushed."

Lexi gripped the steering wheel tighter. "I keep thinking—what if this is what Evelyn wants? What if she's expecting us to go to The Sanctuary?"

"Then we need to be prepared," Kesia said firmly. "Faith is taking the first step even when you don't see the whole staircase."

Lexi exhaled, forcing herself to nod. "You're right. No more second-guessing."

As they approached The Sanctuary, the shift in energy was immediate. What had once felt like a place of healing and knowledge now carried an undercurrent of unease. The towering trees lining the road seemed darker, their branches swaying as if whispering warnings.

The moment they stepped out of the car, Dorian was waiting.

"Thank you for coming," he greeted them as they approached. His expression was serious, his gaze holding the weight of unspoken truths. "I wish the circumstances were different, but we have no time to waste."

Lexi met his gaze. "We believe that Redington's alive. But in great danger. What can you tell us?"

Dorian gestured toward the monastery. "Come inside. We need to talk."

They followed him through the winding stone paths of the Sanctuary of Light, passing monks deep in meditation. The place still carried a powerful presence, but something about it felt off—as if the balance had been disrupted. Lexi couldn't tell if it was her own doubt or something more sinister.

Inside the candlelit meeting chamber, they gathered around a low wooden table. Dorian took a deep breath before he spoke.

"Redington has been undercover for months," he began. "Infiltrating a cult that has been growing in power and influence. This cult, led by Evelyn Stone, is not just dangerous because of its teachings—it's dangerous because it manipulates the very fabric of reality."

Kesia stiffened. "What do you mean?"

Dorian's gaze darkened. "Evelyn has tapped into forces beyond what most can comprehend. She has found a way to weaponize belief—to twist spiritual truths into something that controls rather than liberates."

Lexi's stomach churned. "And Redington was trying to stop her?"

Dorian nodded. "Yes. But his cover is thin. She knows someone close to her is not who they seem, and she's tightening her grip. If we don't move soon, he won't have a chance to escape."

"We need to get him out," Isabella said, her voice resolute. "Before it's too late."

Dorian studied them for a moment, his gaze unreadable. Then, he leaned forward.

"It's not just about Redington. This is about stopping Evelyn before she becomes unstoppable."

Silence fell over the room.

"Her power is growing," Dorian continued. "She's using it to control minds, to erode free will. And if she's not stopped, the consequences could be catastrophic—not just for Redington, but for everyone she's ensnared."

Lexi's mind raced. They weren't just facing a manipulative leader. They were facing something… darker.

"What do we do?" she asked.

Dorian's expression hardened. "You have to confront her. But you can't do it alone. Stone's power comes from the dark energy she's tapped into, but your power comes from the light. You've spent months cultivating your gifts, deepening your faith, and now it's time to use what you've learned."

He let the words sink in before continuing.

"She will try to exploit your fears, your doubts. She will try to turn your own minds against you. But remember—the power of faith is stronger than any darkness she can summon. Your belief in each other, in the light, is your greatest weapon."

Kesia swallowed hard. "What if we're not strong enough?"

Dorian placed a hand on her shoulder. "You are stronger than you know. The trials you've faced, the losses you've endured—they've prepared you for this moment. Trust in yourselves, and you will prevail."

Isabella took a deep breath, strengthening herself. "What's our next step?"

Dorian stood. "We need to lure Stone out. She's too powerful within her stronghold, surrounded by her followers. But if we can get her alone, we can confront her directly. Redington has been feeding her information that he's close to discovering a powerful artifact—something she desperately wants. We'll use that to draw her out."

Lexi nodded, determination hardening in her chest. This was happening.

"And when she comes," she said, "We'll be ready."

Dorian met her gaze. "Then go. Gather your strength. Tonight, we set the plan in motion. Remember—your faith is your shield, and your light is your sword."

Lexi took a steadying breath. No more doubts. No more hesitation.

It was time to face Evelyn Stone.

Chapter 33

The shadows in Evelyn Stone's sanctuary stretched long across the candlelit chamber, flickering against the walls like restless spirits. Redington sat perfectly still, his posture relaxed, his breath steady—but his mind was running calculations at an unrelenting pace. He had infiltrated deep into the cult. Maybe too deep.

He wasn't sure how much longer he could maintain his cover.

The past few months had been a slow descent into madness—watching as Evelyn manipulated her followers, twisting their faith into chains of obedience. What had started as an elite spiritual movement had evolved into something more dangerous.

Something darker.

He had been careful. Always careful. But he could feel the shift in Evelyn's demeanor. She was watching him more closely now, testing his loyalty in ways that left no room for doubt.

Something inside of her must have told her he wasn't truly one of them.

And she wasn't wrong.

Tonight, he had been summoned.

The great hall of Evelyn's stronghold was dimly lit, lined with statues of deities from every tradition—twisted in ways that made them feel unnatural. The room smelled of incense and something more pungent, something metallic. Blood. A sacrifice had been made here tonight.

Evelyn sat at the head of a massive stone altar, her presence commanding, her dark eyes piercing. Around her, followers sat in a near-trance, some chanting in low, rhythmic tones, others whispering unintelligible words.

Redington knelt before her, playing the role he had perfected, 'the faithful disciple.'

"You are devoted," Evelyn mused, her voice smooth like silk over steel. "And yet, I sense something in you, Rhoan."

She only called him Rhoan in front of the others—a name assigned to him the day he joined them.

"Something hesitant. Something… resisting."

Redington held her gaze, keeping his breathing even. Do not flinch. Do not react. "I have no doubts, High Priestess. Only the will to serve."

A slow smile spread across Evelyn's face. "Then prove it."

A woman stepped forward from the shadows, her hands bound in front of her, her face streaked with tears. Redington felt the slightest tightening in his chest—he had seen this before.

A loyalty test.

"She betrayed our cause," Evelyn said lazily. "She sought to leave us. To warn others about what we do here." Her gaze flickered to him, a trap hiding in the warmth of her expression. "Show your devotion, Rhoan. End her."

The dagger was handed to him. The weight of it was familiar, cold in his palm.

He had been through hell before. But this? This was a different kind of war.

He stepped forward, the woman looking up at him with wild, pleading eyes. She was young, no older than twenty, and shaking uncontrollably. Fear was an ugly thing to witness.

His mind raced. Think. Think. There was no way out of this that didn't end in his own death—unless…

Unless he played her game.

Redington lowered himself until he was at eye level with the woman. He pressed the blade against her throat just enough to break the skin— blood trickled down, warm against his fingers.

Her breath came in short, gasping sobs.

He whispered so quietly that only she could hear. "Fall."

The woman's eyes widened in shock. "Trust me."

Then, with a swift movement, he threw her backward, slicing at her bonds instead of her flesh.

She collapsed onto the stone floor, motionless.

For a long, agonizing moment, no one breathed.

Evelyn's eyes gleamed in the candlelight, studying him. Waiting.

Redington turned back to her, stepping away from the body. "She is dead." His voice was cold, empty. "She was weak. She fell."

The room was silent.

Then Evelyn laughed.

It was low, amused, almost delighted. "Ah, Rhoan. You surprise me."

Her followers cheered, seeing the blood, believing. None of them questioned the motionless girl lying on the cold floor.

Evelyn's eyes, however, never left his.

She knew.

She might not have figured out what he was, but she sensed it now—he was dangerous.

He had won tonight. But his time was running out.

That night, he slipped away to his one safe place—a small chamber hidden within the stronghold's underground halls. There, beneath the stone floors, he had stashed a burner phone, knowing one day he might need it.

That day had come.

His fingers trembled as he typed.

Chapter 34

The city was still in the dead of night, wrapped in a heavy silence that felt unnatural. Even the wind, which usually carried soft whispers through the trees, had stilled.

Lexi lay on her comfy mattress, staring at the ceiling, her body exhausted but her mind racing. Something felt… off.

A familiar pull, deep in her chest, told her that sleep would not be just sleep tonight. Something—or someone—was calling her.

She closed her eyes, surrendering to the weight pressing on her consciousness.

And then—

Lexi stood on the edge of a vast abyss, a canyon so deep she could not see the bottom. Across the chasm, a towering city of golden light shone, floating above the earth, untouched by time. It pulsed like a heartbeat, calling to her.

A bridge of pure energy stretched from her feet toward the city, but it was incomplete—broken in the middle, the gap impossibly wide.

"You cannot cross it alone."

The voice was both thunderous and soft, commanding and gentle.

Lexi turned, already knowing who she would find.

Archangel Pistis Sophia.

She stood there, glowing as before, her robes shimmering between white and gold, her eyes endless pools of knowing. She was not just an angel. She was an archangel.

Lexi felt the weight of her presence settle into her bones. "I don't understand," Lexi whispered.

Pistis Sophia stepped closer, her expression calm but urgent. "There is a path ahead that you cannot walk alone, Lexi. If you try, you will fall. Faith is not just believing—it is knowing when to reach for the hands beside you."

Lexi swallowed, glancing back at the broken bridge. "I've always had faith."

Pistis Sophia tilted her head, her gaze sharp but not unkind. "Have you?"

Suddenly, the ground beneath Lexi shifted. The canyon widened, the golden city seeming farther away. Shadows coiled at the edges, whispering doubts in voices she knew.

"You always push too hard—you're going to break."

"You can't fix this—it's too late."

"You'll lose yourself trying to save me."

"You're not ready for this."

Lexi's chest tightened. She recognized these voices.

Her father.

Her mother.

Redington.

Herself.

The whispers turned into a roar. She clutched her head, dropping to her knees.

"No," she gasped. "This isn't real."

Pistis Sophia knelt beside her, placing a hand over Lexi's heart. "Neither is fear. But you let it guide you anyway."

Lexi felt the warmth of Pistis Sophia's touch seep into her, pushing back the cold. The shadows hissed and recoiled, but they did not vanish.

Pistis Sophia gestured to the bridge. "You are strong, Lexi, but strength alone is not enough. You cannot walk this path by yourself."

Lexi looked up, her throat tight. "Then what do I do?"

Pistis Sophia smiled. "You trust."

A flash of light erupted from her chest, and suddenly, Lexi saw them.

Kesia.

Isabella.

Redington.

They stood at the edge of the canyon beside her, hands outstretched.

She hesitated for only a moment.

Then, she reached for them.

The moment their hands connected, the bridge mended itself. The golden city blazed even brighter, its light banishing the last of the shadows.

Pistis Sophia's voice rang out, echoing across the void.

"The final trial is not one of strength, but of surrender. Find the lost, and you will find the way."

She bolted upright in bed, gasping for air.

Her heart pounded in her chest. The vision was fading, but the feeling remained—a deep knowing.

She wasn't meant to do this alone.

Something small and cool pressed against her palm. She looked down—

A stone etched with the same symbol she had seen on the bridge.

Her breath caught.

It hadn't been a dream.

She clutched the stone to her chest, the last words of Pistis Sophia's prophecy ringing in her ears.

Find the lost, and you will find the way.

She didn't know what it meant yet.

But Lexi knew one thing—she had to go back to the monastery in Nepal.

Chapter 35

The flight to Nepal had been long and tense, the silence between them weighted with unanswered questions. Lexi sat by the window, watching the jagged peaks of the Himalayas break through the thin veil of clouds as the plane began its descent into Kathmandu. Isabella sat beside her, arms crossed and eyes closed, while Kesia absentmindedly twisted the silver ring on her finger, her gaze distant.

None of them had spoken much since they left New York. The shock of what had happened still hung heavy in the air—the girl murdered in front of them, the burner phone, and the name that kept resurfacing like a dark tide.

Evelyn Stone.

The clues had led them back here—to the monastery in Nepal—where it all began. And though none of them could say it out loud, they all felt the same creeping unease. Whatever Evelyn had set into motion, it was unraveling into something far darker than they could imagine.

They had secured last-minute flights out of JFK airport. It had been a risk—leaving New York with so many loose ends—but Lexi knew they wouldn't get answers back home. The truth was waiting for them here, in Nepal.

It was evening by the time they arrived. A familiar sense of heaviness settled over Lexi as they approached the monastery, perched high overlooking the small town. The stone walls, weathered from centuries of wind and prayer, loomed against the backdrop of the mountain.

The heavy wooden gates were slightly ajar when they arrived, a thin stream of light spilling through the crack. Lexi pushed them open and stepped inside, the familiar scent of incense and aged stone washing over her.

Brother Timothy was waiting in the entryway. His lined face was more drawn than Lexi remembered, the deep furrows in his brow speaking of sleepless nights. His eyes sharpened when they met hers.

"You came," he said quietly.

Lexi nodded. "We need answers."

Brother Timothy's gaze swept over them. "Answers are not always kind."

They followed him through the stone corridors, the sound of their footsteps swallowed by the cool, heavy silence of the monastery.

Monks moved through the halls like shadows, heads bowed, whispers trailing behind them. Lexi could feel it in the air—a subtle shift, like the monastery was holding its breath.

Brother Timothy led them into a small chamber off the main hall. Candles flickered against the cold stone walls. He closed the door behind them.

"There have been… disturbances," he said carefully.

"What kind of disturbances?" Lexi asked.

Brother Timothy hesitated. "Monks disappearing for hours without explanation. Whispers of sacred texts are being stolen from the archive. And rumors that an outsider has infiltrated the monastery."

Lexi's stomach tightened. "Do they know who?"

Brother Timothy shook his head. "No. But the fear is growing."

Lexi glanced at Isabella and Kesia. The same thought passed between them without needing to be spoken.

Evelyn.

Lexi's mind drifted back to Pistis Sophia's prophecy. Find the lost, and you will find the way.

If Evelyn had taken something from the monastery, it meant she was somehow connected to this place.

And if they could trace it back to her—
They might finally stop her.

That night, Kesia suggested something reckless.

"We need to follow the monks who keep disappearing."

Lexi and Isabella exchanged looks.
"And if they catch us?" Isabella asked.

Kesia's mouth tightened. "Then we'll know we're onto something."

Still, when the monastery quieted for the night, they waited in the shadows—watching.

It was just after midnight when a small group of monks slipped out from their quarters.

Lexi's pulse quickened as she gestured for them to follow.

They moved silently through the darkened monastery halls, trailing the monks down a narrow corridor lined with faded murals of angels and demons locked in battle. Lexi's fingers brushed the cold stone wall as they turned a corner.

Then the monks stopped in front of an archway Lexi had never noticed before. One of them pressed a hand to the wall. With a low, grinding sound, a hidden door slid open.

Lexi's breath hitched—a hidden chamber.

They slipped inside, the dim flicker of candlelight revealing an underground room lined with ancient carvings. In the center, a wooden chest sat on a pedestal, covered in an ornate cloth embroidered with ancient symbols.

One of the monks stepped forward, his voice hushed but sharp.

"This is the last of them," he said, placing something inside the chest. "Now, we wait."

Kesia's hand brushed against Lexi's arm. "Wait for what?" she whispered.

Lexi shook her head. "I don't know."

Then—

A soft knock echoed through the chamber.

The monks turned toward a side door hidden within the stone wall.

And a voice, smooth as silk, slipped through the darkness.

"You have done well."

Lexi's breath hitched.

From the flicker of candlelight, a figure emerged. The glow danced across the edge of a dark hood as it slipped back, revealing sharp, calculating eyes and a cold smile.

Evelyn Stone.

She was here.

Not just influencing from afar.

Standing in the flesh, shadowed and dangerous.

She had walked into the monastery itself.

Another figure stepped through the shadows—a tall, imposing man with sharp, calculating eyes. The flicker of candlelight caught the angles of his face as his hood slipped back, revealing familiar features that sent a jolt through Lexi's body.

Redington.

His gaze swept over the room, lingering for half a second too long on Lexi and the others hidden in the shadows. His expression remained cold—empty—as though he didn't see her at all.

Lexi's pulse hammered painfully against her chest.

Evelyn smiled faintly.
"Soon," she said.

Then she reached out—and the monk nearest to her placed the chest in her hands.

Lexi's heart clenched. *What was in that chest? And more importantly—*
Why had the monks given it to her willingly?

As Evelyn turned to leave, her gaze flicked toward Lexi's hiding place.

Her smile deepened.
"I see you."

Lexi's breath caught—
But it wasn't Evelyn's gaze that made her freeze.

It was Redington's.

For a brief second, his eyes met hers across the flickering candlelight. His face remained cold, unreadable—but the flicker of recognition in his gaze was unmistakable.

Then he turned and followed Evelyn without a word.

Kesia grabbed Lexi's arm. "Lexi, we need to move."

But Lexi's legs felt rooted to the stone floor as Evelyn's words echoed in her mind.

I see you.

Evelyn knew they were there.
And Redington had seen her too.
He wasn't a captive.
He had *chosen to walk away*.

Chapter 36

The underground chamber grew colder, the air thick with unseen energy as Evelyn Stone's voice cut through the dim candlelight.

Lexi's pulse pounded in her ears as she pressed deeper into the shadows, watching the scene unfold.

She's here.

Not a distant threat.

Not a whispered danger lurking beyond reach.

She had walked into the monastery itself.

The weight of her power.

The way she twisted energy around her like an unseen force.

Lexi couldn't believe that it was one of the monks—one of their own—who had stepped forward, his face illuminated by candlelight.

Lexi's stomach tightened at the memory.

She knew him.

Brother Elias.

A man who had once spoken of faith with such unwavering devotion that Lexi had admired him.

Now, he was with Evelyn.

Lexi's fingers dug into Isabella's wrist. "They're working with her," she whispered.

Her jaw tightened. "Not all of them. But enough."

Enough to tip the balance.

Enough to destroy the monastery from within.

The three ladies followed Evelyn.

Lexi barely dared to breathe as Evelyn slowly lifted the cloth, revealing what had been hidden inside the chest.

A sacred text.

Ancient.

Bound in worn, handwritten pages, its leather cover darkened with age.

Lexi recognized it immediately.

She had studied its teachings.

Had prayed over its words.

It was one of the monastery's most sacred volumes—one that should never have left the archives.

Kesia's voice echoed in her memory.

"If they start believing the monastery is tainted… they'll crumble from the inside."

This was the final move.

Not brute force.

Not destruction.

Corruption.

And Evelyn was winning.

Lexi clenched her fists.

Not if we stop her.

Lexi barely had time to process the gravity of what was happening when Isabella shifted beside her.

Her muscles tensed.

She recognized the look in her eyes.

Determination.

Calculated risk.

Reckless intent.

No—

She grabbed her arm, but she was already moving.

Stepping from the shadows.

Into the candlelight.

Into Evelyn's line of sight.

Lexi's breath caught in her throat.

The monks staggered back, startled.

Elias' eyes went wide.

Evelyn simply smiled.

"Ah," she murmured, tilting her head. "I was wondering when you'd stop hiding."

Isabella's stance remained rigid, her expression unreadable. "We both know why I'm here."

Evelyn exhaled softly as if amused. "Yes," she agreed. "You're here because you still don't understand."

She reached for the book, turning its delicate pages with reverence. "You think I'm corrupting faith," she mused. "That I'm distorting what is sacred."

Her gaze lifted, meeting Isabella's directly.

"You're wrong."

Lexi stepped forward, heart pounding. "You're manipulating them. Twisting their beliefs to serve your agenda."

Evelyn smiled again—a knowing, patient smile.

"As all leaders do."

Her voice was calm.

But power rippled beneath it.

Lexi felt it in her bones.

The way the energy shifted.

The way Evelyn's presence commanded the air itself.

"You don't like the truth, do you?" Evelyn continued, her voice almost gentle. "That belief is… fluid. People crave structure. They crave something bigger than themselves. And when they find it… they will follow."

Lexi's hands curled into fists.

This wasn't just about power.

It was about control.

And Evelyn had mastered it.

The monks were listening to her.

Some of them were nodding.

No.

Lexi's breath shuddered.

She thought of Pistis Sophia's words—

"Faith is not the absence of fear. It is the courage to move forward despite it."

She stepped in front of Isabella, her voice steady.

"You're right," Lexi admitted. "Faith is powerful."

She let the words linger.

"But faith built on fear isn't faith at all."

Something flickered in Evelyn's gaze.

For the first time, a crack in her perfect certainty.

Lexi pressed forward.

"The ones who follow you?" she continued. "They're not free. They're afraid. And you… you need their fear."

The candle flames flickered violently.

Lexi wasn't just speaking words.

She was shifting the energy in the room.

Evelyn's grip on the book tightened.

"You're stronger than this," Lexi said, turning to Elias. "All of you are. You don't need her."

The monks hesitated.

A single moment of doubt.

And in that moment—

Evelyn moved.

A sharp, forceful wave of energy exploded outward, knocking Lexi, Isabella, and Kesia off their feet.

Lexi barely had time to brace herself as she hit the cold stone floor.

Evelyn's voice rang out, laced with power and fury.

"I offered you a choice," she hissed. "And you reject it?"

She raised a hand—

Lexi felt the force pressing against her chest, constricting.

Redington stepped forward. "Let her go!"

Evelyn's gaze snapped to him.

"Ah, Agent Redington," she murmured. "Always so eager to save someone else."

A dark smile curled at her lips.

"But who will save you?"

The air seemed to shatter.

Lexi's vision blurred.

Darkness swallowed the chamber.

And then—

Chapter 37

The next room was bathed in darkness, yet Evelyn saw everything.

The flickering candles cast dancing shadows, their movement rhythmic, alive—whispering secrets only she could hear.

She knelt before the sacred altar, her fingers tracing the lines of an ancient text. Its ink faded, but the meaning was clear.

The prophecy was nearly complete.

She had seen it in her visions.

The world was on the brink of evolution.

But first—

The old had to be destroyed so the new could be born.

Evelyn exhaled, lifting her gaze toward the towering blackened statue in the corner of the chamber. It depicted a faceless figure, hands outstretched, welcoming the future.

The true Enlightened One.

The world did not understand.

They called her a cult leader.

They called her dangerous.

They whispered that she was mad, that her teachings were twisted, that her path led only to destruction.

But they were blind.

She alone had the vision to see beyond illusion.

The weak clung to faith, to outdated myths of "light" and "salvation."

But true enlightenment was not found in the light.

It was in embracing the shadow.

Only through chaos could the world be reborn.

And yet—

For all her certainty, there were moments… whispers in the night…

A creeping unease that slithered through the cracks in her mind.

She had been told long ago that there were two interpretations of the prophecy.

Two sides.

She had chosen hers.

But was it right?

Evelyn's fingers tightened into a fist, nails digging into her palm.

She couldn't afford doubt.

Not now.

Not when she had come so far.

Not when Lexi and her misguided faith stood in the way.

Lexi.

The girl who was meant to stand beside her, not against her.

She had seen her in visions for years—

Another woman, filled with light, guided by faith, who would one day challenge her.

It had always been Lexi.

It had always been this battle.

But Evelyn would not lose.

She was stronger.

She understood what needed to be done.

Lexi still clung to foolish ideals—faith, love, trust—weaknesses that would break her in the end.

Evelyn rose to her feet, her resolve hardening like steel.

She would finish this.

Lexi had her faith.

Evelyn had the truth.

One would survive.

One would fall.

And Evelyn knew which side was destined to win.

Chapter 38

The chamber erupted with energy.

As Lexi entered, she gasped, struggling for air as an invisible force pressed against her chest—crushing, suffocating, like unseen hands wrapping around her lungs.

Evelyn's dark presence loomed, her fingers twitching as if she were controlling the very air around them.

"Faith can move mountains," Evelyn whispered mockingly. "But what happens when the mountain moves against you?"

Redington lunged.

Faster than Lexi thought possible, he threw himself forward, aiming to break Evelyn's focus.

But with a flick of her wrist, he froze mid-air, suspended as if gravity had betrayed him.

"You think brute force will change anything?" Evelyn murmured, tilting her head. "I expected more from you, Agent Redington."

She clenched her hand.

Redington crashed to the floor.

The impact was brutal—his body colliding hard against the cold stone. He groaned, rolling onto his side, pain written across his face.

Lexi fought against the invisible force holding her down, every instinct screaming to move—but Evelyn's power was suffocating, like a weight pressing her deeper into darkness.

This wasn't just energy manipulation.

This was domination.

Pure, unchecked control.

Evelyn smiled.

"You came here thinking you had power," she said, walking forward, her movements slow, deliberate. "That your faith would protect you."

She crouched beside Lexi, her voice soft and venomous.

"But faith without understanding?" Evelyn whispered. "That's just... blind obedience."

Lexi's chest ached.

The pressure tightened—her lungs burned—her vision blurred—

No.

This wasn't how it ended.

Lexi clenched her fists, forcing herself to remember—

The warmth of Pistis Sophia's light.

The strength of her friends.

The truth buried beneath fear.

She closed her eyes.

And let go.

Not of her fight.

Not of her purpose.

But of her fear.

The moment she did, something shifted.

A pulse of pure energy exploded outward from within Lexi like a shockwave of light.

Evelyn staggered back, her eyes flashing in surprise.

The force around Lexi vanished.

She gasped, inhaling deep, ragged breaths.

Evelyn's gaze darkened. "Interesting," she mused. "You're stronger than I thought."

Lexi rose to her feet, her body trembling but unbroken.

Redington pushed himself up beside her, wiping blood from the corner of his mouth.

"You okay?" he muttered.

Lexi nodded, eyes locked on Evelyn.

Something was different now.

She could feel it.

The energy in the chamber wasn't just Evelyn's.

It was theirs, too.

Kesia.

Isabella.

Redington.

And the monks who had lost their way.

They were all here, woven together in something greater.

Evelyn's power had been built on fear and control.

But Lexi's?

Lexi's power came from faith, trust, and light. And that difference…

That was Evelyn's greatest weakness.

Evelyn's expression shifted—for the first time, a flicker of uncertainty.

"You think your faith makes you invincible?" she scoffed. "Let's see how far that gets you."

She raised her hands, energy crackling between her fingertips.

Lexi didn't hesitate.

She reached inside herself—not for power, but for connection.

For the light, Pistis Sophia had shown her.

For the faith that didn't require sight.

The chamber shuddered, energy colliding in unseen currents.

Evelyn's darkness surged.

Lexi's light rose to meet it.

Chapter 39

The chamber shook as opposing forces clashed—light and darkness colliding in a battle far greater than any of them had imagined.

Evelyn's power lashed out, tendrils of shadow twisting toward Lexi like living serpents. The air crackled with energy, its force making the very ground tremble.

Lexi stood firm.

Not because she wasn't afraid.

But because faith isn't the absence of fear—it's the decision to move forward despite it.

She remembered Pistis Sophia's words, the vision, the warning…

And she knew what had to be done.

Kesia, Isabella, and Redington formed a protective triad of energy, their collective force pushing against Evelyn's shadows, holding the darkness at bay.

But Evelyn was stronger than they anticipated.

Redington moved swiftly, attempting to get behind her, but with a flick of her wrist, he was flung backward, slamming into the stone wall with a sickening crack.

"No!" Lexi cried out, reaching toward him.

Evelyn's laughter echoed through the chamber. Cold. Mocking. Endless.

"You're all so predictable," she sneered. "You think love and faith make you powerful? They make you weak."

Lexi gritted her teeth, her heart pounding.

No.

Love wasn't a weakness.

It was the reason she was still standing.

And she would prove it.

A sudden memory of Pistis Sophia's dream flooded Lexi's mind—

The light battling the darkness—
The moment when everything would hinge on a single choice—
The mark she hadn't understood… until now.

Lexi glanced down at her hands—

A faint golden symbol was glowing on her palm.

The same one Pistis Sophia had pressed into her dream.

A gift.

A key.

The realization slammed into her.

This was never about fighting Evelyn with force.

This was about overcoming her with something she could never understand—faith without fear.

Lexi's eyes lifted, and she walked straight toward Evelyn.

Evelyn's power lashed out at her, shadows surging forward like a storm—

But they never touched her.

The moment they reached Lexi's aura, they dissolved into light.

Evelyn staggered back, eyes wide.

"No—" she hissed. "That's not possible."

Lexi kept walking.

Closer.

Evelyn's control was slipping.

Lexi could see it.

The cracks in her certainty.

The panic beneath the power.

"You don't understand, do you?" Lexi whispered, stopping just a breath away.

Evelyn tried one last time—her power surged, desperation in her every move—

Lexi reached forward.

And touched her palm to Evelyn's chest.

Light exploded.

A wave of pure faith.

Evelyn screamed—her shadows shattering like glass.

Her form began to dissolve, her darkness unraveling into nothingness.

And then—

Silence.
The energy died down.
The room was still.
Lexi stumbled back, breathing hard.
The others stared in shock.
Evelyn Stone… was gone.
Only a faint echo of darkness remained, fading into nothing.

Lexi swayed, exhaustion crashing into her like a tidal wave—but before she could fall, Redington was there, catching her.

His arms wrapped around her, steady and strong.

"You did it," he whispered.

Lexi leaned into him, her heart still racing.

"We did it," she corrected, looking at all of them.

Isabella, Kesia, Redington, the monks.
The ones who had fought beside her.
Who had never let go of their faith.
The battle was over.
But their journey?
Was far from finished.

Chapter 40

The monastery's sacred chamber was silent,
save for the slow, rhythmic drip of water from
the stone ceiling. Lexi stood alone, the dim
torchlight flickering against the ancient walls.

She had felt the shift in energy the moment
she stepped inside. This was her trial.

The air grew heavy, charged with something
unseen, something that coiled deep in her chest.

Then—

A figure emerged from the darkness.

Her own face stared back at her.

But it wasn't her.

It was Evelyn Stone.

But no.

It was Lexi, twisted into Evelyn's form.

Her own voice—smooth, confident, cold—
spoke from the figure before her.

"You already know the truth, don't you?"

Lexi's stomach twisted.

"You feel it. That power inside you."

"You think you're different from me, but you're not."

The figure stepped closer, eyes gleaming with knowing.

"How long before you realize that faith is just another way to control?"

Lexi shook her head. "I'm not like you."

"Aren't you?" The reflection smiled. "You crave power, Lexi. And the more you use it, the more you'll realize—it was never faith that made you strong. It was always you."

Lexi staggered back, her breath unsteady.

Was it true?

Had she relied on her own will instead of true faith?

The room blurred, shifting around her. She saw visions—herself standing atop a burning city, followers kneeling before her, waiting for her command.

It was terrifying.

And intoxicating.

She felt it pulling at her, an invisible force beckoning her forward.

Then—

A voice cut through the illusion.

"Faith is not about power, Lexi. Faith is surrender."

The words rippled through her.

The voice—Pistis Sophia.

Lexi's heart steadied.

She wasn't Evelyn.

She never would be.

Her power wasn't meant to control—it was meant to heal.

Lexi took a breath, lifted her hands, and let go of the fear.

The reflection shattered like glass, the illusion dissolving into golden light.

She had passed her trial.

Chapter 41

Kesia stood alone before the ancestral shrine, her heart pounding. The stone carvings around her seemed to pulse with an energy she could not explain, as if the very walls of the monastery were watching her, judging her.

Her trial had begun.

A cold wind rushed through the chamber, though no doors had opened. The flickering light of the oil lamps dimmed until only shadows remained.

Then—

A voice, clear and piercing.

"You do not belong here."

Kesia turned sharply.

A woman stood before her, wrapped in ceremonial robes, her posture rigid, her expression unreadable. Her presence commanded authority, yet there was something deeply familiar about her.

Kesia knew instantly who this was.

Her ancestor.

The air grew thick, pressing down on her chest.

"You have strayed too far from your roots," the woman said, her voice carrying an eerie weight. "You have forgotten the wisdom of those who came before."

Kesia's throat tightened. "That's not true. I honor my past."

The woman's gaze darkened. "Do you?" Shadows flickered across her face. "Or have you abandoned it in favor of illusions?"

Kesia took a step forward, but the ground beneath her cracked, splitting into jagged fragments. A deep chasm yawned before her, separating her from the woman.

Then—

The visions began.

The Ghosts of Her Past

Images flashed through Kesia's mind—scenes from her past unraveling like an old film.

She saw herself as a child, sitting at her grandmother's feet, listening to stories of ancient wisdom—stories she had dismissed as superstition.

She saw the day she turned away from a spiritual path, too skeptical to embrace the teachings of her ancestors.

She saw the moments she had ignored her intuition, where she had chosen the easy path instead of the right one.

She saw her greatest failure—a moment when she had hesitated when she should have acted.

Then, the visions shifted.

She saw herself in the future—alone, wandering, lost in a fog of regret.

No connection to her past. No guiding light. No purpose.

The weight of it crushed her.

"You think you have power?" The woman's voice was like a thunderclap. "It is nothing compared to what you have lost."

The shadows deepened, swallowing Kesia's surroundings.

"You will fail." The voice resonated all around her. "Just as I did."

The words hit like a blow, knocking the air from Kesia's lungs.

The Breaking Point

A great weight pressed down on her, forcing her to her knees.

Doubt crawled into her mind, whispering the fears she had long avoided.

"You are not strong enough."

"You will never live up to your ancestors."

"You were never meant to succeed."

The voices grew louder, circling her like a storm.

The chasm widened, and her ancestor turned away, her back disappearing into the void.

Kesia reached out—but stopped.

Her breath shook.

This was it.

The moment that defined her.

Would she surrender to the weight of her past?

Would she allow it to chain her forever?

Or—

Would she forge her own path forward?

A memory surfaced—one she hadn't thought of in years.

A Voice from the Past

Her grandmother's voice, gentle but firm,

"Strength is not in never falling, Kesia. Strength is in standing up again."

Tears pricked at Kesia's eyes.

How many times had she let herself be held back by fear?

How many times had she refused to trust herself?

She had spent years looking outward for validation, for proof that she was worthy of her gifts.

But now—

She understood.

Her power wasn't something granted to her by others.

It had always been hers.

And it always would be.

Kesia lifted her head.

The doubt was still there, lingering like smoke.

But she refused to let it control her.

She pressed her hands together, feeling the warmth of her own energy building.

"I will not be bound by the past."

A golden light began to pulse from her palms, soft at first, then brighter, burning away the darkness around her.

The shadows recoiled, their whispers turning to static before fading completely.

The chasm sealed. The ground beneath her grew steady once more.

Kesia exhaled, the weight lifting from her shoulders.

For the first time, her ancestor smiled.

"Then walk forward, child. And carry our wisdom with you."

The trial was over.

A warmth spread through Kesia's chest—not just relief, but something stronger.

A clarity she had never known before.

She had passed.

And she would never doubt herself again.

Chapter 42

Redington stepped into the darkness.

No torches. No walls.
Just the weight of silence.
Then—
A voice.
"You let us die."
The shadows shifted, forming figures.
Redington's breath caught in his throat.
He knew them.
Faces from past cases—victims he had failed
to save.
They stood before him, their expressions
vacant, their eyes hollow.
"You swore to protect us."
"You swore you'd find the truth."
"Where were you?"
The voices layered over each other, growing
louder. Angry.

Redington's chest tightened. He had carried this guilt for years, but standing before them, it was suffocating.

"I tried." His voice was hoarse. "I did everything I could."

The crowd shifted, revealing a small child at the center.

A girl.

Her pale face was streaked with dirt. Her wide, unblinking eyes stared into his soul.

"Was it enough?"

The words hit like a punch.

No.

It had never been enough.

The shadows thickened, wrapping around his legs like chains, pulling him down.

"You failed us."

"You abandoned us."

"You let them win."

The whispers became screams, pounding against his skull.

Memories flooded his mind—

—A woman begging him to save her child.

—A suspect he had let slip away—only to kill again.

—A case that had gone cold, the family left broken.

The faces in the shadows multiplied, surrounding him.

He could feel their pain, their anger, their hopelessness.

And the worst part?

They weren't wrong.

Redington fell to his knees, his breathing ragged.

This was what haunted him.

Not the killers.

Not the cases.

But the people left behind.

"I should have done more," he whispered, his fingers curling into fists. "I should have been stronger."

The girl stepped forward, her bare feet silent against the void.

She reached out, touching his forehead.

A chilling wave of grief coursed through him.

The years of regret, the endless weight of loss— threatened to consume him.

"And what will you do now?"

The question froze him.

Because he didn't know.

For years, his guilt had driven him—chasing justice, trying to balance the scales.

But he had never found peace.

And if he couldn't let go of the past, how could he fight for the future?

Redington closed his eyes.

He breathed in. Steady. Strong.

The answer came—not from logic but from something deeper.

"I cannot change the past."

The shadows wavered.

"But I can fight for the future."

His words rippled through the darkness like light breaking through storm clouds.

The shadows hesitated, then began to dissolve.

One by one, the figures vanished.

The voices faded.

Only the girl remained.

She smiled.

"Then go, Redington. And do not carry our weight anymore."

Her small hand lifted, pressing against his heart.

The darkness shattered.

A rush of warmth flooded his chest—like the first breath of air after drowning.

He opened his eyes.

He was alone.

The trial was over.

But for the first time in years—

Redington felt lighter.

Chapter 43

The morning air was crisp, carrying the scent of damp earth and pine as Lexi, Isabella, Kesia, and Redington set out from the monastery. Their steps were quiet, deliberate. There was no idle chatter between them—only the shared understanding that Sophea was missing.

And wherever she was, she had left them much of a trail to follow.

The direction they took led them through the dense forest, the towering trees arching overhead like silent sentinels. Sunlight filtered through in broken streams, painting shifting patterns on the ground. The damp earth beneath their feet was uneven, the trail narrow and winding.

Lexi followed Redington, walking with steady confidence though her mind was a storm of thoughts. Sophea wouldn't have left without reason. She was more than just a spiritual guide—she was a pillar of strength. If she had disappeared, it meant one of two things, she was either in danger or searching for something she couldn't share.

Redington kept scanning their surroundings with the instincts of a detective. He had been in countless situations like this before—tracking missing people, chasing leads—but this was different. There was an energy here, something beyond logic. He could feel it pressing against the edges of his mind.

They walked for hours, the silence between them thick, charged with anticipation.

Isabella, usually quick to offer a sharp remark or observation, was uncharacteristically quiet. She had never been one to put faith in unseen forces, but Sophea's absence unsettled her in a way she couldn't explain. She should be here.

Kesia trailed slightly behind Lexi, her thoughts heavy. She was still reeling from her trial, from the visions that had tested the foundation of her beliefs. But there was no time to dwell on self-doubt. Sophea was part of their journey, part of their spiritual bond, and she wasn't about to let uncertainty keep her from finding her.

The trees thinned as they reached a plateau, and the valley below stretched out before them—a vast expanse of rolling hills, the river winding like a silver vein through the landscape. Nestled between the trees stood a temple.

A solitary structure, carved from stone and aged by time.

Lexi exhaled, feeling a strange sense of both relief and unease.

"She's been here," she murmured. "I know it."

Their pace quickening.

The air changed as they stepped onto the temple grounds. It was still—too still. The kind of silence that didn't just feel peaceful but expectant.

The temple itself was simple. No doors. No locks. Just open stone pillars holding up the structure, the scent of incense lingering in the air. It had once been a place of sanctuary, but today, it felt like something was waiting beneath the surface.

Isabella swept the area with her gaze. "If she came here, why leave? This place feels…" She hesitated, searching for the word.

"Abandoned," Redington supplied.

Lexi shook her head. "No. She left something."

Her eyes scanned the temple until they landed on the altar.

A small, polished stone rested on its surface, its smooth black surface reflecting the candlelight. A symbol was etched into it—one she recognized instantly.

Kesia stepped closer. "Isn't that—?"

Lexi picked it up, running her fingers over the familiar carving. "Yes. It's one of the sacred waypoints. Markers for those who walk the spiritual path."

Redington crossed his arms. "Then she left it here for us."

Lexi nodded, her grip tightening around the stone. "She's guiding us."

But to what?

The realization sent a shiver through her.

Sophea wasn't just missing—she was leading them toward something.

And whatever it was…

It wasn't over yet.

Chapter 44

The sun dipped lower on the horizon, casting a golden glow over the path as Lexi, Isabella, Kesia, and Redington pressed deeper into the wilderness. Each step forward felt like walking into the unknown, guided only by the stone marker Sophea had left behind.

Lexi absently ran her fingers over the smooth surface of the polished stone in her pocket, feeling its cool weight against her palm. This was no ordinary path. It was deliberate, intentional—leading them toward something Sophea had wanted them to find. But what?

The ancient forest surrounding them was alive in ways that words couldn't capture. It whispered. Not in an audible way, but in something deeper—in the rustling of the leaves, the shifting of the wind, the strange pull beneath their feet as though the earth itself guided them forward.

The feeling was unmistakable.

They were being watched.

Redington's sharp gaze swept the treetops. He walked ahead, his body language alert, his instincts on high. Years as an investigator had honed his senses—there was someone, or something, out there. But what unsettled him most was that he couldn't tell whether the presence was hostile or waiting.

Isabella broke the silence first. "Does anyone else feel that?"

Kesia's brow furrowed. "Like we're not alone?"

Lexi inhaled deeply. "I feel it, too."

A sound.

Not footsteps. Not a voice. A murmur. A sound that wasn't quite there, yet unmistakable in the way it curled at the edges of their consciousness.

Redington turned sharply, his hand instinctively reaching toward his belt. No gun. He wasn't carrying one here. He exhaled, forcing his mind back to the present. "There's something ahead," he murmured.

They had no choice but to follow.

The whispering grew clearer as they climbed a narrow, rocky trail, their steps echoing against the stone.

The trees thinned, revealing a breathtaking vista—a vast valley stretching beneath them, a silver river carving its way through the landscape. But Lexi barely noticed.

Because Sophea was standing there.

She stood at the edge of the outcrop, her back to them, staring out over the valley. The orange light of sunset silhouetted her form, her simple robes fluttering slightly in the breeze.

She did not turn immediately when Lexi called out.

"Sophea!"

A pause.

Then, slowly, she turned to face them.

Lexi felt something shift in the air—a presence, an energy, something beyond explanation.

Sophea looked... different.

She was still the woman they had known—the wise teacher, the steadfast guide—but there was a sadness in her gaze, a weight that had not been there before.

Lexi stepped closer, cautious. "Sophea... what's happening?"

Sophea smiled softly, but it didn't reach her eyes. "You came."

Lexi's chest tightened. "Of course we did. We've been looking for you. Why did you leave the monastery?"

Sophea lowered her gaze, her hands folding together. "Because there were answers I could not find within the monastery's walls."

Isabella's arms crossed, her suspicion evident. "Answers about what?"

Sophea sighed, turning her gaze back toward the valley. "This forest… it speaks to those who know how to listen. It has whispered to me of things that are yet to come. Things that cannot be ignored."

Redington stepped forward. "What kind of things?"

For a moment, Sophea did not answer. Then—

"The war has already begun."

Lexi's breath hitched. "What war?"

Sophea turned fully to face them now. Her eyes held something ancient. Something knowing.

"The war for the soul."

Silence.

Then—

Kesia swallowed. "You mean Evelyn's cult."

Sophea nodded. "Their reach is growing. But it is not just them. The monastery is not the only place where the balance is being tested. There are forces beyond what you or I have prepared for."

Lexi shook her head. "If you knew this, why didn't you tell us?"

Sophea stepped closer, looking directly into Lexi's eyes. "Because you were not ready."

A shiver ran through Lexi's spine. "And now?"

Sophea's smile was faint but resolute. "Now, you are."

Sophea gestured toward the valley below. "This is where I have come to listen. The answers are not in books, not even in the sacred texts. They are in the energy that flows through all things."

Isabella's skepticism flared. "And what have you heard?"

Sophea's face grew somber. "The bonds that hold faith together are being tested. Fear is spreading. Doubt is being sown. This is how corruption begins—not with violence, but with hesitation. With division."

Redington exhaled sharply. "Then we need to move fast."

Sophea nodded. "Yes. But first, you must understand—this fight is not only external. It is internal."

Lexi swallowed. "What do you mean?"

Sophea's gaze was piercing. "The battle for faith is fought in the heart before it is fought in the world."

Her words settled over them like a weight.

Kesia spoke, her voice quiet. "And what happens if we lose?"

Sophea's smile was almost imperceptible.

"Then the world loses, too."

A chill ran through them.

Lexi, her fingers tightening around the stone marker in her pocket, finally asked, "What do we do now?"

Sophea stepped back, her presence as steady as the earth beneath them.

"Return to the monastery."

Kesia frowned. "And then?"

Sophea's eyes darkened slightly. "Prepare."

Chapter 45

The journey back to the monastery felt profoundly different than the one that had led them into the forest. The fear and uncertainty that had lingered over them like a storm cloud had been replaced by something steadier—purpose.

With Sophea walking among them once more, the tension that had once gnawed at the edges of their resolve had eased. Yet, in its place, a new weight had settled in. They had uncovered truths in the forest—truths that had set them on an irreversible course.

The whispers that had once carried an eerie, unknowable energy now seemed softer—not warnings, but reassurances. The rustling leaves, the sway of the branches overhead, the cool breeze curling around them—it was as though the land itself acknowledged their newfound understanding, offering silent encouragement.

Lexi felt a deep connection to it all. She had always known that energy flowed through all things, but here, in the presence of something greater than herself, she felt it—a living current weaving through the world, unseen but undeniably real.

Her gaze drifted to Sophea, who walked a few steps ahead, serene but unreadable.

Had she always known? Had she foreseen this journey from the very start?

As the sun began to set, streaking the sky in shades of gold and violet, the monastery's silhouette emerged in the distance. What should have brought relief instead sent a wave of unease crawling up Lexi's spine.

Something was wrong.

Brother Timothy stood at the entrance, waiting for them. The relief in his expression was immediate, but so was the exhaustion lining his face.

"You've returned," he said, his voice thick with emotion. "Thank the heavens."

Sophea offered a gentle, knowing smile. "We had to seek answers in the forest, Brother Timothy. There are forces at work that we must confront together."

Timothy's gaze darkened. "I fear you are right. Things have only grown worse in your absence."

Lexi's stomach tightened. "What's happened?"

"The monks are on edge. Paranoia has taken hold. Small disputes have turned into conflicts, whispers of distrust growing among those who were once brothers. And… the disturbances continue."

Sophea's eyes flashed with understanding as if she had expected nothing less. "Then we must act quickly."

Brother Timothy nodded. "Come. Everyone is waiting."

The monastery halls felt different.

The silence was tense, no longer the sacred stillness of a meditative refuge but something fractured. They passed monks moving through the corridors, their nods polite but cautious, their eyes carrying a weight of suspicion.

By the time they entered the main hall, the tension had thickened like smoke.

The monks were already gathered, their hushed conversations ceasing as Sophea stepped forward. All eyes turned to her.

She did not hesitate.

"My brothers," she began, her voice calm but carrying a quiet authority. "We are facing a trial unlike any other."

She let the silence settle before continuing.

"The disturbances we have seen are not random. They are not a coincidence. They are deliberate. Someone, or something, is working to unbalance us—to drive wedges between us, to turn our own fear against us."

Murmurs spread, flickering like embers in dry grass.

Sophea raised a hand. The room fell silent again.

"We must remember that our strength has never come from isolation nor from fear. Our strength comes from unity. From faith."

Lexi felt a subtle shift in the room. Hope trying to push through doubt.

Redington stepped forward next. "We have reason to believe that some of the new initiates may be involved—whether knowingly or as pawns in a larger scheme. But we must be careful. Reckless accusations will only serve the very forces trying to divide us."

Isabella followed, her tone measured but firm. "The first step is rebuilding trust. We must move forward not in fear but in awareness. We cannot fight darkness with darkness."

Kesia, quiet up until now, lifted her gaze. "This is only the beginning."

The words sent a chill through Lexi's spine.

Kesia's voice was steady. "This is not just about this monastery. What we are experiencing here is a reflection of a much larger battle. One that is not just physical, but spiritual."

A ripple of understanding passed through the room.

Sophea nodded. "And that is why we must stand firm. We will begin with what has always made us strong—our practices, our discipline, our unity. We will meditate together. We will eat together. And we will face the unknown not with fear, but with clarity.”

She turned to the monks, her gaze filled with certainty.

“The choice is ours. We can fall into the chaos that seeks to consume us. Or we can stand together and emerge stronger.”

For a moment, silence.

Then—

A single nod.

Another.

A ripple through the crowd as a shared determination took root.

They were not broken.

They were not divided.

As the monks dispersed, Sophea’s expression shifted.

She turned to Lexi, Isabella, Kesia, and Redington, lowering her voice.

“There is something I haven’t shared with the others yet,” she said quietly.

Lexi’s pulse quickened. “What is it?”

Sophea hesitated only a second before speaking.

“While I was in the forest, I received a vision. A warning.”

Redington’s jaw clenched. “What did you see?”

Sophea's eyes darkened. "A final trial. A test that will determine everything. It will not come from outside. It will come from within."

Lexi felt the weight of those words settle in her chest. "Within… you mean—"

Sophea nodded. "The enemy was not just Evelyn. The final teacher is on their way. And when they arrive, our greatest battle will begin."

Kesia exhaled sharply. "Who is this final teacher?"

Sophea's voice was solemn.

"I do not know their face. Only their presence."

She looked toward the monastery doors, where the last light of day faded into the night.

"And they are almost here."

Chapter 46

The following days at the monastery carried an air of renewed purpose. With Sophea's guidance, the community had returned to their sacred practices—daily meditations, communal meals, and open discussions meant to rebuild trust. The disturbances that had once shaken the monastery had lessened, but an unspoken tension still hung over them. It was the kind of stillness before a storm, a breath held in anticipation of something inevitable.

Lexi, Isabella, Kesia, and Redington immersed themselves in monastery life, learning and observing as much as they could. Yet, beneath the routines, they never lost sight of the warning Sophea had given them. The final trial was coming.

And then, it began.

One afternoon, during a quiet meditation session, a knock at the monastery's main doors echoed through the hall.

Brother Timothy, his brows furrowing, rose to answer. Visitors were rare.

When he returned, his expression was unreadable—a mix of surprise, reverence, and something else entirely.

"There is someone here to see you," he announced. "He says he's been sent to guide you."

Lexi and the others exchanged glances. They weren't expecting anyone.

They rose to follow Brother Timothy, stepping into the dimly lit hallway—and froze.

A man stood at the entrance, dressed in dark robes, his posture effortless yet commanding. His presence filled the space like a quiet storm.

Lexi's breath caught.

Dorian.

"Dorian?" Lexi's voice was barely above a whisper, but the shock in it was undeniable.

Isabella and Kesia exchanged stunned glances while Redington's expression hardened into curiosity.

"What are you doing here?" Redington asked, his gaze sharp. "We left you back in the States. How did you find us?"

Dorian smiled—not in amusement, but in knowing.

"I told you before, Lexi, our paths are intertwined. I may have been in the United

States when we last spoke, but this journey is not bound by geography."

Lexi felt a shiver crawl up her spine. She knew Dorian was more than he appeared, but this? This was something else.

Sophea, who had never met him before, observed the interaction with quiet intrigue. "You know each other?"

Lexi nodded. "Dorian was a spiritual guide for us back in the U.S. He helped us when we needed him most."

"And now you need me again," Dorian said, his eyes locking onto hers. "The work we started isn't finished. Your journey has led you here, and so has mine."

Redington's eyes narrowed. "How did you know we were here?"

Dorian's smile deepened. "The journey of the soul is not linear, Redington. It is guided by forces beyond our understanding. The same forces that led you here led me as well."

Sophea studied him for a long moment, then nodded. "If Lexi and the others trust you, then I trust you as well."

A quiet certainty settled over the group.

Dorian was meant to be here.

Dorian took his place at the center of the hall, facing them.

"I have come to offer guidance," he said. "But also to prepare you. The final trials are approaching, and they will test you in ways you cannot yet imagine."

Lexi's stomach tightened. She already knew this.

"What kind of trials?" Isabella asked.

Dorian's gaze darkened slightly. "Both external and internal. You will face not only the challenges before you but the ones within you—the doubts, the fears, the shadows that linger in your souls."

A heavy silence settled between them.

"The monastery itself will become a crucible," Dorian continued. "Each of you has grown in strength and wisdom, but there is more to learn. The first trial will begin here."

Sophea stepped forward. "We have faced many tests, but this… this feels different."

Dorian met her gaze. "Because it is."

Lexi took a steadying breath. "What do we do?"

Dorian's expression softened slightly. "First, you must understand that this is no ordinary trial. This is a test of faith, of trust, of unity. You must be willing to see beyond your own perceptions."

Kesia, her voice quiet but firm, spoke next. "If we're going to do this, we need to be fully honest with each other."

Dorian nodded in approval. "Exactly. The path to enlightenment is paved with truth. Doubt and secrecy will only weaken you."

Redington exhaled, rolling his shoulders as if preparing for battle. "Then let's get started."

Dorian's gaze lingered on him. "You are ready."

But then, his eyes shifted to Lexi.

"Are you?"

Lexi's heart pounded.

She was ready.

But something deep inside whispered,

The hardest part is yet to come.

Chapter 47

The morning after Dorian's arrival, the monastery was charged with an eerie stillness. The group knew their journey was entering a critical phase, but something still felt unresolved—like a shadow lingering just beyond sight.

For Lexi, that shadow had a name.

David.

The young monk had been avoiding eye contact ever since he buried the talisman in the garden.

The previous night, Lexi had spoken with Isabella, Kesia, and Redington about it, and they had all agreed—David wasn't the enemy, but he was hiding something important.

The time had come for the truth.

Lexi found David standing apart from the others in the main hall. His usual calm demeanor had been replaced with anxious tension—his hands fidgeting, his breath coming too fast.

She stepped toward him, her voice gentle but firm.

"David."

He flinched but didn't turn away.

"We need to talk."

His eyes darted to her, then to the others. "I…" His throat bobbed as he swallowed hard. "I know."

Lexi lowered her voice. "We know about the talisman. But I don't think we know everything, do we?"

David exhaled shakily, then gave a slow nod. "No. You don't."

Lexi gestured for him to follow her to a quieter part of the hall. The others gathered nearby, giving him space but making it clear— they were here to listen.

David sank onto the bench, rubbing his hands together. "It's not just a symbol of protection as you may believe," he admitted. His voice trembled. "It's something much darker."

Lexi's heart thudded in her chest. She had suspected this.

"Go on," she urged.

David closed his eyes for a moment. Then the truth spilled out.

"The Evelyn Stone's cult approached me before I ever came here," he said, his voice thick with emotion. "I was lost… I had nothing. They told me the talisman would give me strength, that it would help me control my emotions, protect myself from harm."

He let out a bitter laugh. "But I didn't know it was also controlling me."

Lexi leaned forward, her stomach twisting. "Controlling you how?"

David's fingers clenched into fists. "It fed my fears. The more I used it, the more I felt like I had to hide—like if anyone found out who I really was, they'd reject me. I became paranoid. I thought if I let go of it, I'd be nothing."

Kesia inhaled sharply, understanding dawning in her eyes. "It was never protecting you, David."

He nodded, shame flickering across his face. "I know that now."

Lexi reached out, placing a steady hand over his. "You're not alone."

David finally met her gaze—for the first time in what felt like weeks.

"I want to make things right," he said, his voice stronger now. "I want to undo the damage I've done."

"You will," Lexi assured him. "But we need to deal with the talisman first. You buried it in the garden, right?"

David nodded. "Yes. I was afraid of what it could do if I kept it, but… I didn't know how to destroy it."

Lexi exchanged glances with the others.

This was beyond them.

"We need Sophea and Dorian," she said decisively. "They'll know how to neutralize it."

David exhaled in relief—as if the burden had already begun to lift.

They found Sophea and Dorian in one of the monastery's inner chambers. The moment Sophea saw David's face, her expression softened.

"What's going on?" she asked, her gaze flicking to Lexi for an answer.

David straightened his spine. "I need to tell you the truth about the talisman."

He confessed everything—his meeting with the cult, how they had manipulated him, how he had clung to the talisman out of fear rather than faith.

When he finished, the silence was heavy.

Sophea let out a slow breath. "Thank you for your honesty, David."

Dorian stepped forward. "The talisman's power must be neutralized." His tone was calm, but his words carried weight. "It was given to you by someone with ill intent. Its energy has been used to feed fear, not dispel it."

David looked anxious. "But how? I don't know how to get rid of it."

Dorian placed a reassuring hand on his shoulder. "You won't do it alone."

Sophea stepped into the center of the chamber. "We will cleanse it together. This is part of your trial, David—facing the consequences of your actions and transforming them into something pure."

David swallowed. "What do I have to do?"

Sophea's eyes were steady. "Trust in the process."

That evening, many of the monks gathered in the sacred chamber.

A low fire burned at the center, illuminating the faces of those who had come to witness the ritual. The talisman, now placed on an altar, seemed to pulse—as if resisting what was about to happen.

Dorian held out his hands, closing his eyes. A shift in energy rippled through the room.

Lexi felt it deep in her chest—a force being drawn out, something ancient and unsettled.

David stepped forward, his hands trembling.

"Repeat after me," Sophea instructed gently.

"I release the fear that binds me."

David's voice wavered, but he repeated it.

"I release the power that is not my own."

A shudder passed through the talisman.

"I walk forward in faith, not in shadows."

A loud crack echoed through the chamber— the talisman split in two.

A rush of wind blew through the room, then— stillness.

The darkness was gone.

David's knees buckled, but Lexi caught him before he could fall.

"You did it," she whispered.

His breath came out in short bursts, but for the first time in months—his eyes were clear.

Dorian bent down, examining the talisman's broken remains. He traced the split stone with a finger, then looked up at David.

"You were never powerless."

David blinked.

Dorian smiled. "You only thought you were."

A deep silence settled over the chamber—not one of fear, but of understanding.

David had been tested.

And he had prevailed.

Chapter 48

The monastery lay cloaked in silence as night descended, the soft glow of candlelight flickering through the windows of the sacred chamber. Outside, the crisp mountain air carried the scent of incense and earth, a quiet contrast to the weight of the ritual about to unfold.

Lexi, Isabella, Kesia, Redington, Sophea, and Dorian stood in a tight circle around the altar. At its center lay the broken talisman—small, seemingly innocuous, but charged with a history of fear and deception.

It looked ordinary, yet everyone present knew otherwise.

Dorian broke the silence first.

"This ritual is not just about cleansing an object. It is about cleansing ourselves."

His voice carried power, steady and deliberate, drawing their focus back to the purpose of the night.

"This talisman is a manifestation of the shadows we carry—our doubts, our fears, our vulnerabilities. We do not destroy it tonight. We transform it."

Sophea nodded, stepping forward. "And we do this together."

Lexi reached out, squeezing her hand. "We're with you."

The others joined hands, their energy interwoven, creating a circle around the altar. The air inside the chamber thickened, charged with the anticipation of what was to come.

Dorian began to chant, his voice low and resonant, carrying the weight of ancient words— not in English, not in any language Lexi recognized, but in something older, deeper.

The flames on the candles flickered, stretching taller as if reaching toward the ceiling. Their shadows danced against the walls, growing and shifting like unseen watchers.

Lexi, Isabella, Kesia, and Redington joined the chant, each of their voices blending into a single, harmonious vibration. The monastery itself seemed to respond, the very stones humming beneath their feet.

The talisman reacted.

David, standing in the shadows, stepped forward, his breath shaky.

Dorian gestured. "Place your hands on it."

David hesitated, then pressed his palms against the cold, smooth surface.

A shock jolted up his arms.

A dark whisper slithered into his mind—insidious, familiar.

"You are nothing without me."

David's jaw clenched.

"You need me."

For months, those words had kept him trapped. But tonight, he saw the truth.

He was never powerless.

The fear, the doubt, the self-loathing—it had never come from the talisman. It had always been inside him.

"I release you," he whispered.

The talisman pieces shuddered beneath his hands.

"I release the fear. The doubt. The darkness."

His voice grew stronger.

"I choose light. I choose faith."

A sudden warmth spread through his fingers—a pulse of golden energy, like the first light of dawn.

The dark aura wrapped around the talisman recoiled, resisting, trying to sink back into him.

But David stood his ground.

Sophea raised her arms. "Focus your energy, David! Do not fight the darkness—transform it!"

Lexi, Isabella, Kesia, and Redington tightened their grip on each other's hands, sending their own energy into the circle. The glow intensified, their combined faith pushing against the tainted energy.

The talisman began to change.

Its dark glow softened—fading, shifting—until the pieces in David's hands no longer felt like a threat.

It was just pieces of glass now.

No whispers. No power. No hold over him.

Dorian lifted his hands, signaling for silence.

The chanting stopped.

For a long moment, there was only stillness.

David slowly opened his eyes.

He gasped.

The talisman lay motionless, neutralized.

Tears blurred his vision.

"It's over."

Sophea stepped forward, her voice warm. "You did it, David. This was your trial, and you met it with courage."

Lexi smiled, the relief in her chest almost overwhelming.

Redington gave David a small nod. "Proud of you, kid."

David let out a small, choked laugh. "I feel… lighter. Like something that's been weighing me down for years is finally gone."

Dorian placed a hand over the talisman's remains. "It is no longer a tool of darkness. It has been cleansed and transformed. Now, we return it to the earth."

The monastery's sacred ground was quiet as the group stood beneath the stars, the night air crisp against their skin.

David knelt before the soft earth, holding the pieces of the talisman one last time.

He pressed it into the soil.

Covered it with his hands.

And let it go.

As the group walked back to the monastery, Lexi looked up at the sky.

The stars shone brighter than before.

Chapter 49

The days following the cleansing ritual were marked by a profound shift in the monastery. The once palpable tension that had gripped the community began to dissipate, replaced by a quiet but steady sense of renewal.

The darkness that had crept in—the doubt, the fear, the division—had been acknowledged and confronted, leaving behind something stronger.

A collective understanding had taken root.

They were not merely surviving the trials—they were learning from them.

For Lexi, the recent trials had deepened her understanding of faith—not as blind trust but as a force of transformation.

She had seen firsthand how fear could creep into a community, how doubt could fracture trust, and how true faith was found not in perfection but in the ability to rise after falling.

She committed herself to ensuring that faith was not just something spoken—it had to be lived.

Each morning, she rose before dawn to lead meditation—not just as a practice of stillness but as a way to integrate their experiences into their daily lives.

She led small reflection circles, where monks and initiates could discuss their fears, their struggles, their lessons—and how they could carry the faith into real-world choices.

More than ever, she understood that faith was a bridge—between the spiritual and the practical, between belief and action.

Lexi also initiated outreach efforts, traveling with small groups to nearby villages—offering not just spiritual guidance but also practical support.

She was no longer just learning the lessons.

She was living them.

Isabella had spent years grieving the life she lost—her son, Hans, her career, the identity she once held.

But now, she saw something new.

She was not confined to the past.

Her worth was not in who she had been but in who she was becoming.

She turned her passion for storytelling into something meaningful—leading creative expression workshops, helping others find their own voices through writing, movement, and art.

She encouraged initiates and monks to use journaling and storytelling to process their emotions—to turn their experiences into narratives of growth rather than wounds that never closed.

Through mentorship, she guided younger monks in understanding their struggles through a new lens—that their faith was not about never falling but about always getting back up.

In those quiet moments, helping others find their voice, she realized something profound.

She hadn't lost her purpose.

She had simply found a new way to use it.

For Kesia, the greatest revelation had been the power of vulnerability.

She had once believed that strength meant facing battles alone—but the trials had shown her otherwise.

True strength was in allowing others in and recognizing that healing was not isolation, but connection.

She began to document her journey, writing reflections that explored the intersection of faith, healing, and personal growth.

Her writings quickly became a source of inspiration within the monastery, passed from monk to monk, each passage resonating in its own way.

She led healing circles, small gatherings where individuals could speak openly about their doubts, their wounds, their fears—and, together, transform them into wisdom.

For the first time in her life, she understood:

Healing was not just something she did for others.

It was something she had to embrace for herself.

Redington had spent years viewing the world through the lens of logic, evidence, and control.

But the trials had forced him to confront something deeper.

Not everything can be solved through analysis.

Some things had to be felt.

Some things had to be trusted.

Yet, his skills as an investigator were not wasted. He used them to strengthen the monastery's security, ensuring their sacred space would remain protected.

He also applied his analytical mind to the monastery's future direction—helping identify vulnerabilities, organize resources, and plan ahead for challenges that had yet to unfold.

But in his own personal practice, Redington did something he had never done before.

He stopped chasing justice—and started seeking balance.

Justice wasn't just law and order.

It was harmony.

And for the first time, he wondered—was that what faith had been teaching him all along?

As the group continued integrating their lessons, they began to see the changes in the monastery itself.

The monks, inspired by their example, began applying their own spiritual growth in practical ways—offering new ways to serve the surrounding villages, expanding their teachings, and embracing a renewed sense of unity.

The fear that had once gripped them was fading.

In its place, something stronger was taking root.

Faith. Purpose. Trust.

One evening, after a long day of teaching, healing, and reflection, Lexi, Isabella, Kesia, and Redington found themselves together in the monastery courtyard.

Above them, the sky stretched wide and infinite, stars glittering like a promise of something greater.

They sat in companionable silence, the weight of everything they had faced settling not as a burden but as a foundation.

A new chapter of their journey had begun.

There were still trials ahead—still, mysteries to uncover, still battles to fight.

But for now, beneath the quiet sky, they allowed themselves a moment of peace.

Because for the first time, they truly understood—

The journey wasn't about reaching enlightenment.

It was about learning how to walk the path, step by step, together.

And they were exactly where they needed to be.

Chapter 50

The integration of their lessons had strengthened Lexi, Isabella, Kesia, Redington, and the entire monastery, but the journey was far from over.

The trials they had faced were not the end, merely steps on a growing path—one that was becoming increasingly demanding and complex.

The final tests would require not just knowledge but wisdom.

Not just faith, but action.

Not just trust in themselves, but trust in each other.

And they had to be ready.

One morning, as the group gathered in the meditation hall, Dorian's voice cut through the stillness, his tone carrying a weight they had never heard before.

"The time has come to face the final level of your journey."

His gaze swept across them, steady and knowing.

"Each of you has grown—in wisdom, in strength, in faith. But now, you must apply everything you've learned. The final tests will challenge not just your individual abilities but your ability to work as a unified force. The enlightenment you seek is not just personal—it is collective."

The group exchanged glances.

They had faced many trials, but this felt different—

More profound. More demanding.

That same day, a group of travelers arrived at the monastery.

They were tired, ragged, and desperate—seeking shelter and guidance.

At first, they seemed like pilgrims.

But something felt off.

Dorian made it clear, "This is your first trial. True compassion is not just kindness—it is discernment. See beyond appearances and understand the true needs of those who come to you."

So, Lexi, Isabella, Kesia, and Redington offered food, water, and rest.

But as the hours passed, they noticed subtle inconsistencies in the travelers' stories.

"Something's not right," Isabella murmured. "They're saying all the right things, but… I can feel it. They're hiding something."

"We should be careful," Redington added. "Compassion doesn't mean naivety."

Lexi thought of Dorian's words.
Compassion was not just about helping.
It was about understanding what help was truly needed.

That night, she approached the youngest traveler, a girl who had been quiet, tense, and nervous.

She knelt beside her.

"You don't have to be afraid," Lexi said gently. "You're safe here."

The girl's eyes filled with tears.

And suddenly, the truth came spilling out.

They weren't pilgrims.
They were refugees.
Fleeing a powerful criminal group that had taken their village.
They were too afraid to tell the truth, fearing they would be turned away.

The first trial had revealed its true lesson.

Compassion was not blind generosity.

It was seeing the truth—even when it was hidden beneath fear—and responding with both heart and wisdom.

The monastery took them in without hesitation.

The first trial was passed.

Days later, a sacred relic—one believed to hold great spiritual significance—vanished from the monastery's inner sanctum.

The monks were devastated.

Panic spread like wildfire.
Suspicions flared.
Faith crumbled.

Dorian gathered them again.

"This is your second trial. Faith is not just belief in the divine—it is trust in each other, especially in times of crisis. This challenge will test your ability to hold onto faith when doubt surrounds you."

But this wasn't just about finding the relic.

It was about restoring what had been broken—
The faith between them.

So, instead of hunting for the relic, Lexi gathered the monks.

She encouraged them to speak—
To share their fears.
To acknowledge their doubts.

And slowly, the fear lessened.
Suspicion faded.

"Let's meditate together," Isabella suggested. "Not on the relic. Not on what's missing. But on trust and unity."

And as they did, something extraordinary happened.

A young novice began to cry.
He confessed.

He had been cleaning late at night.
Had accidentally broke the relic.
And in his fear, he had hidden it away, terrified
of being banished.
The monks forgave him without hesitation.
Their faith in one another was restored.
The second trial was passed.

The final challenge came unexpectedly.
A severe drought had struck the local village,
threatening their entire water supply.
The villagers were divided—
Some wanted to use what little they had to
save the crops.
Others argued that it should be saved for
drinking water.
A decision had to be made.
Dorian spoke to the monks.
"This is your final trial. Wisdom is the ability
to see beyond the immediate and understand the
broader implications. The right choice is not
always clear. How will you lead?"
They traveled to the village together.
And for days, they listened.
They mediated heated debates.
They spoke to the farmers, the elders, the
children.
And then—
Kesia spoke first, drawing from her mother's
illness.

"We need a plan that preserves both immediate needs and long-term survival."

Redington used logic and strategy.

"If we ration carefully, we can save both some of the crops and some of the water—enough to sustain both for the time being."

Lexi and Isabella helped mediate, encouraging cooperation over division.

And finally—

The village agreed.

The water was rationed.

New wells were dug.

Rainwater was collected.

It wasn't a perfect solution.

But it was the right one.

The third trial was passed.

Chapter 51

The monastery's main hall was cast in flickering light, the glow of oil lamps stretching their shadows against the stone walls. The air was thick with silence, anticipation settling deep in the spaces between them.

David stood at the center of the room.

His hands clasped tightly.

His shoulders were rigid with tension.

His face was a mixture of apprehension and resolve.

Everyone waited.

Then, his voice broke the silence.

"I owe you all the truth."

A hush fell over the group.

"I've been hiding something—not just about the talisman but everything it represented. I didn't know how to tell you before because… I wasn't sure if I fully understood it myself."

Lexi leaned forward, her gaze steady but kind. "Take your time, David. We're here to listen."

David nodded, taking a deep breath as if trying to steady the weight pressing on his chest.

"The talisman wasn't just an artifact—it was part of something much larger."

His words carried an energy, shifting the air around them.

"I found it years ago, long before I became part of the cult. Buried in the ruins of an old temple in the Himalayas. At the time, I thought it was just a relic of a forgotten faith. But the moment I touched it, I felt… something.

A presence.

A power.

It was as if the talisman was alive, calling out to me."

A heavy stillness filled the room.

Isabella exchanged a glance with Kesia, both sensing the gravity of his words.

David swallowed hard, then continued.

"I didn't understand what it was—not until I came here. The teachings of the monastery helped me see that the talisman was tied to the Nine Spiritual Gifts."

His hand lifted, remembering the etched symbols on the talisman's surface.

"Each symbol corresponded to one of the gifts, and legend says it held the wisdom of those who've mastered them."

Redington's voice cut through the silence.

"Then why did you bury it?"

His sharp gaze locked onto David.

"Why hide it instead of sharing it with the monks?"

David's shoulders sagged, shame flickering in his expression.

"Because I was afraid."

The words hung between them, heavy with undeniable truth.

"The talisman wasn't just a source of knowledge—it was also a test. It revealed the truth of one's soul. It could amplify the light within you… or the darkness."

His voice dropped to a whisper.

"I buried it because I didn't feel worthy of its power."

Lexi's heart clenched. She knew that kind of fear—the terror of not being enough.

David's fists tightened at his sides.

"And then, when the disturbances started happening here, I thought the talisman might be the cause. I thought hiding it would protect everyone."

Kesia spoke softly, her voice steady but piercing.

"But it didn't stop anything, did it?"

David shook his head.

"No. It only got worse."

Then—

His eyes darkened with remorse.

"Sophea… she came to me last night before she left."

Lexi stilled, her breath catching.

"She asked me about the talisman. She said she still felt its energy. She told me that she needed to leave—that the answers she sought couldn't be found here."

A long pause.

"She didn't say much else, but I think… I think she went looking for the source of the talisman's power."

Lexi's stomach twisted.

Sophea—

Alone.

Searching.

Chasing something far beyond their understanding.

"Did she say where she was going?" Lexi asked, urgency tightening her voice.

David hesitated, then nodded.

"She mentioned an ancient site in the mountains, hidden deep in the forest. She said it was where the talisman was meant to be. She believed that the answers she needed lay there."

The group exchanged troubled glances, the weight of his words pressing down on them.

The talisman was no longer just a buried mystery.

It was a key—a beacon leading them toward something far greater than they had anticipated.

Redington's voice was firm.

"If Sophea is out there searching for this place, we need to find her."

A pause.

"And we need to understand what this talisman is really about. If it's tied to the Nine Spiritual Gifts, it could be the final piece of the puzzle we've been trying to solve."

Lexi felt her resolve harden.

"This isn't just about us anymore."

She turned to where the pieces of the talisman were buried, watching the way the light shimmered against its surface.

"If it truly had the power to test and reveal the truth of the soul, then it's part of our journey.

We follow its clues.

Not just for Sophea.

Not just for answers.

But for ourselves."

David stepped forward, his hands trembling slightly as he extended a piece of the talisman toward her.

"I trust you with this," he whispered.

Lexi reached out, looking towards where it had been buried, fingers closing around the smooth surface.

The moment she touched it—

A faint warmth pulsed beneath her fingertips. Like a heartbeat.

Like it recognized her.

The symbols etched into its surface seemed to glow, pulsing faintly with energy.

Lexi exhaled, her grip tightening.

"We'll find the truth."

"And we'll find Sophea. Together."

Chapter 52

Sophea moved through the dense forest with deliberate steps, the cool earth beneath her feet grounding her as she pressed forward. The morning was thick with silence, broken only by the occasional whisper of wind through the trees. She had left the monastery in secrecy, following the pull of something unseen—an energy that resonated through her very bones, calling her to a place she had never been but somehow knew existed.

She clutched a piece of the talisman in her palm, its warmth pulsing in time with her heartbeat. She had spent years meditating on the gifts, teaching others their wisdom, but never had she felt the depth of connection she did now. The talisman was guiding her, revealing a path only she could follow.

Hours passed, or perhaps days. Time had lost its meaning as she moved deeper into the wilderness. The trees grew taller, their canopies weaving a dense web that allowed only slivers of moonlight to touch the ground. Hunger gnawed at her stomach, and exhaustion tugged at her limbs, but she continued on, compelled by something greater than herself.

Then, she saw it.

A clearing stretched before her, its heart dominated by a circle of towering stones. They stood in perfect symmetry, ancient symbols carved into their surfaces. In the center, a raised altar of smooth black stone gleamed under the moonlight. Energy crackled in the air, thick with the weight of forgotten wisdom.

Sophea approached, her breath shallow. She placed the talisman piece onto the altar, and the symbols along the stones ignited with an ethereal glow, their light illuminating the night like a constellation brought to earth. A hum filled the air—a vibration so deep it resonated in her bones.

Then came the voices.

Not in words but in energy and feeling. A thousand whispers layered atop one another, blending into a single harmonic sound. It wasn't frightening, it was overwhelming. A rush of visions flooded her mind, images she could barely comprehend.

She saw Lexi, Isabella, Kesia, and Redington standing at a crossroads, the talisman between them, its light wavering as darkness threatened to consume it. She saw the monastery, its walls trembling as an unseen force pressed in. And she saw herself—standing where she was now—but different. Frail, exhausted, but with eyes that held the depth of all she had seen.

Then came the trial.

The energy surged, forcing her to her knees. The whispers grew louder, crashing into her like waves against the shore. The visions shifted, no longer showing her the outside world but turning inward—showing her herself.

She saw every moment of doubt she had ever carried, every hesitation that had held her back. She saw the weight of leadership she had borne, the sacrifices, the fears she had never spoken aloud. And then, she saw something deeper— something she had buried long ago.

Her past.

She was a child again, standing at the edge of a village in flames. Smoke curled into the sky, the scent of burning wood and despair thick in the air. She could hear the cries, the panic. She saw herself, young and helpless, reaching for hands that never came.

She had always spoken of faith, of surrender, of trusting in the path laid before them. But in this moment, she saw the truth—she had never truly surrendered. She had carried the past like a stone in her heart, shaping every decision she had ever made. Even now, she was trying to control the outcome, trying to lead rather than follow.

The realization hit her with the force of a storm. The lesson was clear.

Faith wasn't about guiding others—it was about letting herself be guided.

Tears streamed down her face as she bowed her head. She let go. Of the pain. Of the past. Of control. And in that moment, the light from the stones surged, enveloping her in warmth. The energy lifted her, wrapping around her like a cocoon.

Then, silence.

The glowing symbols faded. The air stilled.

Sophea remained on her knees, her body trembling. The weight she had carried for so long was gone, replaced by something lighter, purer. Strength, but not the kind she had known before. This was something deeper—something unshakable.

The path was clear now.

She took the talisman piece and pressed it to her heart, whispering a silent prayer of gratitude. The journey had changed her. When she returned, she would not be the same.

She rose to her feet, her steps slow but steady, and turned toward the monastery. Her body felt weak, but her soul had never been stronger.

It was time to go home.

Chapter 53

The two talisman pieces rested on the table in the monastery's study room, its faint glow illuminating the ancient symbols etched into its smooth surface.

Sophea, Dorian, Lexi, Isabella, Kesia, and Redington stood around it, their faces a mixture of curiosity and apprehension.

The air in the room was thick with anticipation, heavy with the weight of what they were about to uncover.

Lexi traced her finger over one of the symbols, feeling the intricate carvings beneath her touch.

"Each of these corresponds to one of the Nine Spiritual Gifts," she murmured, voice filled with reverence.

But—

Her brows furrowed as she noticed something else.

"Look—these smaller markings… they form a pattern."

Redington leaned closer, his detective instincts kicking in.

"It's like a map," he noted, pointing to a faint series of interconnected lines between the symbols.

"Not a literal map, but a guide. If we can decipher it, it might lead us to something."

Isabella, ever the methodical thinker, pulled out her notebook, sketching the talisman's surface.

"Let's work systematically," she suggested. "Each symbol could be a clue—a step toward whatever this talisman is meant to reveal."

For hours, they studied the talisman—Cross-referencing its symbols with the monastery's ancient texts.

Each gift was represented:

✓ Prophecy

✓ Healing

✓ Miracles

✓ Wisdom

✓ Knowledge

✓ Faith

✓ Discernment

✓ Tongues

✓ Interpretation

But something stood out—

The markings between them seemed to connect the gifts, almost like they were pieces of a greater whole.

"Here," Kesia pointed at a specific section.

Her voice was hushed but certain.

"This point—it's marked differently. Almost like a focal point."

Lexi's eyes widened with realization.

"The meditation chamber," she said.

The words felt right as if they had always known.

"It's the heart of the monastery. The place where all the teachings converge."

The group exchanged determined glances.

Without hesitation—

They gathered the talisman pieces and headed for the chamber.

The meditation chamber was quiet.

Dimly lit, filled with the scent of incense.

Its walls—lined with intricate carvings— depicted scenes from the monastery's history.

Redington scanned the stone walls, searching for anything unusual.

"There," he said, pointing to a carving.

A circular design—eerily similar to one on the talisman.

Lexi stepped forward, holding the talisman up to the carving.

As its glow intensified—

The wall trembled.

The sound of stone grinding against stone echoed through the chamber.

Then, slowly—
A hidden doorway appeared.
Beyond it, a narrow staircase descended into the depths of the monastery.
For a moment, no one spoke.
Then, without hesitation—
They stepped into the unknown.
The staircase opened into a vast chamber, its walls lined with,
Shelves of ancient texts.
Artifacts untouched for centuries.
Symbols matching those on the talisman.
The air was cool, still, as if time itself had paused in this hidden sanctuary.
"Look at this," Isabella whispered, picking up a scroll.
She unrolled it, eyes scanning the delicate script.
"It's a record of the Nine Spiritual Gifts—written centuries ago."
Her breath hitched.
"These aren't just teachings… they're accounts of how the gifts were used."
Of those who carried them.
Of what happened when the gifts were misused.
Kesia's fingers brushed against an ornate box.
Inside—A collection of glowing crystals, each one pulsing faintly.
"These must correspond to the gifts," she said.
"Each one tied to a specific aspect of spiritual energy."

They explored deeper—
Their curiosity mounting.
Lexi froze.
A strange sensation—
A pull.
A presence.
As if the talisman was guiding her.
She stepped forward—
And placed it on a central pedestal.
Light exploded from the talisman.
The room was bathed in a warm, radiant glow.
Everything shifted.
The group blinked.
Suddenly—They were somewhere else.
A vast, barren plain stretched before them.
Above—Dark storm clouds swirled.
Ahead—A figure cloaked in shadow waited.
Radiating power.
Radiating menace.
Around them—Fragments of the gifts—
scattered like broken shards of glass.
Lexi's voice rang clear and steady.
"We must face this together."
A pulse of energy surged through them—
An understanding settling deep in their bones.
"Only through unity can we overcome what
lies ahead."
The vision shattered like a pane of glass.
They staggered back, gasping as reality
returned.
The underground chamber was silent once
more.

But the talisman's glow had dimmed—Its presence felt stronger than ever.

It had passed its knowledge to them.

For a long moment, no one spoke.

"This is what we're being prepared for," Redington said, his voice low but certain.

The final test.

And it wasn't just about them.

"It's about everything the gifts stand for."

Lexi exhaled, her resolve solidifying.

"We need to understand this place.

These teachings.

What they mean for us."

She turned to the group. "The talisman has shown us the path. Now—It's up to us to walk it."

With renewed purpose, the group ascended from the chamber.

The talisman was safely tucked away.

But its lesson—

It's warning—

Still lingered.

They had been given a glimpse of the challenge ahead.

A shadow waiting to be confronted.

Chapter 54

The monastery was unusually quiet, the late afternoon sunlight filtering through the stained-glass windows, casting intricate patterns on the stone floor.

Lexi, Isabella, Kesia, and Redington sat in the meditation chamber, their minds still reeling from the profound vision shown to them by the talisman.

The air felt heavy, thick with anticipation—
As if the monastery itself was holding its breath.

A soft knock at the chamber door.

Brother Timothy.

His face was pale, eyes wide with disbelief.

"You need to come to the courtyard. Now."

His voice trembled.

The group exchanged wary glances before hurrying out of the chamber.

As they stepped into the courtyard, their breath caught collectively.

Because standing there—
Sophea.
Unsteady.
But unmistakably, Sophea.
Lexi's heart pounded.
Sophea was thinner, her once-vibrant complexion pale, her movements slower, as though she had aged years in just a few weeks.
Her presence radiated power.
A force beyond physical strength, an undeniable aura of spiritual energy that rippled through the air.
"Sophea," Lexi whispered, rushing forward.
She stopped just short of embracing her—Sensing that something profound had changed within her.
Sophea met her gaze.
And smiled.
Faint, tired—Yet knowing.
Isabella and Kesia joined Lexi, their expressions of concern.
Redington hung back, his instincts telling him that Sophea's presence carried a significance they were only beginning to understand.
Lexi swallowed hard.
"What happened?
Sophea took a deep breath, steadying herself against the edge of a stone bench.
"I was guided to a sacred site deep within the forest—

A place I didn't even know existed until the day I left."

Her gaze grew distant as though she were reliving it.

"The forest itself opened a path for me."

The group leaned in, hanging onto her every word.

"The site was ancient—Older than this monastery. Older than any structure I've ever seen."

A circle of stones, each etched with symbols—Like those on the talisman.

"At its center was an altar…
And when I placed my hands on it, I was overwhelmed by visions—

Visions of us."

Kesia's breath hitched.

"Us?"

Sophea nodded.

"Yes. Each of you was there. The visions showed trials, challenges, and choices."

Her voice grew stronger despite the exhaustion in her body.

"We will face something powerful—
Something that will test every aspect of our faith and our unity."

Her next words landed heavily—

"The talisman is central to this challenge. It's a guide… but it's also a key."

"Without it, we can't unlock the wisdom we'll need to overcome what's coming."

The group sat in stunned silence, the weight of her words settling over them.

Isabella studied her. Her brows knitted with concern.

"And you? What happened to you there?"

"You look… different."

Sophea gave a small smile tinged with sadness.

"The site wasn't just a place of visions— It was a crucible."

Her words sent chills through them.

"It tested me. Stripped away everything I thought I knew about myself… and my faith."

"I'm not the same person who left here."

She glanced down at her hands.

"My body feels weaker… But my spirit? My spirit has never been stronger."

Lexi knelt beside her, eyes searching Sophea's face.

"Why didn't you tell us before you left?"

"Why did you face this alone?"

Sophea's expression softened.

"Because it wasn't your time yet."

"I needed to prepare myself so that I could prepare you."

A pause.

"What I learned at the site wasn't just for me—It's for all of us."

Redington, who had been silent until now, finally stepped forward.

"Then tell us. What do we need to know?"

Sophea locked eyes with him—

Her gaze was piercing. "We need to embrace everything we've learned. The gifts, the trials, the unity we've built. The final test will demand all of it."

She exhaled deeply, her next words firm, unwavering. "This isn't just about overcoming external challenges—It's about confronting the deepest truths within ourselves. And we must do it together."

The group sat with her words, the magnitude of what lay ahead settling over them like a heavy cloak.

There was also clarity.

A realization.

Their paths had been leading them to this moment all along.

Kesia placed a hand on Sophea's arm.

"We're ready." Her voice was steady despite the uncertainty in her eyes. "Whatever comes next, we'll face it together."

Sophea's smile grew, and for a moment—Her exhaustion faded. "Then let's begin. The path ahead won't wait for us."

As the sun dipped below the horizon, casting the courtyard in a golden glow—The group felt the stirrings of something greater than themselves.

Sophea's return wasn't just a reunion—It was a call to action.

Chapter 55

The monastery held its breath.

The usual sounds of life—the rustling of trees, the distant chants of monks, the calls of morning birds—were absent, swallowed by a heavy stillness that settled over the stone walls like a shroud. It was the kind of silence that came before something broke.

Inside the meditation chamber, Lexi, Isabella, Kesia, Redington, and Sophea stood around the talisman pieces, its glow pulsing steadily atop the central pedestal. A heartbeat of energy, waiting.

The door creaked open, and Dorian stepped inside, his presence filling the space like a coming storm. He scanned the group, his gaze lingering on Sophea before settling into quiet certainty.

"You've been prepared for this," he said, his voice calm but carrying an unmistakable weight. "What lies ahead will test not just your faith but your ability to act as one."

No one spoke, but Lexi could feel the shift in the room—a shared understanding.

"Trust in each other."

"It will be your greatest weapon—and your greatest challenge."

Then, as if summoned by the force of his words—

The bell tolled.

Its clang ripped through the monastery, urgent and unrelenting. The sound vibrated through the stone walls, sending a cold shiver through Lexi's spine.

Brother Timothy appeared in the doorway, his face drained of color.

"There's a disturbance at the outer gate," he said, his voice tight with urgency. "A group of people—armed. They're demanding to speak with those who hold the talisman."

By the time they reached the outer courtyard, the monks had already gathered, tension thick in the air.

Beyond the gate stood a cluster of figures, their faces shadowed beneath dark hoods. They weren't soldiers, but their stance—the way they held their weapons, the way their eyes flicked from one side to the other—spoke of experience.

A man stepped forward.

Tall. Broad-shouldered. His lips curved into a smile, but there was no warmth behind it. Only patience. And certainty.

"We know you have it," he said, his voice smooth, almost amused.

Lexi felt the heat of Redington's presence beside her. His entire body tensed, waiting.

"The talisman," the man continued. "Hand it over, and no one gets hurt."

Lexi didn't move. Didn't blink. "It's not yours to claim."

The man tilted his head as if assessing her. "Power can always be claimed. The only question is—who holds it?"

A pause.

Then his voice sharpened, cutting like a blade. "Give it to us—or we'll take it."

It happened too fast.

One of the hooded figures flicked their wrist, and something small and metallic arced over the gate.

It hit the ground with a dull clink.

Boom.

The explosion was blinding.

Smoke billowed through the courtyard, thick and suffocating. The monks scattered, coughing and stumbling. Lexi's vision blurred as she instinctively raised an arm, trying to see through the chaos.

Then—movement.

Through the haze, shadows slipped past the iron gate.

They were inside.

Redington grabbed her wrist, his grip firm. "We need to regroup—NOW."

She didn't hesitate.

They ran, pushing through the confusion, dodging stumbling monks and the shifting silhouettes of their attackers. The monastery had become a battlefield.

They barely made it inside the meditation chamber before the heavy doors slammed shut behind them.

Redington threw the bolt.

Outside, fists pounded against the wood. The door shuddered but held.

Inside, the talisman glowed brighter as if sensing the impending danger.

Sophea's voice was calm, unshaken. "This is the trial."

Lexi turned to the others, heart hammering. "We have to fight."

But not with force.

Kesia clutched the talisman pieces. "We can't let them have it. But we also can't fight them physically. This isn't about force—it's about faith."

Lexi exhaled sharply. "Each of us has our own gifts. If we combine them, we can protect the talisman—and the monastery."

One by one, they linked hands, forming a circle around the pedestal.

Sophea began to chant, her voice weaving through the chamber like an unbreakable thread.

Lexi's *Prophecy* flared behind her eyes. She saw the attackers' movements before they made them. Every step. Every plan.

Redington's *Discernment* sliced through the noise. The leader—he wasn't a man of evil. He was desperate. Searching. Lost.

Isabella's *Healing* radiated outward, wrapping the monastery in warmth. A quiet calm spread through the walls, seeping into the hearts of even those who sought to destroy them.

Kesia's *Faith* anchored them all. Unwavering. Absolute. She strengthened their light, pushing back the creeping darkness.

And the talisman responded.

The glow erupted outward—not in an explosion, but in something softer.

Something deeper.

The attackers outside the door hesitated.

The first man staggered, his fingers loosening around his weapon.

Then another.

And another.

One by one, they dropped their weapons.

Their expressions shifted, confusion flickering through their eyes.

Then—the leader stepped forward.

He was trembling.

His hands shook. His breath came uneven.

His lips parted, but it wasn't a demand that left them.

"What… is this?" His voice cracked. "I came for power… but… this is something else."

Dorian's voice was steady. Certain.

"It's faith."

He took a step closer, no fear in his stance.

"True faith."

"Something you can't take."

"Something you have to find within yourself."

The man crumpled to his knees.

His followers did the same.

The light from the talisman dimmed, its purpose—fulfilled.

As the monks escorted the intruders away, the courtyard was silent once more.

Lexi turned to the others.

"That wasn't the end."

Her voice was quiet. Steady.

"It was only the beginning."

Sophea nodded, her gaze sharp with understanding. "The true test is still ahead. But now—" She looked at each of them in turn. "We know we're ready for it."

As they stepped out of the meditation chamber, the golden light of dusk spilled over the monastery, casting long shadows across the stone.

The battle had been fought.

The talisman was safe.

But the real war was still waiting.

Chapter 56

The first rays of dawn kissed the monastery's stone walls, bathing them in gold as if the heavens themselves acknowledged the journey about to unfold. The crisp morning air carried the scent of damp earth and incense, a lingering presence of prayers whispered over centuries.

Yet, beneath the monastery's serene facade, the echoes of the previous day's events still hummed—a quiet reminder of the battle they had fought, the test they had endured, and the deeper challenge that still lay ahead.

Lexi, Isabella, Kesia, and Redington gathered in the meditation chamber, standing once more before the talisman. Its glow was softer now, subdued, but its presence was no less profound. It had been their guide, their teacher, and their catalyst for change. And now, it was time to decide what came next.

Sophea stood at the center of their circle, her hands clasped before her, the weight of her decision reflected in the steady calm of her gaze.

"I've thought deeply about this," she began, her voice firm yet tinged with emotion. "This monastery—it's not just my home. It's my responsibility. The talisman's knowledge is too precious, too powerful to be left unguarded. If it were to fall into the wrong hands again…" She let the unspoken warning linger in the air.

Lexi held her gaze, a quiet understanding passing between them. "You're staying."

Sophea nodded. "I must."

Isabella reached out, squeezing Sophea's hand. "You've always been the heart of this place. The monks, the talisman… they couldn't ask for a better guardian."

Redington exhaled, resting a reassuring hand on Sophea's shoulder. "Your strength is what will hold this place together. But if you ever need us—any of us—we'll come back."

Sophea smiled, gratitude softening her features. "I know. And I have faith that your paths will take you exactly where you are needed. What we've done here… it isn't the end. It's the beginning."

Kesia blinked back tears before stepping forward and embracing her. "You've changed my life, Sophea. I'll carry your lessons with me wherever I go."

Sophea returned the embrace, whispering, "And you'll teach others, Kesia. That is how we keep the light alive."

The room fell into a comfortable silence, the kind that existed between those bound by something greater than mere words. They had walked through trials, faced their deepest fears, and come out stronger—not just as individuals, but as a whole.

Now, it was time to move forward.

The morning passed in quiet preparations. There were no rushed goodbyes, no dramatic moments—only the careful gathering of belongings, the familiar routine of monks moving through the halls, and the occasional exchange of knowing glances.

The monks had gathered at the gates by the time Lexi and the others were ready. Some stood with their hands folded in silent prayer, while others simply watched, their expressions filled with both hope and sorrow.

Sophea stood tall beside Brother Timothy, her posture one of unwavering resolve. She was no longer just a guide; she was a protector, a guardian of something ancient and sacred.

"Remember," she said, her voice clear and steady, "Faith isn't something you carry—it's something you live. Let it guide you, even when the path ahead seems unclear."

Lexi met her gaze, nodding. "We will."

There was no need for any more words.

One last glance at the monastery—the place where so much had changed—and then they stepped beyond the gates.

The forest stretched before them, the sunlight filtering through the canopy like a golden promise. The path ahead was unknown, but it no longer felt daunting. It felt inevitable.

They walked in silence for a while, each of them lost in their own thoughts. The weight of the monastery, of Sophea's decision, of everything they had endured still clung to them like morning mist.

Finally, Lexi spoke. "We'll honor her." She didn't need to say who. They all knew. "We'll take what she's taught us and use it to make a difference."

Redington nodded, his eyes scanning the horizon. "And we'll be ready for whatever comes next. Together."

Behind them, the monastery stood as a silent guardian, a testament to their journey thus far.

Chapter 57

The familiar hum of city life greeted Lexi, Isabella, Kesia, and Redington as they returned to the United States. The vibrant energy of urban landscapes was a stark contrast to the serene tranquility of the monastery, yet it was here, amidst the noise and motion, that their lessons would take root and flourish.

For Lexi, the shift was profound. She had left behind the towering Himalayan peaks and stepped back into the rhythm of a metropolis that never slept, but she was not the same woman who had boarded that plane months ago.

Her new studio, perched on the fourteenth floor of a converted warehouse in downtown New York, was a reflection of her transformation. The industrial charm of exposed brick walls and high ceilings was softened by draped fabrics and racks of her latest designs.

Floor-to-ceiling windows framed the city skyline, but it was the quiet sanctuary within these walls that truly mattered.

The hum of her sewing machine filled the space, a rhythmic meditation in itself. Sunlight streamed through the windows, casting soft patterns on the hardwood floor as she carefully guided a flowing piece of silk beneath her needle. Her latest collection was unlike anything she had created before—every stitch carried intention, inspired by the lessons she had learned at the monastery.

Gone were the days of chasing fleeting trends. Now, her designs embodied something deeper, resilience, faith, and the interconnectedness of all things. She used natural fibers in soft, earthy tones, accented with vibrant embroidery symbolizing energy and transformation. Each garment was an extension of the spiritual journey she had embraced, a tangible reminder of the Nine Spiritual Gifts woven into fabric.

But even in this new creative space, doubt crept in.

Would people understand what she was trying to convey? Could fashion, often dismissed as superficial, carry the weight of something so profound?

Lexi sighed and reached for the worn leather journal she had carried through the monastery. Flipping through its pages, she found the passage she needed:

"Faith is an active force. It shapes how we see the world and how we create within it."

She exhaled, her grip on uncertainty loosening. This was her path now—to create with intention, to allow her work to be a vessel for meaning rather than mere aesthetics.

When she began sharing her designs online, the response was immediate.

Messages flooded in. "Your designs speak to my soul." "This feels like a reminder of who I want to be." "I never knew clothing could hold so much meaning."

Orders poured in from fashion enthusiasts and meditation retreats, spiritual gatherings, and wellness centers seeking to integrate intention into their spaces. A boutique in California featured her collection alongside crystals and incense, and its owner described her garments as "Sacred attire for the modern seeker."

"This isn't just fashion," Lexi explained during an interview with a popular magazine. "It's a way to remind people of their inner strength and the gifts they carry within. Every piece I create is meant to be a gentle nudge toward self-awareness and connection."

Her designs soon found their way into places she never expected. At a retreat in Sedona, attendees meditated in her flowing linen robes, each outfit stitching a silent prayer woven into the fabric. In New York, a renowned yoga teacher donned one of her pieces during a mindfulness seminar, calling it "A second skin for the spirit."

The most surreal moment came when an invitation arrived—an opportunity to showcase her collection at a high-profile spiritual conference. She hesitated at first. She had once designed for glitzy fashion weeks, runways lined with flashing cameras and whispers of industry insiders. This would be different. This was not about status.

It was about purpose.

That night, standing in her dimly lit studio, she surveyed her collection, the racks of garments standing like quiet sentinels of her journey.

Her assistant, Clara, entered, her eyes wide with admiration. "Lexi, your work is incredible. I've never seen fashion like this—so personal, so inspiring."

Lexi smiled, the warmth of Clara's words settling deep within her. "It's not just my work," she said softly. "It's the journey, the lessons, and the people I've met along the way. This collection is a tribute to everything we carry within us—the strength, the love, the faith."

She thought of Sophea, standing in the monastery courtyard, her presence unwavering. Of Isabella, Kesia, and Redington, each finding their own path forward. They were all creating in their own ways—Isabella through storytelling, Kesia through healing, and Redington through his unshakable discernment.

And Lexi?

She was weaving faith into fabric, one stitch at a time.

That night, as she turned out the light and gazed at the city beyond her window, she felt the quiet certainty of purpose settle over her.

She had stepped into the next chapter of her journey.

Chapter 58

The scent of dust and aged velvet filled Isabella's senses as she stepped into the small theater in downtown Manhattan. The glow of the stage lights, the scuffed wooden floors, the quiet hum of anticipation—it was all so familiar, yet entirely different. This time, she wasn't here to play a role. The stage, once the measure of her worth, was no longer her battlefield. Now, it was her classroom.

The rows of young actors sat eagerly before her, their faces a mix of excitement and uncertainty. Some had already tasted the sting of rejection, others were still burning with ambition, but all of them had come for something more than just technique. They had come to understand the heart of their craft—the part that couldn't be taught in scripts or rehearsals.

Isabella let her fingers trail along the edge of a stool at center stage before turning to face them. "Welcome," she said, her voice carrying the quiet authority of someone who had lived through every high and low of the industry. "You're here because you have something to say. But before you can make the world listen, you need to listen to yourself."

The room fell silent.

She took a slow breath, then continued. "Acting isn't just about pretending to be someone else. It's about truth—your truth. The world will tell you to become what's marketable, what sells, what fits their expectations. But real artistry, the kind that moves people, can only come from authenticity. And authenticity takes courage."

A young man in the front row, his arms crossed tightly over his chest, raised an eyebrow. "But isn't acting about… well, acting? Playing a part?"

A knowing smile tugged at Isabella's lips. "Yes, but the best performances don't come from fabrication. They come from connection. When I played my most celebrated roles, I wasn't just saying lines—I was living them. I let myself be raw and vulnerable. And that's what people remember. Not perfection, but truth."

She saw the flicker of recognition in their eyes. They were beginning to understand.

The next few weeks became a whirlwind of movement, emotion, and revelation. Isabella led her students through rigorous exercises—breathwork to steady their nerves before auditions, mindfulness techniques borrowed from the monastery to quiet self-doubt, and movement drills that forced them to step outside their comfort zones.

One exercise, in particular, challenged them to strip away all pretense. Standing one by one before their peers, they had to speak—not as a character, but as themselves. It was uncomfortable at first. The silences stretched, and the nervous shifting of feet filled the room. But then, something shifted. Words poured out—stories of childhood dreams, of insecurities, of why they wanted—needed—to be here.

One student, Elena, struggled the most. A naturally gifted actress, she could transform into any character effortlessly. But when asked to be herself, she faltered.

"I don't know what to say," she admitted, her hands twisting in her lap.

Isabella knelt in front of her. "You don't need to say what you think people want to hear. Just say what's real."

Elena hesitated, then whispered, "I'm afraid... that if I show people who I really am, they won't think I'm enough."

The words hung in the air.

Isabella reached for Elena's hands and squeezed them gently. "That's exactly why you're enough."

Tears welled in the young woman's eyes, and Isabella saw it—the moment of transformation. The shift from acting to being. From hiding to embracing.

By the time the showcase arrived, Elena's performance was breathtaking. She stood before a packed theater, delivering a monologue that wasn't just spoken—it was felt. Every word carried weight. Every pause was electric. The audience held its breath as she laid her soul bare, and when she finished, the applause was thunderous.

Backstage, Isabella watched with quiet pride. She had once lived for this kind of acclaim, had craved it like oxygen. But tonight, it wasn't about her. It was about Elena—about all of them.

Later that night, after the students had gone, Isabella lingered in the empty theater. The stage lights cast a golden glow over the seats, and she imagined the ghosts of her past selves watching from the wings. The ingénue chasing stardom. The woman who had lost herself in the pursuit of perfection. The seeker had found peace in a monastery far from the cameras and flashing lights.

She had played so many roles in her life, but this one—this quiet guide, this mentor—felt the most real.

A soft voice interrupted her thoughts. "You're still here?"

She turned to see Michael, the theater director, leaning against the doorway with an amused expression.

"Couldn't leave just yet," she admitted. "I was… remembering."

Michael nodded, stepping closer. "You know, when you first came back, I wasn't sure what to expect. Thought you might try to reclaim the spotlight."

Isabella chuckled. "That's what I would've done once. But this… this is where I'm meant to be."

Michael studied her for a moment, then smiled. "Well, you're damn good at it."

She glanced back at the stage one last time before turning toward the exit. The night air was cool as she stepped outside, the sounds of the city wrapping around her like an old song.

For years, she had searched for something— fame, fulfillment, belonging. And now, at long last, she had found it.

Not in the spotlight.

Not in the applause.

But in the quiet moments of truth, in the souls she had helped illuminate.

She had spent a lifetime performing. Now, she was finally living.

And that was the greatest role of all.

Chapter 59

Nestled in the heart of her hometown, Kesia's healing center had become a sanctuary, a place where people came not only to find relief but to rediscover themselves. The converted community hall, once a space for town meetings and local gatherings, now carried a new energy—one of peace, renewal, and quiet strength. Sunlight filtered through the wide windows, casting golden streaks onto the polished wooden floors. The scent of lavender and sandalwood lingered in the air, grounding every visitor in an immediate sense of calm.

This place was more than a wellness center—it was an extension of Kesia's soul. Every detail, from the warm-toned tapestries hanging on the walls to the handwoven cushions placed in a circle, was intentional. It was a space of belonging, of transformation.

Her workshops were unlike anything the town had seen before. She wove together guided meditation, hands-on healing, and storytelling, each element seamlessly blending into the next. Inspired by her time at the monastery, Kesia crafted experiences that touched not just the mind and body but the spirit.

The heart of her practice was a workshop she called *Healing the Soul: A Journey Through Faith and Family*. Participants arrived carrying the weight of grief, stress, and disconnection, but they left lighter, their burdens eased by the collective energy of the space. Kesia's voice, steady and reassuring, became the thread that wove them all together.

The workshop always began with grounding. Seated in a circle, her participants closed their eyes as she led them into meditation.

"Feel the ground beneath you," she would say, her tone gentle yet unwavering. "Imagine roots growing from the soles of your feet, reaching deep into the earth. You are supported. You are steady. Whatever you carry, let it rest here for now."

Some came in skeptical, their faith shaken by life's trials. But as the minutes stretched and the silence deepened, something always shifted. Shoulders softened. Breaths steadied. The walls came down.

Next came the storytelling. Drawing from her family's rich oral traditions, Kesia shared tales that blended ancestral wisdom with the lessons she had learned at the monastery. One particular story, about a grandmother's unwavering faith during a time of great loss often left the room hushed in contemplation.

"These stories," she explained one evening, her voice weaving through the quiet, "Aren't just memories. They are maps. They show us where we've been and remind us of the resilience that already exists within us. Every hardship we face is written in the fabric of our lineage, and every triumph is a testament to the strength we carry forward."

She watched as the words settled over her participants, their eyes reflecting not just understanding but recognition.

The most transformative part of the workshop, however, was the hands-on healing. Moving through the circle, Kesia placed her hands gently on the shoulders of each person, channeling the energy she had honed through years of practice. Some felt warmth, a deep sensation of release. Others described it later as a wave of peace, something they hadn't realized they needed.

Her mother, now fully recovered and brimming with quiet wisdom, became an integral part of the space. She prepared herbal teas in the adjoining kitchen, offering words of comfort and insight to those who needed them. Sometimes, she simply sat beside participants as they shared their struggles, her presence a balm all its own.

One evening, as they packed up after a long session, her mother turned to her, eyes filled with something unspoken. "What you're doing here, Kesia… it matters," she said. Her voice was soft but carried a weight that pressed directly into Kesia's chest. "You're not just healing bodies—you're bringing people back to themselves. That's something rare."

The words lingered long after her mother had gone to bed, settling into Kesia's bones like a truth she had always known but never fully acknowledged.

As her practice grew, so did its reach. Word spread beyond the town, and soon, she was leading sessions in nearby communities, even hosting virtual workshops for those too far to travel. What had begun as a deeply personal endeavor had become something greater than herself.

One evening, after a particularly powerful session, Kesia sat alone in the now-empty hall, the scent of incense still clinging to the air. She traced her fingers over the edge of a wooden prayer bead bracelet, a simple yet sacred token she had kept since the monastery.

She thought of the journey that had led her here—the moment she had nearly lost her mother, the solitude of the monastery, the faith that had carried her through it all. And now, here she was, offering that same faith back to the world, one story, one healing touch at a time.

Her journey, she realized, had never been solely about healing others. It was about honoring the interconnectedness of faith, family, and community. It was about remembering that every person who stepped through her doors carried not just their pain but their own untapped strength.

She stood, stretching, feeling a quiet certainty settle within her. The path ahead was still unfolding, but for the first time, Kesia felt truly aligned with her purpose. She was home—not just in a building, not just in a town, but within herself.

With a deep breath, she turned off the lights, locking the doors behind her as the night stretched out before her. Whatever came next, she was ready.

She had faith.

Chapter 60

Back in the world of law enforcement, Redington found himself stepping into familiar shoes—only to realize they no longer fit quite the same way. The precinct still hummed with its usual frenetic energy—phones ringing, officers exchanging hurried words, reports being filed—but Redington moved through it with quiet deliberation. The chaos no longer pulled him in; he had learned to find stillness within it.

His time at the monastery had changed him in ways that weren't immediately visible, but the shift didn't go unnoticed. Colleagues who had worked alongside him for years observed the transformation with curiosity. He still carried the same sharp instincts, the same investigative brilliance that had made him one of the best, but there was something new—a calm, unwavering patience that made him seem more perceptive than ever.

"You're different," his partner, Detective Morales, said one afternoon as they walked out of an interrogation room. "A year ago, you would've gone in there like a bulldog, worn the guy down until he confessed. Now? You actually listen."

Redington chuckled, leaning against the metal railing outside the precinct. "Maybe I learned that people give you more when you stop trying to take."

Morales shook his head, grinning. "That monastery really did a number on you, huh?"

Redington only smiled.

His first major case back on the job was a theft turned armed robbery. The suspect, a young man named Alex Carter, had been caught fleeing the scene, stolen goods still in his possession. On the surface, it was a straightforward case—the evidence was stacked against him, and the legal system was prepared to lock him away. But something about Alex's demeanor during the initial interrogation gave Redington pause.

Sitting across from him in the stark, fluorescent-lit room, Redington didn't lean forward with intimidation or push the case with rehearsed questioning. Instead, he folded his hands and met Alex's gaze, his voice even.

"I'm not here to pin you against the wall," he said. "I just want to understand. Why did you do it?"

At first, Alex scoffed, his defenses high. "What does it matter? You've already got me."

"It matters," Redington replied. "Because this isn't just about what you did. It's about why you did it."

Silence stretched between them, and for a moment, it seemed Alex wouldn't answer. But then something shifted—maybe in Redington's tone or in the way he held himself without judgment.

"My mom's sick," Alex muttered. "Bills keep piling up, and no one will hire me because of my record. I didn't know what else to do."

The confession struck a chord in Redington. He had seen desperation drive good people to dark places before. In the past, he might have focused only on the crime, on closing the case and moving on. But now, he saw something different—not just a criminal, but a young man on the edge of losing himself.

When the case went to court, Redington did something he never would have considered before his time at the monastery—he stood before the judge and advocated for Alex.

"Your Honor," he said, his voice steady, "Alex made a choice that put others at risk and that can't be ignored. But his story is one of many where desperation clouds judgment. If we lock him away, we don't just punish him—we eliminate his chance to make it right."

The courtroom was silent. Redington took a breath before continuing.

"I'm not saying he shouldn't be held accountable. I'm saying there's a different way. A program of rehabilitation—community service, mandatory counseling—gives him a chance to repay what he's taken and find a way forward. Give him a chance to prove he can do better."

The judge, initially skeptical, studied Redington carefully. But in the end, he agreed. Alex was sentenced to a restorative justice program rather than prison time.

Back at the precinct, the decision caused a stir. Morales raised an eyebrow as he passed Redington in the hallway. "You're really pushing the second chances these days, huh?"

Redington smirked. "Justice isn't just about punishment. Sometimes, it's about redemption."

His approach didn't just change the way he handled cases—it changed how he interacted with the world. He began listening more, digging deeper—not just for answers, but for truth. During domestic disputes, he worked to de-escalate tension rather than simply taking statements. He encouraged victims to seek help, offering them resources beyond legal action.

One particular case tested him more than most. A violent altercation between two men had left one hospitalized and the other in handcuffs. It seemed cut and dry—until Redington sat with the accused and discovered that years of resentment and misunderstanding had led to the fight. Instead of filing it away as another act of aggression, he pushed for mediation, helping the two men face their pain, their history, and, ultimately, their own capacity for forgiveness.

Some days were easier than others. Not every case had a clear path to healing. But Redington held onto the lessons he had learned, trusting that even the smallest act of faith could make a difference.

In quiet moments, he found himself turning a small stone over in his hand—the one he had kept since the monastery, a reminder of the trials that had shaped him. He had once thought faith belonged only in sacred spaces, but now, he carried it with him everywhere.

As the weeks turned into months, the ripples of his change began to spread. His team started handling cases with more mindfulness, questioning their own assumptions. The precinct, once rigid in its approach, grew more adaptable. Even suspects and victims alike noticed the difference in how Redington worked.

One evening, after a particularly long day, Redington sat in his office, the city lights twinkling outside his window. He thought of Lexi, Isabella, and Kesia—each of them walking their own path, using their gifts in their own way. They had all changed, but they had also stayed the same—carrying the monastery's lessons into the world, making it better in whatever ways they could.

A soft knock interrupted his thoughts. Morales leaned against the doorframe, holding a file. "Got another case for you. Repeat offender, theft charge. But, uh… thought you'd want to talk to him first before we throw the book at him."

Redington smiled, standing. "Yeah. Let's talk to him."

He wasn't just an investigator anymore. He was a guide. A reminder that even in the darkest corners of human nature, light could still find its way in.

And that was faith, in its truest form.

Chapter 61

The city buzzed with life outside Lexi's studio, the neon lights casting long shadows against the streets below. Inside, however, the space was a sanctuary—warm, filled with the scent of jasmine tea and the quiet hum of deep conversation.

Lexi's studio had become more than just a workspace. It was a reflection of her evolution—a place where her creativity and spirituality intertwined. Swaths of fabric in muted earth tones and vibrant gold hung from wooden racks, each design infused with intention. The delicate embroidery on some of the garments held patterns reminiscent of the monastery's ancient carvings, symbols of faith, wisdom, and unity.

Tonight was one of their monthly gatherings, something she, Isabella, Kesia, and Redington had promised to uphold despite the separate paths they had taken. The ritual had become an anchor, a reminder that no matter where life led them, they were bound by something deeper than circumstance.

Lexi moved around the studio, arranging cushions on the floor as Isabella ran her fingers over a draped gown.

"This is exquisite," Isabella murmured, admiring the fine stitching. "You've always had an eye for beauty, but there's something… different now. It's like these designs tell a story."

Lexi smiled, brushing a stray curl from her face. "That's the goal. I don't just want to make beautiful things—I want people to feel something when they wear them. To feel connected, empowered."

Kesia, sitting cross-legged on one of the cushions, nodded. "You've taken everything we learned at the monastery and woven it into your work, Lexi. That's rare."

The words settled deep within Lexi, stirring something unspoken. She had changed—there was no denying that. The monastery had unraveled her stripped her down to her essence, forcing her to redefine success, ambition, and even love. Now, every choice she made, every stitch, was an extension of her faith, a testament to what she had come to believe.

Redington leaned against the edge of her desk, arms crossed. "So, what's next for you?"

Lexi hesitated, turning the question over in her mind. The truth was, she didn't know. She had poured herself into her work, but there was an undercurrent of restlessness as if something was still waiting to be discovered.

"I have an opportunity to expand," she admitted. "A boutique in Paris reached out. They want to feature my designs, maybe even partner on a collection."

Isabella's eyes lit up. "That's incredible! Paris, Lexi—this is what designers dream of."

But Lexi hesitated. "It is…, but I keep wondering if it's the right path. If I say yes, I'll be traveling constantly, managing a team. It's everything I once wanted, but now… I don't know. I've spent so much time making sure my work has meaning, but what if this pulls me away from that?"

Redington studied her, his detective instincts always sharp. "What are you really afraid of?"

Lexi exhaled, crossing her arms. "Losing myself again."

The confession hung in the air.

She had spent years chasing something— fame, recognition, an identity that had always felt just out of reach. The monastery had stripped away those illusions, leaving her raw but real. She had found purpose in creation, in stillness, in faith. But could she carry that into the world beyond the sanctuary she had built here?

Kesia placed a hand over hers. "You're not the same person you were before. You won't lose yourself, Lexi. You've found yourself."

Lexi nodded, but doubt still lingered in the back of her mind.

The conversation shifted as they shared updates from their lives—Kesia's growing healing practice, Isabella's mentorship program, and Redington's evolving approach to law enforcement. They laughed, reminisced, and leaned into the comfort of familiarity. But even as she smiled, Lexi felt that restlessness gnawing at her.

As the night wound down, Isabella raised her glass of tea. "To faith," she said, her eyes glinting with warmth.

"To faith," Redington echoed, lifting his glass. "And to all the lessons we've learned—the easy ones and the hard ones."

"And to the future," Kesia added with a grin, "Because I'm pretty sure it's going to keep throwing us curveballs."

Lexi smiled, feeling the warmth of their bond filling the room. She lifted her glass last. "To the journey ahead—because I feel it's far from over."

They clinked glasses, the sound ringing softly in the studio.

Later, after her friends had left and the studio had settled into silence, Lexi stood by the window, gazing at the city below. The streets pulsed with life, people moving through their own stories, their own searches for meaning.

She pressed a hand against the glass, her reflection staring back at her.

What was she searching for?

The answer felt just out of reach, lingering in the space between who she had been and who she was becoming.

Paris.

The thought sent a thrill through her—of possibility, transformation, and something new calling her forward. But it wasn't just about Paris. It was about stepping into the unknown again, trusting that faith wasn't about standing still. It was about movement. Growth.

With a deep breath, Lexi turned away from the window.

She wasn't afraid of the journey ahead.

She was ready for it.

Chapter 62

The streets of Paris unfolded before Lexi, a city alive with an effortless blend of history and modernity. The air carried the scent of fresh bread from corner boulangeries, mingling with the faint floral notes of early spring. The move had been swift—her designs had taken off in a way she hadn't fully anticipated, and the boutique's offer had been too tempting to ignore.

Now, standing in the heart of the Marais district, just outside her new apartment, she felt a strange mix of exhilaration and unease. This was a fresh start, a dream she had once longed for. But dreams had a way of shifting and evolving. And she wasn't sure this was still the one she wanted.

Her apartment was small but beautiful, with wrought-iron balconies and floor-to-ceiling windows that overlooked the quiet street below.

Sunlight bathed the space in a golden glow as she set down her suitcase and took it all in. The studio space she had rented was only a short walk away, inside a historic building filled with artists and designers, each chasing their own creative aspirations. It should have been perfect.

But as she unpacked her things, a nagging sensation settled in her chest.

Something—or someone—was missing.

She busied herself setting up her workspace, draping swaths of fabric over chairs, and pinning sketches to the walls. The boutique owner, a woman named Élodie, had been generous in her praise, insisting that Lexi's designs had something special—something that went beyond fashion and into the realm of storytelling.

And yet, as she worked, she felt untethered. The vibrant city around her pulsed with energy, but she felt strangely removed from it as if she were merely an observer rather than a participant.

That night, she took a long walk along the Seine, her hands tucked into the pockets of her coat. The Eiffel Tower glittered in the distance, its reflection shimmering on the water's surface. Lovers strolled hand in hand, their laughter light and effortless. The sight made something tighten in her chest.

She had told herself she was fine being alone. That her work, her faith, and her purpose were enough.

But as she leaned against the cool stone railing, watching the city move around her, a familiar face ghosted through her thoughts.

Redington.

She hadn't expected to miss him so soon.

And yet, she did.

It was a quiet ache, not all-consuming, but ever-present, like a song playing softly in the background of her mind.

She missed the way he listened, how his silence had always been more grounding than most people's words. She missed the steady presence he carried, the way he had always been able to see through her defenses.

She had thought leaving for Paris would be a new beginning and that it would be easy.

Instead, she felt like she had left something unfinished.

With a sigh, she turned from the river and began walking back toward her apartment, the city's lights glowing softly around her.

Tomorrow, she would throw herself into work.

Tomorrow, she would focus on the opportunity she had been given.

Tomorrow, she wouldn't think about Redington.

At least, that's what she told herself.

But as she lay awake in bed that night, staring at the unfamiliar ceiling, she knew it wasn't true.

And for the first time since she had arrived, she wondered if she had made a mistake.

Chapter 63

Paris had always been a city of inspiration, a place where history and faith intertwined with art and beauty. Now, as Lexi wandered through its ancient streets, she found herself drawn not to the designer boutiques or bustling cafés but to something deeper.

She had spent the morning at Notre Dame, standing beneath the shadow of its restored stained-glass windows, watching as the colored light danced across the scaffolding and newly repaired stone floors. After the devastating fire in 2019, the cathedral underwent extensive restoration and officially reopened on December 8, 2024. The cathedral, scarred but resilient, remained a monument of faith—its very walls echoing prayers of centuries past.

Lexi closed her eyes and inhaled the scent of melted wax and old wood, remembering the days when she had sat in church pews as a child, her mother's rosary beads clutched between her fingers. Catholicism had been the foundation of her spiritual upbringing, the framework through which she had first learned of miracles, saints, and divine grace.

But now, after everything—after the monastery, after the talisman, after discovering the Nine Spiritual Gifts—her faith had expanded beyond the bounds of a single doctrine. She no longer saw spirituality through the lens of just one religion but as something vast, limitless, and interwoven with every culture and every belief system.

Still, standing near the great cathedral, she couldn't ignore the pull of nostalgia. She stood staring, letting the silence envelop her.

"Was I wrong to walk away from this?" she wondered. "To follow a path that led me beyond the traditions I was raised in?"

A familiar voice, warm and teasing, pulled her from her thoughts.

"You always did overthink things."

Lexi's head snapped up, her breath catching. *Susannah.*

Her sister stood beside her, looking just as she had in life—blonde curls cascading over her shoulders, her hazel eyes bright with mischief and wisdom. She wore the same locket she had always worn, the one Lexi now kept tucked away in a jewelry box back in New York.

Lexi's hands trembled. "You're not real," she whispered.

Susannah smiled. *"And yet, here I am."*

Lexi exhaled shakily, her heart pounding. It had been years since she had lost Susannah, but the pain had never fully faded.

"Why now?" she asked.

"Because you need me," Susannah said simply. She gestured around them. *"You came here looking for something. Maybe answers. Maybe peace. Maybe just a reminder of where you started."*

Lexi swallowed, nodding. "I thought coming here would help me reconnect with something. But now I just feel… lost."

Susannah tilted her head. *"You're not lost, Lexi. You're just in between. That's the hardest place to be—between who you were and who you're becoming."*

Lexi looked down at her hands. "I keep thinking about the Nine Spiritual Gifts. About everything we learned at the monastery. And I wonder if I've let go of my faith too much."

"Faith isn't about holding on or letting go," Susannah said gently. *"It's about allowing yourself to evolve. To trust that Spirit is leading you, even when you don't know where."*

Lexi felt her throat tighten. "I just want to know I'm on the right path."

Susannah smiled knowingly. *"Then stop looking outside yourself for the answer."*

A gust of wind blew through the cathedral, flickering the candles along the altar. When Lexi turned back, Susannah was gone.

Lexi stood motionless for a long time, her sister's words echoing in her heart.

The next day, she made her way to the Sainte-Chapelle, a place she had always wanted to visit. The chapel's famed stained glass—fifteen towering panels that told the story of the Bible—filled the space with a celestial glow. Standing beneath them, Lexi felt as if she had stepped into a living vision.

She let her gaze wander over the intricate designs, her mind drifting to the concept of divine guidance. She had seen visions before—messages from Spirit that had come in moments of stillness or dreams. Perhaps the stories in these windows weren't so different.

As she stood there, she felt a strange sensation, like an unseen presence brushing against her mind.

Then, in an instant, the chapel seemed to melt away.

She was somewhere else, bathed in golden light.

A figure stood before her—tall, radiant, wrapped in flowing robes of shimmering white.

"Pistis Sophia."

Lexi recognized her instantly.

The archangel's voice was both powerful and soothing as it filled the air around her.

"You seek clarity, child, but clarity does not come from questioning your past. It comes from embracing your present."

Lexi felt her breath hitch. "Then why am I so conflicted?"

"Because you believe you must choose between the faith of your childhood and the wisdom you have gained. But truth is not found in choosing one over the other. It is found in allowing them to exist together, in harmony."

Lexi closed her eyes. She had spent so long thinking of faith as something separate from herself, something to be found in places—churches, monasteries, sacred sites. But faith had never been about a location. It had always been within her.

As she opened her eyes, she was back in Sainte-Chapelle, the golden light gone, but the feeling of warmth lingering in her chest.

She took a deep breath, feeling lighter than she had in weeks.

Her journey in Paris wasn't just about her career.

It was about rediscovering herself.

And for the first time since she had arrived, she knew she wasn't lost.

She was exactly where she was meant to be.

Chapter 64

Lexi buried herself in work.

Paris had a way of making everything seem grander, more intoxicating—the pastries, the architecture, the way the Seine shimmered under golden lamplight. But for all its magic, the city couldn't silence the ache she carried inside her.

She had come here for a fresh start, throwing herself into designing a new collection inspired by the Nine Spiritual Gifts. Her designs were fluid and ethereal, blending elegance with subtle spiritual symbols. The fashion world in Paris was already taking notice, and invitations to exclusive events and showcases flooded in.

Yet, no matter how busy she kept herself, the silence of her apartment at night was deafening.

She missed Redington. She missed her friends.

She didn't allow herself to say it out loud, but the truth was there, wrapped around her like an invisible thread she couldn't untangle.

So she worked harder.

Mornings were spent in her studio, afternoons in meetings, and evenings at networking events. She convinced herself she was thriving. She convinced herself she was happy.

But Paris had a way of forcing truths to the surface.

One evening, after a particularly high-profile event at a designer's loft in Le Marais, she found herself walking along the Seine, her heels clicking against the cobblestones. The party had been lively—full of artists, models, and wealthy investors eager to be part of something new.

And there at the party had been a man.

Julien.

Charming, confident, with the kind of easy French allure that women fell for effortlessly. He had spent the night engaged in playful banter with her, leaning in a little too close, offering to show her his version of Paris.

It should have been exciting.

Instead, it had made her feel empty.

Julien had leaned against the railing of a balcony, watching her with a knowing smirk. "You're in the most romantic city in the world, yet you seem somewhere else entirely."

She had forced a smile. "Just taking it all in."

He had studied her then, his expression shifting. "Or thinking about someone who isn't here."

Lexi's breath had caught in her throat.

She had laughed it off, thanked him for the conversation, and left soon after.

Now, as she strolled along the river, she exhaled slowly. Maybe Julien had seen something she had been trying to ignore.

The ache in her chest wasn't just loneliness. It was missing someone.

She stopped at a bridge, leaning against the cool metal railing. The reflection of the Eiffel Tower shimmered on the water, distorted and wavering.

Had Redington ever been to Paris?

Had he walked these same streets, leaned against this very railing, and watched the same moonlit ripples on the Seine?

The thought made her throat tighten.

She reached into her bag and pulled out her phone. She hadn't spoken to him since she left. They had parted on good terms, promising to keep in touch. But the reality was, they hadn't.

Maybe it was easier that way.

Or maybe she had been running from the truth.

She scrolled to his name.

Her thumb hovered over the screen.

Then, with a sigh, she locked the phone and slipped it back into her purse.

She wasn't ready.

The next morning, she arrived at her studio early, determined to drown herself in work. The light streamed through the tall windows, illuminating fabric swatches and unfinished sketches. She pulled out her journal and jotted down ideas—fluid silhouettes delicate embroidery that mirrored sacred symbols from different cultures.

She was in the middle of pinning fabric to a mannequin when a knock sounded at the door.

Her assistant, Clara, peeked in and announced in her thick French accent, "A lettair 'as arrived for you."

Lexi frowned. "A letter?"

Clara tilted her head slightly, her French accent lilting as she said, "Zere is no return address, but it arrived by special couriér."

Lexi's heart started hammering before she even opened it.

She turned it over, fingers grazing the unmarked seal.

Something told her this wasn't just any letter.

With a deep breath, she tore it open.

Her eyes scanned the page, her pulse quickening with every word.

And then, she froze.

It was from Redington.

Lexi swallowed hard, her fingers trembling as she read the first line again.

"Lexi—" She inhaled sharply.

Paris, it seemed, was done letting her hide.

Chapter 65

The letter sat unread on Lexi's desk, its crisp envelope stark against the clutter of sketches, fabric swatches, and notes strewn across the polished surface. She had stared at it for the better part of an hour, her fingers hovering over the first word, yet something inside her resisted. It had arrived without a return address, hand-delivered by a special courier, and though she told herself it could be anything—but a friendly note—her gut knew better.

It was from him.

Redington.

Her heart pounded at the thought, but she pushed it down, as she had been doing since she arrived in Paris. The city had become her sanctuary, a place where she could throw herself into her work, where every sunrise over the Seine and every late-night walk past Notre Dame offered her the illusion of distance—from the past, from herself, from him. But the truth lingered like the scent of espresso in the air: she missed him.

And now, here was a tangible piece of him, staring back at her.

Clara, sensing Lexi's hesitation, had already disappeared from the doorway, leaving her alone with whatever words Redington had sent. With a steadying breath, Lexi unfolded the letter.

His handwriting—bold, deliberate—was unmistakable.

Lexi,

I don't know if you'll read this. Part of me wouldn't blame you if you didn't. I wasn't sure I should send it at all, but there are things I need to say, things I should have said before we left the monastery.

Paris suits you, I have no doubt. I can almost picture you walking along the Seine, lost in thought, lost in your work. You were always meant for something grander, something bigger than any one place. And yet, I wonder if you feel it too—that pull, that unfinished thread between us.

I won't pretend to have answers. I've spent months trying to untangle what happened, trying to make sense of where we left things. I keep telling myself that the life I chose—the work I do—demands my full attention and that I can't afford to be distracted. But that's a lie, isn't it?

Because you were never a distraction.

You were the only thing that ever made me stop and truly see.

I don't know what this letter is supposed to accomplish. Maybe I just needed you to know that I miss you that I think about you more than I should. That no matter how far I go, some part of me still walks beside you.

Be well, Lexi.

Redington

Lexi's breath hitched as she finished reading. She gripped the letter tightly as if it might disappear the moment she let go.

A strange mix of emotions rushed through her—relief, longing, frustration, warmth. She had spent so much time convincing herself that moving on was the right thing to do, that throwing herself into her work, into a new city, was the answer. But here, in the quiet of her Parisian workspace, with Redington's words curling around her heart like a whispered confession, she realized she had been running.

Slowly, she set the letter down, smoothing out its creases.

Her gaze drifted to the window, where the lights of Paris flickered like distant stars, and for the first time since she arrived, she let herself feel it.

The missing.

The ache of what they had left unfinished.

And the quiet, undeniable truth that no matter how far she had come, her heart had never really let him go.

Chapter 66

The letter haunted her.

Lexi had folded it neatly, placed it in the drawer beside her bed, and told herself she wouldn't think about it again. That had been three days ago. And yet, she found herself reaching for it in quiet moments—after long meetings, before drifting off to sleep as she sipped her morning coffee on the balcony overlooking Paris.

Redington's words clung to her mind like a bittersweet melody, soft yet insistent, threading their way through her thoughts no matter how much she tried to drown them out with work.

She needed a distraction.

That morning, she buried herself in designing a new collection, sketching furiously in her sunlit studio. The fabric samples Clara had gathered lay untouched on the table, her mind too restless to focus on materials and textures. Every time she tried to lose herself in her work, the memory of Redington's letter pulled her back.

Maybe she needed a change of scenery.

That evening, she accepted an invitation to a gallery opening—an elegant affair in the Marais district. It was the kind of event she used to thrive in, dazzling, fast-paced, filled with creatives, socialites, and intellectuals discussing art, fashion, and philosophy over glasses of champagne.

Yet, as she moved through the gallery, offering polite smiles and nodding at acquaintances, she felt disconnected. The hum of conversation, the clink of crystal glasses, the flashes of camera lights—none of it stirred her. The room buzzed around her, but she wasn't really present.

"Lexi."

A deep, velvety voice, tinged with the unmistakable cadence of a French accent, pulled her back.

She turned, surprised to see Marc, the effortlessly charming French designer she had met at a previous event. He was dressed in a sleek, charcoal-gray suit, perfectly tailored to his lean frame, his wavy dark hair slightly tousled, as if he had just stepped out of a passionate conversation or, perhaps, out of bed. More than once, Clara had hinted that he was interested in her.

Marc's lips curved into a knowing smile as he took her in. "You look… magnifique tonight."

Lexi returned the smile, "You always say that," she teased.

"Ah, but I only speak the truth, ma chère." He tilted his head, his eyes dark, and assessed. "But tonight, you are… how do you say? Elsewhere?"

She considered brushing it off, pretending she was simply tired or distracted by work. But something about Marc's easy confidence, his ability to see beyond the surface, made her admit, "Just a lot on my mind."

Marc took a flute of champagne from a passing waiter and handed it to her, his fingers brushing hers lightly. "Then perhaps a walk after this? Paris has a way of bringing clarity."

She hesitated. The idea of walking the city with Marc, of allowing herself to be drawn into his world—even if just for a night—was tempting. But then again, everything about Paris was tempting.

Finally, she nodded. "A walk sounds nice."

Later that night, they strolled along the Seine, the city lights reflecting in the rippling water. The cool air carried the scent of freshly baked bread and espresso from a nearby café, and for the first time in days, Lexi felt a little lighter.

Marc's presence was effortless, his conversation fluid. He was witty, charming, and disarmingly perceptive, moving between deep philosophy and playful flirtation with the ease of someone who had spent his life weaving between art and passion.

They spoke about creativity, about inspiration, about how Paris had shaped them both.

Then, casually, he asked, "And what is truly on your mind, Lexi?"

She hesitated. She had spent weeks pretending she was perfectly fine, that Paris had healed her. But tonight, with the soft glow of street lamps casting golden shadows on the cobblestone, she found herself saying, "Someone from my past."

Marc's expression was unreadable. "Someone important?"

She let out a quiet laugh, shaking her head at her own foolishness. "Yes."

They walked in silence for a moment before he stopped and turned to face her, his gaze steady. "I do not know much about love, Lexi, but I do know this—Paris is a city of clarity. We may come here to escape, but in the end, this city always reveals the truths we try to ignore."

Lexi looked at him, touched by his sincerity. "And what if the truth is complicated?"

Marc studied her for a long moment before lifting his hand lightly brushing a strand of hair from her face. His touch was feather-light, intimate but not demanding. "Then you must decide, ma belle… do you run from it? Or do you face it?"

Her breath hitched. The answer should have been simple, but it wasn't.

Marc's lips quirked into a small, knowing smile. "No matter what you choose, I hope you find what you are looking for."

Lexi smiled back, grateful. But deep down, she already knew—she wasn't looking for something.

She was looking for someone.

Chapter 67

The soft hum of the Parisian morning filtered through the sheer curtains of Lexi's apartment. The scent of freshly brewed coffee mingled with the distant aroma of warm croissants from the café below. She sat at her small marble bistro table, staring at the city bathed in the golden glow of the rising sun. The streets of Montmartre were already alive—laughter from vendors, the melodic notes of an accordion drifting from a busker, and the occasional ringing of a bicycle bell.

Yet, despite the city's vibrancy, a hollow feeling settled deep in her chest.

She had spent the night replaying Marc's words in her head.

Paris reveals the truths we try to ignore.

She had tried to ignore Redington. She had thrown herself into her work, into the charm of the city, into the embrace of fleeting distractions.

But none of it could silence the truth ringing in her heart—she missed him.

With a sigh, she pushed away from the table, the ceramic clink of her coffee cup breaking the silence. Work. That was the answer. If she could just keep herself busy, maybe the ache in her chest would lessen.

She slipped into her atelier, a spacious studio with vaulted ceilings and sprawling windows that overlooked the bustling Rue de Rivoli. Fabrics in soft hues and rich textures draped over mannequins, half-finished sketches cluttered her desk, and swatches of intricate embroidery spilled across the worktable.

Clara, her ever-efficient assistant, was already waiting, a bundle of notes tucked beneath her arm. "The final fittings for your collection are scheduled for this afternoon, and the press preview is set for next week. Oh—" she hesitated, then smirked. "Marc sent flowers."

Lexi let out a soft laugh. "He doesn't give up easily, does he?"

Clara shrugged. "French men. They are romantic… persistent. You should let him charm you."

Lexi shook her head, waving off the thought. "I don't need charming right now."

"No?" Clara raised an eyebrow. "Then what do you need, boss?"

Lexi hesitated. What did she need?

Before she could answer, Clara pulled a crisp envelope from her pile of notes. "This came this morning. Special courier. No return address."

Lexi stilled. A strange sense of déjà vu washed over her as she took the letter. The last time she had received a letter without a sender, it had been from Redington.

With careful fingers, she broke the wax seal and unfolded the letter.

The handwriting was neat, unfamiliar—not Redington's. But as she read the first line, her breath caught.

"You are being watched."

Her fingers tightened around the paper, her heartbeat spiking.

The letter continued,

"They know about the talisman. They know you were at the monastery. You must leave Paris. You are not safe."

Lexi's mind reeled. The talisman? No one here knew about it. No one outside the monastery even understood its significance.

Her pulse thundered as she read the final words.

"Trust no one."

A gust of wind rattled the windows, sending a shiver down her spine.

"Lexi?" Clara's voice was softer now, concerned. "What's wrong?"

Lexi folded the letter, slipping it into the pocket of her silk robe. "Nothing. Just another distraction."

But deep down, she knew—this wasn't just a distraction.
This was a warning.

Chapter 68

The warning stayed with Lexi long after she had tucked the letter away.

By the time she left the studio that evening, the usual charm of Paris had dimmed. The streets were still alive with their effortless beauty—the glow of lamplights casting golden reflections on the cobblestone roads, the faint murmur of lovers strolling along the Seine—but everything felt different now.

The letter had rattled her.

She wasn't paranoid—at least, she didn't think she was—but as she walked through the lively streets, she couldn't shake the feeling of being watched.

At first, she convinced herself it was just her nerves. The cryptic words had unsettled her, and she was merely imagining things.

But then, as she crossed a quiet street in Le Marais, she caught a glimpse of movement in the reflection of a shop window.

A man.

He was tall, dressed in dark clothing, his gaze sharp.

She turned quickly—but he was gone.

Her heart pounded.

Lexi forced herself to walk normally, refusing to look over her shoulder. She could hear Dorian's voice in her head, calm and steady. Fear is a doorway. Choose carefully what you let in.

She took a breath, inhaling the cool Parisian night air, grounding herself. If someone was watching her, what did they want? The letter had warned her about the talisman, but the talisman was safe—wasn't it?

Her steps quickened, her thoughts racing. She needed to think.

By the time she reached her apartment, her body was tense with anticipation. The elevator ride to her floor felt agonizingly slow, and when she stepped into her flat, she immediately locked the door behind her.

The silence inside was suffocating.

She flicked on the lights, scanning the room, half-expecting to find someone lurking in the shadows.

Nothing.

With a shaking breath, she pulled out the letter and read it again.

"Trust no one."

She sank into the couch, rubbing her temples.

This wasn't just a coincidence. Someone out there knew about her past, about the monastery, about the talisman.

And that meant someone wanted something from her.

Her phone buzzed, startling her.

Marc.

She hesitated before answering.

"Bonsoir, Lexi." His voice was smooth, laced with its usual charm. "You disappeared so quickly the other night. I was beginning to think I'd offended you."

Lexi closed her eyes, forcing a smile into her voice. "No, not at all. I've just been… distracted."

A pause.

"You sound tense," he noted. "Why do I get the feeling you are not alone?"

She glanced around the apartment, a chill running down her spine. "Because I don't feel alone."

Marc's tone shifted, losing its playfulness. "Tell me what happened."

Lexi hesitated. The letter's warning echoed in her head. Trust no one.

Could she trust Marc?

She barely knew him, yet something in his voice—his quiet intensity, his concern—made her want to confide in him.

"I received a letter. Anonymously delivered." She exhaled. "It was a warning."

Silence.

Then, "What kind of warning?"

She swallowed. "That I'm being watched. That I should leave Paris."

Another pause, longer this time.

"Where are you now?"

"Home."

"Stay there. I'm coming over."

"Marc—"

"Don't argue, Lexi." His voice left no room for protest. "Just stay inside."

The call ended.

Lexi stared at the phone in her hand, her mind racing.

Was she making a mistake trusting him?

Maybe.

But right now, she wasn't sure she wanted to be alone.

Chapter 69

The minutes ticked by with agonizing slowness.

Lexi sat curled up on her couch, knees drawn to her chest, fingers gripping her mug of now-cold tea. The city hummed outside her apartment, but inside, everything was unnervingly still.

She kept glancing at the letter on the table, its stark warning playing over and over in her head.

"Trust no one."

And yet, Marc was on his way.

She didn't know if it was intuition or desperation that had made her pick up the phone. Maybe both. She wasn't sure which was the greater risk—trusting him, or being alone.

A knock at the door.

Lexi's heart lurched.

She set her mug down carefully, rising from the couch, her bare feet making no sound against the hardwood floor.

Another knock—firmer this time.

She hesitated for a split second, then checked the peephole.

Marc.

Dressed in dark clothes, his sharp features shadowed under the dim hallway light.

Lexi unlocked the door but kept the chain in place. "Say something," she murmured.

His lips quirked into a smile, but his eyes were serious. "I told you I'd come."

She studied him for a beat longer before unlatching the chain and stepping aside. Marc entered without hesitation, closing the door behind him.

The air between them was charged, thick with unspoken tension.

He took in her small apartment—a minimalist space filled with soft neutrals, a few sketches pinned to the walls, an unfinished design draped over a dress form in the corner. His gaze flickered to the coffee table, where the letter lay, then back to her.

"What exactly did it say?" he asked.

Lexi handed him the letter without a word.

Marc took his time reading it, his expression unreadable. When he finally looked at her, his voice was lower, rougher.

"This isn't a joke."

"I know."

"Have you told anyone else?"

She shook her head. "Just you."

A flicker of something—concern? Frustration?—crossed his face before he exhaled sharply and ran a hand through his hair.

"Lexi," he said slowly, deliberately, "Whatever this is, it's bigger than a simple warning. Someone doesn't just send a letter like this unless they have a reason."

She swallowed. "You think it's about the talisman?"

He studied her, his sharp gaze searching. "You tell me. Does anyone in Paris know about it?"

"No."

Not that she had told, anyway.

Marc tapped the letter against his palm, thinking. "If someone went through the trouble of finding you and sending this, they don't want to scare you off without purpose. They want to rattle you. Keep you distracted. And that means—"

"They're not done."

Marc nodded.

A shiver ran down her spine.

She wasn't new to danger. The monastery had tested her. Redington had warned her of the things lurking in the world, things not everyone could see.

But this was different.

This was targeted.

Marc's voice cut through the tension. "If you want my opinion—"

"I do."

He smirked, just a little. "Then you're not safe here."

Lexi exhaled, dragging a hand through her hair. "I can't just leave Paris, Marc."

His smirk faded. "Why?"

She hesitated because leaving would feel like running because she had built something here, something of her own. Because a part of her was still waiting for a sign that Redington would find her again.

Instead, she said, "Because I need answers."

Marc watched her for a long moment, then exhaled through his nose, shaking his head with a wry smile. "You're stubborn, Lexi."

"So I've been told."

He studied her, his expression thoughtful, then finally nodded. "Then we do this carefully."

She frowned. "What do you mean?"

Marc set the letter down. "I mean, if someone is watching you, we need to watch them back."

Lexi's stomach tightened. "You mean… set a trap?"

A slow, dangerous smile spread across his face. "Exactly."

For the first time in days, Lexi felt something other than fear.

She felt…

Chapter 70

Lexi sat frozen.

The realization struck her like a sudden gust of cold wind.

How did Marc know where I live?

She had never given him her address. They had met at events, at cafés, and in public places. He had never been to her apartment—never even asked. Yet, when they spoke on the phone, he had simply said, "I'll come over."

And he had without hesitation.

Her heartbeat thudded against her ribs, a slow, creeping unease curling in her stomach.

Marc stood near the table, fingers lightly tapping the ominous letter, his posture relaxed as if he didn't sense her shift in energy. But now, she was watching him differently.

His presence had always been easy, comforting in a way that disarmed her, but now?

Now, she felt like prey, realizing too late that she had stepped into a snare.

She took a slow breath, keeping her voice even. "Marc, how did you find my place?"

He glanced up, his expression unreadable. Then, after the briefest hesitation, he smiled. "Paris isn't so big, ma chérie."

The answer was too smooth. Too practiced.

Lexi narrowed her eyes. "That's not an answer."

Marc exhaled, rubbing a hand across his jaw, and for the first time, she saw a flicker of something beneath his usual charm. Annoyance? Frustration? Guilt?

"I asked someone," he admitted finally. "Clara."

Lexi's brows shot up. Clara?

He sighed. "I was worried about you, Lexi. I knew you were troubled after the gallery, and when we talked—" He paused, his gaze softening. "I wanted to be there for you."

Lexi studied him, her mind racing. Clara wouldn't just give out her address—not without a reason. But maybe Marc had convinced her. Maybe Clara had thought she was helping.

Or maybe… this was bigger than just Marc.

The letter. The warning. The perfectly timed appearance of someone she had barely trusted enough to let into her world.

Was it all connected?

Lexi crossed her arms. "And if I had said I didn't need your help? Would you still have come?"

Marc tilted his head, watching her carefully now. "What are you implying?"

She didn't answer. Not yet.

The air between them shifted, something subtle but undeniable.

Marc's smile returned, but it didn't quite reach his eyes. "Lexi, I understand. You've been through a lot. You have every reason to be cautious." He picked up the letter and turned it over between his fingers. "But you're not the only one who's concerned. Whoever sent this, they're trying to shake you. I don't want to see that happen."

The words were reasonable. Reassuring, even.

But something still didn't feel right.

Lexi forced herself to relax, nodding as if she accepted his explanation. "You're right," she murmured. "I'm just… on edge."

Marc stepped closer, his presence warm, steady. "Then let me help."

Lexi met his gaze, searching for something—a crack, a flicker of truth, a sign that she wasn't imagining this.

She found nothing.

And that, more than anything, scared her.

Because if Marc was lying, he was very, very good at it.

Two Hours Later

Lexi sat on the edge of her bed, watching the city lights flicker through the sheer curtains.

Marc had left an hour ago after another round of reassurances and promises that they would "Figure this out together." She had smiled, played along, and pretended to believe him.

And then, as soon as the door had closed behind him, she had locked it. Twice.

She needed answers.

Not tomorrow. Not when it was convenient. Now.

Lexi grabbed her phone, hesitating only for a moment before dialing Clara's number.

It rang twice before a sleepy voice answered. "Lexi? What—?"

"Clara," Lexi cut in, keeping her voice low. "Did you give Marc my address?"

A pause. A beat too long.

Then, softly, "…Yes."

Lexi closed her eyes. "Why?"

Clara sighed. "He called me the night of the gallery. Said he was worried about you, that you had been acting distant. He asked where you lived because he wanted to check on you."

Lexi gritted her teeth. "And you just told him?"

"I—" Clara hesitated. "He sounded genuine. And I know you, Lexi. You never let people in. I thought maybe… maybe you needed someone."

Lexi exhaled slowly, willing herself to stay calm. "Did he ask anything else?"

A longer pause.

Then, more hesitant this time, "Yes."

Lexi's grip on the phone tightened. "What else did he ask, Clara?"

"He wanted to know about the monastery."

A cold wave crashed over her.

Lexi shot to her feet, her mind racing.

Marc wasn't just some charming designer.

He had been watching her.

And now, she had no idea who he really was.

Chapter 71

Lexi didn't sleep.

She spent the night curled up in the corner of her bed, staring at the faint glow of her phone screen as she replayed her conversation with Clara over and over in her head.

Marc had asked about the monastery.

Why?

It wasn't just casual curiosity. Not anymore.

The realization slithered through her, cold and sharp. Marc had never been interested in her work, not really. He had asked the right questions, said the right things, and played the role of the effortlessly charming Parisian.

But now, the pieces weren't fitting.

Had he been watching her from the beginning? Had he sought her out deliberately?

Or worse—was he connected to the letter?

A knock at the door jolted her from her thoughts.

Her pulse spiked.

3:12 AM.

No one should be here.

She slid off the bed as silently as possible, creeping toward the door, careful not to let the floorboards creak. Peering through the peephole, she saw only darkness.

Another knock. Firmer this time.

Lexi swallowed, her breath shallow.

No. She wasn't opening it.

Backing away, she grabbed her phone with shaking fingers and texted Clara.

Lexi: *Tell me the truth. How well do you know Marc?*

She waited, every second stretching unbearably long.

Three dots appeared. Then disappeared.

Lexi's stomach dropped.

The knock came again—harder, more insistent.

She spun toward the kitchen, grabbing the heaviest thing she could find—a thick metal candlestick from her countertop. Clutching it with both hands, she backed into the shadows of the living room, watching the door.

The knocking stopped.

Silence.

Then—footsteps retreating.

Lexi remained frozen, listening until she was sure whoever it was had gone.

The weight of the moment crashed over her.

She wasn't safe here.

She had to leave. Now.

By 5:00 AM, she was packed.

A single suitcase, light and efficient. She didn't know where she was going yet, only that she couldn't stay.

Marc had crossed a line. Whether it was a coincidence or something darker, she wasn't going to sit around waiting to find out.

She booked a train ticket south, toward Nice. It wasn't far enough to disappear, but it would give her space—distance to think, to plan.

As she left her apartment, she checked her phone again.

Still no reply from Clara.

That alone told her everything she needed to know.

Hours Later—A New City.

Nice was different from Paris in every way.

The warmth, the slow rhythm, the scent of salt in the air—everything felt lighter here as if the very atmosphere rejected the weight she had been carrying.

But even as she walked the sunlit streets, she couldn't shake the feeling that she wasn't alone.

She kept catching glimpses—a figure disappearing around a corner, a shadow lingering too long in a café window.

Paranoia? Maybe.

But Lexi had learned long ago that intuition was rarely wrong.

That evening, she checked into a boutique hotel near the waterfront, a charming place with ivy-covered walls and an old-world charm that reminded her of the monastery.

She locked her door. Bolted it. Pulled the curtains shut.

Then she pulled out her phone and did what she should have done days ago.

She called Redington.

It rang once.

Twice.

Then—his voice, rough with sleep.

"Lexi?"

The sound of his voice hit her harder than she expected.

For a moment, she couldn't speak.

Then, in a whisper, she said, "I think I'm in trouble."

Chapter 72

The line crackled with silence for half a second before Redington's voice sharpened, suddenly wide awake.

"Where are you?"

Lexi sat on the edge of the hotel bed, gripping the phone like a lifeline.

"Nice." The word came out shakier than she wanted. "I left Paris this morning."

She heard rustling—him moving, getting up. He was already in motion.

"Tell me everything."

Lexi exhaled slowly, forcing herself to think clearly. "It started with Marc. He—he knew things about me that I never told him. About the monastery. About the letter."

A pause. Then, "What letter?"

Her stomach twisted.

He didn't send it.

That realization solidified something terrifying inside her.

"I got a letter, Redington. No return address, just your name signed at the bottom." She rubbed her temple, feeling the weight of the past few days pressing down on her. "I thought it was from you. But now…"

Now, she wasn't sure of anything.

Redington swore under his breath. "Lexi, listen to me. You need to stay inside. Lock the doors, don't go anywhere alone."

"I already did."

"Good. I'm coming to you."

Her breath hitched. Redington was coming.

She hadn't expected that. She had wanted his help, his advice, but the thought of him dropping everything to get on a plane—

"Oh my God, I can't ask that of you—"

"Too bad," he cut in. "You call me if anything happens. If you hear something, see something out of place, even if it feels small. Understand?"

She nodded, then realized he couldn't see her. "Yeah."

Redington hesitated. For a moment, neither of them spoke. Then, softer, "You should've called me sooner, Lex."

She swallowed past the lump in her throat. "I didn't know if I should."

"Always."

The quiet certainty in his voice made something inside her crack.

She closed her eyes, gripping the phone tighter. What if she had never left? What if she had fought for him instead of running?

But it was too late for that now.

Wasn't it?

"I'll be there soon," Redington said. "Sit tight."

And then he was gone.

Lexi didn't sleep.

She sat by the window instead, the glow of the streetlights washing over her as she watched the quiet streets below.

Nice was supposed to be safe—a refuge.

But now, every unfamiliar face felt like a threat. Every shadow felt like it was watching her.

She picked up her phone, checking for a message from Clara.

Still nothing.

She knew something. She had to.

Lexi hesitated, then sent one last message.

Lexi: *I don't know what's happening, but I need the truth. Please, Clara. If you know something, please tell me.*

No response.

Outside, a figure moved at the edge of her vision.

Lexi's heart slammed against her ribs.

She stood so fast the chair scraped against the floor, her pulse hammering.

The figure paused under the glow of a street lamp.

Marc.

She stumbled back a step, pressing herself against the wall.

How did he find her?

Her phone buzzed in her hand.

A new message.

From Clara.

Clara: *Lexi, I'm sorry. You need to leave. NOW.*

Her breath caught.

Outside, Marc lifted his head.

And then, slowly, he smiled.

Chapter 73

$\mathcal{L}$exi's body moved before her mind could catch up.

She grabbed her bag, her passport, her phone—anything within reach—and backed away from the window.

Her pulse pounded against her skull as she reread Clara's message.

You need to leave. NOW.

Marc stood beneath the streetlamp, hands in his pockets, his posture easy, almost amused. Like he knew she'd see him like he wanted her to.

How did he find me?

She had left Paris without telling anyone but Clara. She had booked the hotel under an alias. But now, here he was.

Her phone vibrated again.

Clara: *They know where you are. I didn't tell them, I swear, but I overheard something. Lexi, please—just go.*

Lexi turned toward the door, but something inside her hesitated. *They.*

Who were they?

She could feel the blood draining from her face.

She had trusted Marc. Let him into her world. Had he been watching her all along? Was he the one who sent the letter? Or was there someone else pulling the strings?

Outside, Marc shifted, raising his hand in a slow, deliberate wave.

Lexi's stomach twisted.

She didn't wait.

She threw on her coat, shoved her phone into her pocket, and grabbed the small leather bag she had packed earlier.

She needed a plan. She needed a way out.

The train station.

Redington.

She fumbled with her phone as she reached the door, pressing his name.

The call rang once. Twice.

Come on, come on—

"Lexi?" His voice was rough.

"Redington, he's here."

A pause. Then: "Where?"

"Outside my hotel." She wrenched open the door, peering down the dimly lit hallway. Empty. She forced herself to breathe. "I don't know how he found me, but Clara just warned me to leave. She said they know where I am."

Silence. Then his voice, tight and sharp, "Go. Now. Get to the train station. Do not go straight to the airport—too predictable. I'll meet you at the next stop. Don't look back."

Lexi nodded, already moving.

"I'm sending you a new number," Redington continued. "If your phone goes dark, use it."

"Okay."

"Lexi."

She stopped at the stairwell.

His voice softened. "Don't let him corner you."

Her fingers curled around the railing. "I won't."

She ended the call.

Escape

Lexi took the stairs two at a time, her heart hammering against her ribs.

The lobby was quiet. The night concierge barely looked up from his book as she stepped out into the cool Nice air.

Marc was gone.

That's worse.

She kept her head down and moved quickly, weaving through side streets slipping into crowds when she could.

She could feel the paranoia creeping in— shadows stretching too long, footsteps echoing too close.

She reached the station and bought the first ticket she could get—Marseille.

The train arrived within minutes. She stepped on, found a window seat, and exhaled, watching the city blur past as the train pulled away.

She wasn't safe yet.

But she was moving.

And Redington was coming.

Chapter 74

The rhythmic hum of the train against the tracks did little to calm Lexi's nerves. She sat rigid, her bag clutched tightly in her lap, her fingers curled around her phone. The ticket to Marseille had been a last-minute choice, but even now, she wasn't sure it had been the right one.

The overhead lights flickered as the train passed through a tunnel, and her reflection in the window appeared fragmented, fractured—just like the mess she'd somehow found herself in.

Her mind replayed the last hour on a loop. Marc was standing beneath the streetlamp, watching her. The text from Clara. The way Redington's voice had shifted—sharp, commanding—the moment he realized she was in danger.

She forced herself to breathe, pressing her fingers against her temple.

Across the aisle, a man in a gray coat sipped his coffee, flipping through a newspaper.

In the row ahead, a woman in a dark sweater stared blankly out the window.

They could be anyone. Watching. Waiting.

Her paranoia was getting the best of her. Wasn't it?

She had to stay calm.

A soft chime signaled an incoming message. She glanced down at her phone.

Unknown Number: New line. Memorize it. Destroy the old one. Don't stop moving.

Lexi inhaled sharply.

Redington.

She committed the number to memory before powering down her phone. The SIM card would have to go next, but not here. Not yet.

The train slowed as it pulled into a small station just outside Aix-en-Provence.

Lexi glanced around, her pulse quickening.

The man in the gray coat folded his newspaper but didn't stand.

The woman in the dark sweater was gone.

Where did she—?

The train doors slid open with a mechanical hiss. A few passengers disembarked. Others boarded.

Lexi caught sight of a familiar silhouette moving toward her car.

Marc.

Her stomach lurched.

How the hell had he found her so fast?

She didn't think. She moved.

Grabbing her bag, she slipped into the narrow aisle and headed for the opposite door. The second the train's warning chime sounded, she bolted, stepping off onto the platform just as the doors sealed shut behind her.

She didn't look back.

Lexi walked quickly through the station, forcing herself to blend into the late-night travelers. Her heart pounded against her ribs, but she kept her posture relaxed, her pace natural.

Marc was here. That meant they were close.

The second she reached the exit, she ducked into a side street and pulled her hood up. She needed a new plan. Marseille wasn't safe anymore.

The bus depot was nearby.

She scanned the schedule, searching for something that would throw them off.

Toulouse.

It wasn't perfect, but it would buy her time.

She purchased the ticket in cash and boarded the night bus, settling into a window seat. The doors closed. The engine rumbled to life.

She exhaled.

Then, just before the bus pulled away, she saw him.

Marc.

Standing at the far end of the station. His eyes scanned the crowd.

Looking for her.

A shiver ran down her spine.
He wasn't working alone.
This wasn't just about her.
It was about the talisman.
And now, they knew she had it.

Chapter 75

The night bus pulled out of the station, the hiss of the brakes fading as it merged onto the dimly lit road. Lexi sat rigid, her shoulder pressed against the cold glass of the window, her bag clutched tightly in her lap. The reflection of the passing streetlights flickered against her face, casting shifting patterns across her pale skin.

Her breath fogged the window as she watched the dark silhouette of Marc standing at the edge of the platform disappear into the distance. He hadn't seen her—or at least, she hoped he hadn't.

She could still feel his eyes on her.

Marc had found her too quickly. That meant someone had tipped him off. Someone close. Clara? No. She didn't want to believe it, but how else could Marc have known where to find her?

Her fingers brushed against the glass crystal of a piece of the talisman hidden beneath the folds of her sweater. Its subtle warmth was familiar now, like a heartbeat.

She wasn't sure what terrified her more—Marc's ability to track her or the fact that someone wanted the talisman badly enough to orchestrate this level of pursuit.

She needed to think, to regroup.

The bus rattled along the uneven road, the low murmur of passengers blending into the hum of the engine. Across the aisle, an older man in a battered coat adjusted his scarf. A young couple near the back whispered to each other in rapid French, their faces illuminated by the glow of a shared phone screen.

A quiet calm settled over the bus—but Lexi wasn't calm.

Her hand slipped beneath her sweater, brushing against the smoothness of the talisman. She closed her eyes, searching for the clarity she'd once found so easily in meditation.

Pistis Sophia, she thought, *if you're listening…*

Nothing. Just the steady rumble of the bus beneath her feet.

She opened her eyes. The world outside the window had darkened, the scattered lights of the countryside blurring into a golden haze as the bus picked up speed.

Her phone buzzed once in her pocket.

Lexi stiffened.

She shouldn't have kept it. The SIM card was still active. That was how they were tracking her.

Slowly, she pulled the phone from her pocket and glanced at the screen.

Unknown Number:

We need to meet. Tomorrow. Noon. Montségur.

Her breath hitched. Montségur.

The ancient Cathar stronghold. A place tied to legends of hidden knowledge—and to the Grail.

Her heart began to race. How did they know?

She deleted the message and powered down the phone. Her hands were shaking.

This was more than a coincidence.

Across the aisle, the man in the battered coat shifted, folding his arms across his chest. His eyes were closed, but the tension in his posture suggested he wasn't really asleep.

She had to get off the bus. Now.

Lexi stood, slinging her bag over her shoulder as the bus slowed to navigate a sharp curve. She made her way toward the back door. The driver glanced at her in the mirror.

"Next stop isn't for another twenty minutes," he said in French.

"I can't wait that long," Lexi replied. "Just open the door."

He frowned but pulled the lever. The door of the bus hissed open.

Lexi jumped down into the chill of the night, her breath rising in a thin mist.

The bus's headlights swept over her as it pulled away, disappearing into the darkness.

She was alone now on the side of a narrow road flanked by looming trees. Crickets chirped in the distance. Further ahead, the faint glow of a village nestled in the hills suggested shelter.

She started walking toward it. Her boots crunched against the gravel.

Her thoughts raced.

Marc had been watching her for weeks. She'd ignored the signs—his familiarity with her schedule, the ease with which he always seemed to 'run into' her. He'd even known how to find her apartment.

She had trusted him. Let her guard down.

Fool.

A branch snapped behind her.

Lexi froze.

Slowly, she turned.

The road was empty—just the dark outline of the forest on either side. The wind whispered through the trees.

Her nerves were shot. She was imagining things.

Except...

A figure stood at the edge of the tree line.

Lexi's pulse hammered in her ears.

The figure took a step forward, the glow of moonlight catching on dark hair and the sharp line of a jaw.

Her breath stilled.

Redington.

His dark jacket blended with the night, but she would have known that silhouette anywhere.

She took a shaky step forward. "How did you—?"

"I've been following you since you left the station," he said, his voice low. He stepped toward her, closing the distance between them in three strides.

"I told you to stay put," he said, his hands closing on her arms, his touch firm but careful. "And yet here you are. Standing on the side of the road in the middle of the night."

Her chest tightened. "Marc—he knew where I was. Someone's feeding him information."

Redington's gaze darkened. His grip tightened slightly. "Clara?"

Lexi shook her head, her throat closing. "I don't know. But someone wants my piece of the talisman. And they're willing to do whatever it takes to get it."

Redington's jaw tightened. "Then we need to disappear. Now."

Lexi hesitated. "What about Montségur?"

A muscle worked in his jaw. "That message— someone knew you'd go there. Which means it's a trap."

"But it could also be the key."

Redington's eyes sharpened. "Lexi—"

"I can't run forever," she said, her voice steady despite the tremor in her hands. "If

Montségur holds the answers—if it's the final piece of the puzzle—I have to face it."

Redington's gaze remained locked on hers, his blue eyes cold and calculating. Then, slowly, he exhaled.

"I guess we are going to Montségur."

Her heart thudded painfully in her chest.

He didn't look away. "I'm not happy, you know."

Lexi's breath hitched. She hadn't realized how much she had needed to hear those words until now.

She reached for his hand. He didn't hesitate. His fingers laced through hers, warm and solid.

"Montségur," he said, his voice low.

Lexi nodded. "Montségur."

As they walked toward the village lights, Lexi couldn't help but feel like something was shifting.

The stakes were rising. The truth was closer than ever.

And whatever awaited them at Montségur— Lexi knew that this time, she wouldn't face it alone.

Chapter 76

The drive to Montségur was quiet. Too quiet.

Lexi sat in the passenger seat of the black sedan Redington had 'borrowed' from a sleepy town outside Toulouse. The engine hummed low beneath the tense silence stretching between them. Moonlight filtered through the windshield, illuminating the narrow mountain road that twisted upward through the Pyrenees.

The night outside was absolute—dense forest crowding the edges of the road, the dark silhouette of the mountains looming against the star-flecked sky. Even the steady sound of the tires against the pavement seemed muted as if the world itself was holding its breath.

Lexi's hand drifted to the talisman beneath her sweater, her thumb brushing the surface. Its warmth pulsed faintly beneath her fingers—a heartbeat of quiet reassurance.

Redington's hands were steady on the wheel, his eyes sharp as they navigated the winding road. He hadn't said much since they'd left the village. The tension in his jaw told her everything she needed to know. He was calculating, analyzing, and preparing for whatever lay ahead.

"You're angry," Lexi said quietly, breaking the silence.

Redington's eyes didn't leave the road. "I'm not angry."

She raised an eyebrow. "You look angry."

"I'm… focused," he said. His voice was clipped, precise. "Marc knew where you were. He knew about Montségur. That means someone close to you has been feeding him information."

"Clara?"

Redington's jaw twitched. "It's possible."

Lexi's chest tightened. She didn't want to believe it—but she couldn't ignore the evidence. Clara knew her schedule. She knew where Lexi lived. If Marc had been working with someone inside her circle, it narrowed the list of suspects considerably.

"I trusted her," Lexi murmured.

Redington's gaze softened briefly, but his tone remained firm. "We'll figure it out. After Montségur."

Lexi exhaled and turned toward the window, her forehead resting against the cold glass. They were climbing higher now, the road narrowing as it twisted around the side of the mountain. Below, the dark valley stretched into infinity.

"You know the history of Montségur?" Redington asked.

Lexi nodded. "The last Cathar stronghold. The place where they supposedly hid the Grail."

Redington glanced at her. "And?"

"And some believe the Grail isn't a cup at all—but knowledge. A spiritual key."

Redington's expression darkened. "That would explain why Marc and whoever he's working with want the talisman so badly."

Lexi's fingers curled around the edge of her sweater. "What if the talisman is the key?"

"Then we need to make sure it stays out of their hands."

The road straightened as they approached a weathered wooden sign:

MONTSEGUR 2 KM

Lexi's pulse quickened.

They rounded the final bend, and the ancient fortress came into view. Montségur sat high on a sheer cliff, its stone walls weathered and cracked with centuries of wear. The entrance was partially hidden by overgrown ivy, but the massive iron gate was unmistakable.

Redington pulled the car to a stop at the edge of the dirt path. His hand hovered over the gear shift. "You're sure about this?"

Lexi's breath fogged the glass as she stared at the dark silhouette of the fortress. "I need to know why the talisman led me here."

Redington nodded once. "Then we don't stop until we have answers."

They climbed out of the car, their boots crunching against the gravel path as they approached the gate. Lexi slipped her hand into her pocket, wrapping her fingers around the talisman. Its warmth increased slightly, a subtle pulse that seemed to echo the beat of her heart.

"The gate's unlocked," Redington said, testing the rusted latch.

Lexi frowned. "That's not suspicious at all."

Redington pushed the gate open. It groaned in protest.

They stepped inside.

The inner courtyard was deathly quiet. Moonlight spilled over weathered stone archways and crumbling towers. Shadows pressed in at the edges, and the cool mountain air carried the scent of moss and damp earth.

Lexi's gaze swept the courtyard. At the far end, a set of worn stone steps led upward toward the central keep. A carved symbol marked the archway—a spiral surrounded by smaller, interlocking circles.

Her breath hitched. "That's the same pattern as the talisman."

Redington stepped closer, his gaze sharp. "That's not a coincidence."

Lexi pulled the piece of talisman from her pocket. It pulsed gently in her hand, the symbol etched into its surface, glowing faintly in the moonlight. She held it toward the archway. The carved spiral shimmered in response.

"It's a key," Lexi whispered.

Redington's hand brushed her arm. "We don't know what's on the other side."

Lexi met his gaze. "We didn't come this far to stop now."

He hesitated for a moment, shaking his head, then nodded. "Lexi, one of these days..."

She stepped toward the archway, raising the talisman. The carved spiral brightened, and the ancient stones began to shift. A deep grinding sound filled the air as the stone door slid open, revealing a narrow passageway that descended into darkness.

Lexi swallowed hard.

Redington stepped beside her. "I'll go first."

"No," Lexi said, squaring her shoulders. "It's my path. I have to lead."

Redington's gaze softened. "Then I'll be right behind you."

Lexi took a steadying breath and stepped into the passage. The air was cold and dry, thick with the scent of ancient stone and something else beneath it—something metallic and sharp.

The talisman's glow cast a soft golden light along the walls, illuminating carved symbols and faded murals depicting figures in long robes, hands raised toward the sky. The symbols mirrored the ones on the talisman.

Lexi's footsteps echoed in the confined space. Redington's steady presence behind her kept her grounded, his breath and the occasional brush of his hand against her back a silent reassurance.

They emerged into a circular chamber.

In the center stood a stone altar. Upon it lay a single object—a narrow silver box adorned with the same spiral symbol etched into the surface.

Lexi's heart hammered painfully in her chest.

"It's the same design as the talisman," she said, stepping toward the altar.

Redington's hand shot out. "Wait—"

Before he could stop her, Lexi touched the box.

Light erupted from the altar, blinding and searing. Lexi stumbled backward, shielding her eyes as the chamber filled with swirling golden light. The air hummed with energy, vibrating beneath her skin.

A voice—soft yet powerful—echoed through the room.

"Faith is not the absence of fear."

Lexi's heart froze.

"Faith is stepping forward when you cannot see the path."

Lexi lowered her hands.

In the light stood a figure—a woman with flowing golden hair and piercing eyes that radiated kindness and strength.

"Pistis Sophia," Lexi whispered.

The figure smiled. "You have done well, Lexi. But your journey is not over."

Lexi's throat tightened. "What is this place?"

"The convergence of all gifts. Wisdom. Knowledge. Healing. Faith. Prophecy. Miracles. Discernment. Tongues. Understanding."

Lexi's breath hitched. "The Nine Spiritual Gifts."

Pistis Sophia stepped toward her. "You were chosen to hold the talisman because you understand that faith is not separate from the other gifts—it is the foundation beneath them. Now you must decide how to use them."

Lexi's gaze flicked toward Redington. His expression was hard, but his eyes were soft as they met hers.

"And if I fail?" Lexi asked.

Pistis Sophia smiled. "Faith is not about certainty. It's about walking forward even when you don't know the outcome."

Lexi's hands curled into fists. "I'm ready."

"Good," Pistis Sophia said. "Because you're about to face the greatest test of all."

The light dimmed.

The box sat unopened on the altar.

Lexi reached for it.

Redington's hand closed over hers.

"Together," he said.

Lexi's chest tightened.

"Together."

Chapter 77

The air inside the fortress was thin and charged, humming with an unseen energy that pressed against Lexi's skin.

She stood at the base of the main hall, her breath shallow, the talisman burning hot against her chest. The carvings beneath her feet pulsed faintly with golden light, mirroring the pattern etched into the talisman.

Redington crouched beside her, his gaze sharp.

"It's a key," he said, his voice low.

Lexi's fingers brushed the edge of the talisman.

"If it's a key… then where's the lock?"

A low rumbling echoed beneath them.

Lexi's heart slammed against her ribs as the stone beneath their feet began to shift.

Redington pulled her back as cracks snaked outward from the center of the sigil. Stone grated against stone, and the circular pattern beneath them began to sink.

"Lexi—"

She stumbled back as the floor collapsed inward, revealing a dark, spiraling staircase beneath the hall. The air that drifted up from below was cold and damp, laced with the scent of earth and age.

Redington's hand was already on his weapon as he looked down into the opening.

"You think that's the lock?"

Lexi swallowed hard.

"There's only one way to find out."

They descended the narrow stone staircase, their footsteps echoing down the corridor. The glow from the talisman provided the only light, illuminating symbols carved into the stone walls—spirals, circles, and interlocking patterns.

"These symbols…" Lexi whispered.

"They're Cathar," Redington said. "But some of these patterns—"

"They match the gifts," Lexi finished.

The deeper they went, the warmer the talisman became, pulsing like a second heartbeat against her chest.

They emerged into a vast underground chamber. The ceiling arched high overhead, supported by weathered stone columns. At the far end of the chamber, a stone altar sat beneath a stained-glass window—dusty and fractured but intact.

Lexi's heart hammered painfully.
"That's it."
Redington's hand shot out.
"Wait—"
Lexi stepped toward the altar. The symbols carved into the stone beneath her feet began to glow brighter as she approached.
"You don't know what it will do," Redington warned.
"I don't think I have a choice," Lexi said softly.
She raised the talisman.
The carvings beneath her flared with golden light. The air trembled. The silver box pulsed as the light from the talisman connected with it— threads of energy weaving together.
Lexi's breath hitched.
"It's working."
Then—
The chamber darkened.
Lexi's pulse spiked.
"What's happening?"
Behind them, footsteps echoed through the chamber.
Marc.
Lexi turned, the glow from the talisman reflecting off his dark silhouette as he crossed the threshold.
Marc's gaze drifted toward the silver box. His smile was faint.
"I told you," he said. "It doesn't belong to you."

Lexi's grip tightened on the talisman.

"Then why is it responding to me?"

Marc's gaze sharpened.

"Because you're the bridge."

Lexi's heart stumbled.

"The bridge?"

Marc's eyes glinted.

"The Cathars didn't protect the gifts—they tried to bury them. But the gifts were never meant to be hidden."

Redington's hand rested on his weapon.

"You're saying they were meant to be controlled."

Marc's gaze darkened.

"They were meant to be used."

Lexi's breath hitched as the light from the talisman flared again, connecting to the silver box in a twisting arc of golden energy.

Marc stepped forward.

"Take the box, Lexi. Finish what the Cathars started."

Redington's eyes narrowed.

"Don't listen to him."

Marc's gaze sharpened.

"You don't understand what's at stake."

Lexi's hand hovered over the box.

"What's inside?"

Marc smiled faintly.

"The final gift."

Lexi's chest tightened.

"The ninth gift."

Marc nodded.

"The gift of faith."

Lexi's hand trembled over the box.

"And what happens if I open it?"

Marc's eyes were cold.

"You complete the circle."

The glow from the box intensified. The air trembled.

Redington stepped toward her.

"Lexi—"

Lexi's breath shuddered.

"I have to know."

Marc's voice was steady.

"It's your choice."

Lexi closed her eyes.

Faith isn't the absence of fear.

Faith is the courage to move forward despite it.

Her hand closed over the box.

Redington's hand shot out.

"Lexi, don't—"

Light erupted through the chamber as the box opened.

Lexi's body jerked as golden energy surged through her, wrapping around her like fire and light. Her vision swam. A thousand voices whispered in her mind.

The gifts are not separate.

They are threads of the same tapestry.

Faith is the loom that binds them.

Lexi gasped as the energy from the talisman merged with the light from the box.

Marc's gaze sharpened.

"You see now, don't you?"

Lexi's breath hitched as her feet touched the floor.

"Yes," she whispered.

Marc's expression darkened.

"Then you know what happens next."

The light cut out. The chamber plunged into darkness.

Redington's voice was sharp.

"Lexi!"

Lexi's breath steadied.

"I'm okay."

Marc's voice was sharp.

"For now."

Redington's hand closed over hers.

"We need to leave."

Lexi's gaze lingered on the box—now empty.

"Not yet," she whispered.

Marc's voice sharpened.

"You've started something you can't stop."

Lexi's grip tightened around the talisman.

"Then I guess I better finish it."

Chapter 78

Lexi gasped.

"Lexi?"

A wave of golden light washed over her vision, and she staggered back. The ruins blurred. Time seemed to warp around her.

And then—

She wasn't in Montségur anymore.

Lexi stood in a wide, marble hall bathed in soft, golden light. Vast columns stretched upward into infinity. The air shimmered.

At the end of the hall, a figure stood waiting.

Clad in flowing white robes with golden accents, the figure radiated calm and strength. Her face was ageless, her hair cascading down her back in soft waves. Her eyes—piercing blue—held all the wisdom of creation.

"Pistis Sophia," Lexi whispered.

The archangel smiled. "You have done well, Lexi."

Lexi's chest tightened. "I don't understand. Why are you showing me this?"

"You have reached the threshold," Pistis Sophia said. "You have carried the gifts, mastered them—but faith is the key that will unlock the final purpose."

Lexi stepped forward, confusion stirring beneath the awe. "The talisman—it's tied to the gifts. Why was it given to me?"

Pistis Sophia's eyes softened. "Because you are the bridge."

Lexi frowned. "The bridge?"

"The gifts are not meant to be held—they are meant to be shared." Pistis Sophia's gaze sharpened. "The world stands at a tipping point. Fear and division are growing. People are searching for something they have forgotten how to find."

Lexi's heart hammered painfully in her chest. "Faith."

"Yes." Pistis Sophia extended her hand, and the full talisman appeared in her palm, like new and now glowing with soft golden light. "This is not power—it is a reminder. Faith is not given. It is discovered."

The light pulsed.

"You must show them how to discover it."

Lexi's throat tightened. "But how?"

"Through the gifts," Pistis Sophia said. "Through a school. A sanctuary where others may come to remember what lies within them."

Lexi's breath hitched. "I can't teach people how to have faith."

"You can," Pistis Sophia said gently. "Because you have lived it. You have found faith not through certainty—but through choice. That is what you must teach."

Pistis Sophia stepped forward and placed the full talisman in Lexi's hands. "The gifts are not separate. They are threads of the same tapestry. Faith is the loom that binds them together."

Lexi's hands closed over the talisman. Warmth flooded through her, radiating outward—a deep sense of knowing settled within her chest.

"You are ready," Pistis Sophia said.

Lexi opened her mouth to speak—

—And the vision shattered.

She was back in the ruins of Montségur. Redington was holding her shoulders, his face inches from hers, his eyes hard with worry.

"Lexi," he said sharply. "What happened?"

She blinked. Her breath came in sharp bursts. Her hands were trembling—but the talisman in her palm radiated warmth.

Lexi straightened. Her pulse steadied.

"I know what we have to do," she said.

Redington's brow furrowed. "What?"

"We need to create a school."

Redington's eyes narrowed. "A school?"

"A place where people can learn to unlock the gifts within them," Lexi said, her voice steady despite the whirlwind inside her. "Healing. Prophecy. Discernment. Faith."

Redington's gaze sharpened. "You think that's why they've been chasing the talisman?"

"Yes," Lexi said. "Because the gifts are not weapons—they're meant to heal. To guide."

"And you think they'll let you create something like that?"

Lexi's mouth curved into a small smile. "I think they can't stop me."

Redington's eyes darkened with approval. "Then we'd better get moving before someone tries to stop us."

"No one will, Marc isn't here anymore. He got what he came for."

"And what was that?" Redington asked.

Lexi exhaled, the cool air stinging her lungs. "Me." *Faith is not given. It is discovered.*

She had spent her life searching for answers—seeking proof that faith was real.

Now she understood.

Faith wasn't about knowing.

It was about choosing to believe—even when the path wasn't clear.

She took Redington's hand, her fingers tightening around his.

"Let's go," she said. "We have a lot of work to do."

As they descended the path from Montségur, Lexi felt the weight of the talisman against her chest—no longer a burden but a promise.

Chapter 79

Lexi sat at the edge of the stone fountain back in the Nepal monastery's courtyard, the sound of trickling water mingling with the soft rustle of leaves in the breeze. The mountain air was crisp, carrying with it the scent of moss and pine. Above her, the sky was a watercolor blend of soft blues and streaks of gold as the sun dipped toward the horizon.

It had been three weeks since Montségur. Three weeks since the confrontation, since Marc had vanished into the night like a ghost, and since Redington had stayed by her side as she pieced together the aftermath. The talisman sat heavy around her neck beneath her sweater, a quiet reminder of everything that had happened—and everything that was still to come.

She lifted her gaze toward the monastery's arched windows, where candlelight flickered behind stained glass. Sophea was inside, preparing for the evening meditation. Isabella and Kesia had arrived earlier that day, and Redington… well, he was never far now.

Lexi's thoughts drifted back to the vision. The dream that had woken her in the dead of night two nights ago.

Pistis Sophia had stood before her, radiating golden light. Her wings, vast and shimmering with iridescence, had filled the void around them. Lexi had knelt at her feet, trembling beneath the weight of the archangel's gaze.

"You have walked the path laid before you," Pistis Sophia had said, her voice a song and a storm all at once. "You have received the gifts, learned their power, and now you know their purpose."

Lexi had lifted her eyes. "I still don't understand."

"The gifts were not given to be hidden. They were not meant to belong to a chosen few. Faith is not a prize—it is a path. You have been chosen to show others how to walk it."

Lexi had felt her breath catch. "You're asking me to teach them?"

"Not teach," Pistis Sophia had corrected gently. "Awaken."

Now, sitting at the fountain, the memory left a lingering hum in her chest. She had spoken to her friend, Sophea, about it earlier that morning.

Sophea, always calm, always steady, had simply smiled.

"You've known this was coming," Sophea had said. "This was always your path."

But accepting it was something else entirely.

"Lexi?"

She glanced up to find Redington walking toward her, hands tucked into the pockets of his dark jacket. His hair was slightly tousled from the wind, and his eyes—those piercing blue eyes—were steady and searching.

"You missed dinner," he said, sitting down beside her on the low stone wall.

"I wasn't hungry."

He studied her for a long moment. "You've been quiet since the dream."

"I'm still trying to figure out what it means."

Redington's mouth curled into a slight smile. "You know what it means."

Lexi sighed. "Faith isn't about knowing the outcome. It's about stepping into the unknown and trusting it."

Redington's gaze softened. He reached over, his fingers brushing lightly over hers. "And you've never been good at trusting the unknown."

Lexi laughed despite herself. "No. I like knowing exactly where I'm going."

"Well," Redington said, his thumb tracing the curve of her hand, "Maybe it's time to change that."

She turned toward him fully, her expression serious. "Pistis Sophia showed me the future. No specifics—just a feeling. There's a need—a hunger—for the gifts. People are searching for something, and they don't know where to look."

"Then you show them," Redington said simply.

Lexi hesitated. "I don't know how."

"You will," he said with quiet conviction. "You have all the pieces—you just need to trust yourself to put them together."

Lexi's gaze dropped to where their hands were joined. Her fingers tightened around his.

"I'm scared," she admitted.

"I know."

"And you're not going to talk me out of this?"

"No." His thumb brushed the edge of her wrist. "Because I think this is exactly what you're meant to do."

A shadow passed across the courtyard. Sophea stood beneath the archway, her hair gathered at the nape of her neck.

"It's time," she said, her tone gentle.

Lexi's breath hitched. "Time for what?"

Sophea smiled. "To decide."

Lexi exchanged a look with Redington, then rose to her feet. He followed, his hand lingering at the small of her back as they walked toward the monastery. Isabella and Kesia were already seated in the meditation hall. Candles lined the stone walls, casting soft flickers of gold and amber against the ancient carvings.

Lexi hesitated at the threshold. The weight of the moment pressed down on her.

Pistis Sophia's words echoed in her mind. "The gifts were not meant to be hidden."

Her heart hammered as she stepped into the hall. Sophea stood at the front, waiting.

"You're ready," Sophea said simply.

Lexi swallowed hard. "And if I'm not?"

Sophea's gaze softened. "Faith isn't about certainty. It's about walking forward even when you can't see the path."

Lexi stood between Isabella, Kesia, and Redington—each of them mirrors of her journey. Her gaze settled on the talisman beneath her sweater.

Faith.

Not certainty. Not perfection. Just trust.

She stepped forward, taking Sophea's hand. "I know what I have to do."

"And what's that?" Sophea asked.

Lexi's eyes flashed with quiet certainty.

"I'm going to build something."

She glanced at Isabella and Kesia. "Together."

"And what will you call it?" Redington's voice was low.

Lexi smiled faintly. "I am not sure yet."

Sophea's smile widened. "A School for the Nine Gifts."

Lexi's chest rose and fell with a steady breath. "Not just to teach them," she said. "To help others discover them. To show them how to walk the path."

Redington stepped forward. "And when do you start?"

Lexi's smile grew. "Now."

Sophea's eyes glinted with quiet approval. Isabella took Lexi's hand, Kesia linked her arm through Isabella's, and Redington's hand brushed against the small of Lexi's back.

Faith wasn't knowing the outcome.

Faith was stepping into the unknown.

Chapter 80

Lexi stood at the edge of the monastery's courtyard, her gaze fixed on the rolling hills beyond the stone walls. A cool breeze whispered through the open archway, carrying the scent of lavender and freshly turned earth. The early morning sunbathed the monastery in golden light, illuminating the intricate carvings on the stone walls.

It had been three weeks since Montségur. Three weeks since the truth about the talisman had come to light. Three weeks since Redington had stood beside her as they faced down the threat that had been chasing them across France.

And now, here, she felt like she was home.

The courtyard was quiet. The monastery settled into the peaceful rhythm of early morning prayers and meditations. A few monks were tending to the gardens, their quiet footsteps and soft murmurs blending with the sound of the wind rustling through the trees.

Lexi traced her fingers along the carved pillar beside her, the smooth stone cool beneath her touch. It felt strange being back. Like returning to a place that had once felt sacred—but now felt... different.

"You're thinking too much," Sophea's voice floated toward her.

Lexi turned to see Sophea standing beneath one of the archways, dressed in the simple robes of the monastery. Her expression carried the quiet authority of someone who had made peace with herself.

Sophea crossed the courtyard, her bare feet silent against the stone. "You don't need to carry it all alone, Lexi."

Lexi smiled faintly. "Feels like I've been carrying it for so long, I don't know how to let it go."

"Maybe it's not about letting go," Sophea said softly. "Maybe it's about deciding what to do with it."

Lexi's hand touched the talisman resting against her chest. The stone warm beneath her sweater, a subtle pulse of energy beneath her skin. Ever since Montségur, the talisman had felt... settled. Its chaotic energy had quieted as though it had finally found its purpose.

"What if..." Lexi hesitated, her eyes meeting Sophea's. "We know that the gifts were never supposed to be hoarded or hidden. They were meant to be shared. To help others unlock what already exists inside them."

Sophea's smile was slight but knowing. "Faith is not given. It is discovered."

Lexi's breath hitched. "Pistis Sophia said that to me."

Sophea stepped closer. "Then maybe it's time to stop protecting the gifts… and start teaching them."

Lexi's heart pounded. The idea felt both terrifying and right. "A school."

Sophea's gaze held steady. "A school."

Lexi's mind raced as the pieces began to fall into place. A place where people could come not just to learn about the spiritual gifts—but to embody them. To understand them. To wield them with wisdom and integrity.

She thought of Kesia's healing work. Isabella's ability to teach others to embrace their true selves through art. Redington's gift for discernment and his ability to see the truth beneath the surface. Sophea's quiet strength and faith.

And herself.

"You think I can pull this off?" Lexi asked, her voice quiet.

Sophea's expression softened. "Faith isn't about knowing the outcome. It's about stepping forward even when you don't know where the path will lead."

Lexi smiled. "Sounds like something Pistis Sophia would say."

"Sounds like something you would say." Sophea squeezed her hand. "I'll support you, Lexi. Whatever you need."

Lexi's smile widened, the weight in her chest lifting for the first time in weeks. "Thank you."

They stood in silence for a moment, the breeze stirring the loose strands of Lexi's hair.

A set of footsteps approached, steady and familiar.

Lexi turned to see Redington walking toward them, hands in his pockets. He looked… relaxed. At ease, in a way, he hadn't been in years. His dark jacket was open, and the faintest trace of a smile curved his mouth as his eyes met hers.

"You two look serious," he said, his gaze flicking between Lexi and Sophea.

"We're talking about the school," Lexi said.

Redington raised a brow. "Have you named it yet?"

"Not that I have heard," Sophea supplied. "She is keeping that to herself for now."

Redington's gaze sharpened. "And you both think people are ready for that?"

Lexi lifted her chin. "I think they need it."

Redington studied her for a long moment, the weight of his gaze steady and grounding. Then he smiled. "Then I guess you'll need some security."

Lexi's mouth curved. "Are you offering?"

"Just try and stop me."

Behind them, the sound of approaching footsteps echoed through the courtyard. Isabella and Kesia appeared beneath the archway, their expressions curious.

"Did we miss something?" Isabella asked.

Lexi looked at them—her family, her soulmates, the people who had stood beside her through the darkest moments of her life.

"No," Lexi said. "You're just in time."

Isabella and Kesia joined them beneath the archway. Lexi turned to face them, feeling the gravity of the moment settle into place.

"I want to create a school," she said. "Not just to teach the gifts—but to help others unlock them. To guide people toward understanding their faith. Their purpose. The way we've found ours."

Isabella's smile widened. "I'm in."

Kesia nodded, her eyes shining. "Me too."

Lexi turned toward Redington, whose blue eyes were already focused on her.

"I'm not going anywhere," he said softly.

Lexi swallowed against the sudden swell of emotion in her throat.

"Good," she whispered.

A light breeze stirred the air, carrying the scent of lavender and jasmine. The sun broke fully over the hills, bathing the monastery in golden light.

It wasn't just a new day. It was the beginning of something bigger.

Lexi reached for Redington's hand. His fingers curled around hers.

"Let's build something that lasts," she said.

Redington smiled, his gaze steady. "Let's."

Sophea stepped toward the carved archway, placing her hand on the stone. "This monastery was built to protect the gifts. Now, it will be used to share them."

"And faith?" Lexi asked.

Sophea smiled. "Faith is what brings us here."

Lexi's heart steadied.

For the first time in her life, the path ahead felt clear.

"Let's get started," she said.

And as they walked back toward the monastery, Lexi knew—this was going to be something exciting.

Chapter 81

Lexi stood at the edge of the courtyard, her breath catching as the early morning light filtered through the arched windows of the monastery. The cool stone beneath her bare feet grounded her, but the weight of what lay ahead settled heavily on her chest.

The school was almost ready.

The last few months had been a blur of movement and creation—gathering resources, writing teachings, and shaping a curriculum that could hold the weight of the Nine Spiritual Gifts. She had drawn from her time at the monastery, from the lessons with Dorian, from the trials she had endured with Isabella, Kesia, Sophea, and Redington. And yet, as she stood on the threshold of making it real, doubt crept beneath her skin.

Was she ready for this?

Would it work?

Would the world listen?

The crisp morning air stirred the loose strands of her hair as she watched the courtyard below. Monks moved through the grounds with quiet purpose, preparing the space for the school's inaugural ceremony. White linen banners bearing the symbols of the Nine Gifts fluttered in the breeze—each one representing the lessons that had brought her here.

Faith. Knowledge. Wisdom. Healing. Prophecy. Miracles. Discernment. Tongues. And the Interpretation of Tongues.

Her gaze drifted toward the far end of the courtyard, where Redington was speaking with Kesia and Sophea. Kesia's calm, grounded presence was palpable even from a distance, and Sophea's serene expression reflected a quiet strength. Redington, arms crossed, looked as sharp and composed as ever, but when he glanced toward Lexi, his eyes softened.

He started toward her.

Lexi's heart picked up speed, but she didn't move.

"Couldn't sleep?" Redington's voice was low, carrying the same knowing tone he had used since the beginning.

"I didn't try," Lexi admitted.

Redington leaned casually against the stone column beside her. "Because you're overthinking again?"

Lexi's mouth twitched into a faint smile. "It's not overthinking if the stakes are this high."

Redington arched an eyebrow. "You faced down Marc. You held off a cult. You survived Sophea's trials. And you're worried about this?"

Lexi's smile faded. "Teaching is different. I can't just rely on instinct. What if I fail them? What if the gifts can't be taught?"

Redington's gaze sharpened. "You think this is about teaching?"

Lexi frowned. "Isn't it?"

Redington shook his head. "No. This isn't about passing down knowledge. This is about showing them what's already inside of them. Faith isn't taught—it's revealed."

Lexi swallowed. "And if they don't see it?"

"Then you'll remind them. You're the living proof of what faith can become."

A familiar voice drifted toward them. "He's right, you know."

Lexi turned to see Isabella standing a few feet away, her expression warm. She wore flowing robes of soft blue and gold, reminiscent of the ceremonial wear from the monastery.

"Of course I'm right," Redington said dryly.

Isabella smirked. "And so humble."

Redington rolled his eyes, but Lexi's chest tightened at the warmth of their exchange.

Kesia and Sophea joined them a moment later, completing the circle. Kesia's calm energy anchored them, while Sophea's gaze seemed to pierce through Lexi's uncertainty.

"You've already built it," Sophea said softly. "You've already succeeded. They just need a place to begin."

Lexi's hand drifted toward the talisman hanging beneath her sweater. The metal was warm against her skin, humming faintly with a quiet pulse of energy.

She had dreamed of Pistis Sophia again the night before—standing at the threshold of a great hall, golden light spilling through stained-glass windows. The archangel's voice had been steady and clear.

"Faith is not the absence of fear. It is the choice to believe despite it."

Redington touched her hand gently. "It's time."

Lexi inhaled deeply, letting the cool morning air settle into her lungs. She nodded once.

They descended the stone steps together, moving toward the courtyard where rows of monks and students were beginning to gather. The students ranged from young to old, some wearing robes, others dressed in simple clothes. Their eyes reflected quiet curiosity and hesitant hope.

Lexi stopped in the center of the courtyard, her heart pounding.

Kesia stood to her left. Sophea to her right. Isabella and Redington flanked them.

Dorian stepped forward, his expression calm but reverent. He inclined his head. "Lexi?"

Lexi's gaze drifted toward the horizon, where the sun was rising, washing the courtyard in gold. Her hands brushed the edges of the talisman as warmth spread through her chest.

She turned toward the gathered students.

"I'm not here to give you answers," Lexi began. Her voice was steady, carrying easily through the courtyard. "The gifts have always been within you. My role is to help you uncover them—to understand them, to trust them, and to use them for good."

She walked toward the first row of students, her gaze soft. "Faith is not a certainty. It's not having all the answers. Faith is stepping into the unknown when the path isn't clear. It's trusting that even when you fall, you will rise."

Her gaze swept the crowd. "The Nine Gifts are not just tools. They are reflections of the divine. They are pathways back to yourself. They are how you carry faith into the world."

A hush settled over the courtyard.

Lexi extended her hands, closing her eyes as the talisman pulsed warmly against her chest. The familiar, quiet hum of energy built beneath her skin. It expanded outward, threading through the circle of students like sunlight through glass.

Kesia's hand brushed against her arm, her energy grounding the flow. Sophea's steady presence bolstered it. Isabella's quiet strength and Redington's focused calm acted as anchors.

The students stirred as the energy reached them. A ripple of light passed over them—a shimmering pulse of warmth and clarity.

Lexi opened her eyes.

One of the younger students—a girl no older than ten—stepped forward. Her small hand reached toward Lexi's.

Lexi knelt, meeting the girl's eyes.

"You already have the answers," Lexi said softly. "Let's find them together."

The girl's eyes widened, and her hand closed around Lexi's fingers.

And just like that, the energy shifted.

A quiet hum resonated through the courtyard—a shared pulse of understanding. The Nine Gifts were no longer separate—they were threads of the same tapestry.

Faith. Wisdom. Healing. Prophecy. Knowledge. Miracles. Discernment. Tongues. Interpretation.

Lexi stood. The girl smiled, and Lexi squeezed her hand.

"You are exactly where you're meant to be," Lexi whispered.

From the edge of the courtyard, Dorian watched, his expression filled with quiet pride.

Lexi stepped back, her heart thudding in her chest.

She met Redington's gaze. His expression was calm, steady.

The light had returned to his eyes.

Lexi turned toward the gathered students.

"Welcome," she said.

The gates to the monastery opened behind them.

One by one, the students began to walk through.

Lexi's chest tightened as the last of them disappeared beyond the gate.

She smiled.

They had begun.

Chapter 82

The afternoon sun filtered softly through the stained-glass windows of the monastery's main hall, scattering jewel-toned light across the stone floor like blessings from above. Lexi stood at the front of the room, barefoot, her toes curling against the cool, polished stone. The talisman, now worn openly on a braided cord around her neck, rested gently against her heart.

Outside, the wind had stilled. The fluttering of the Nine Gifts banners had quieted. Even the monks had paused in their movements, sensing a shift in the air—a calm before something greater.

Classes had started.

Three days had passed since the gates opened, and students from around the world entered. Each one brought something different, pain, doubt, curiosity, and longing. Many didn't know what they were searching for. But Lexi recognized it in their eyes—what she herself had carried for so long.

The search for faith.

She moved slowly down the hall, past a group of students seated in meditation. The sound of breath rose and fell like an ocean, rhythmic and grounding. One student trembled slightly, emotions welling up. Lexi knelt beside her, placing a gentle hand over her heart. The trembling eased.

"You're safe to feel," she whispered.

In the far corner, Redington sat with a group of older students, guiding them through the Discernment teachings. He glanced up as she passed, their eyes meeting in quiet solidarity.

Later that evening, the council gathered in the high tower room—Lexi, Redington, Kesia, Isabella, Sophea, and Dorian.

Candles flickered in the low light, their flames dancing with the rising mountain wind that pushed against the shutters.

"We've had three requests from outside monasteries," Sophea said, her voice calm. "They want to send students."

Isabella smiled. "It's spreading already."

"Word of miracles always does," Kesia said gently. "But we need to be careful. This isn't about spectacle. This is about stewardship."

Lexi nodded, but her fingers twitched slightly against the stone table.

"There's something else," she said.

The group fell silent.

Lexi reached beneath her robes and pulled the talisman free. It shimmered faintly, brighter than it had in days. The hum it gave off was… different now. Not just vibration—but sound. Words, almost, that hadn't formed yet.

"Last night," she said, "I dreamed again."

Dorian leaned forward. "Pistis Sophia?"

Lexi met his gaze. "Yes. But this time, it wasn't a vision. It was a calling."

The others stilled.

"She said the Nine Gifts were never meant to be mastered separately. That the final gift… the one not written, not spoken… is Unity. That Faith is the doorway to it. That only through complete surrender—not to her, not to doctrine—but to Spirit itself, can the tapestry be completed."

Sophea's brows drew together. "A tenth gift?"

"No," Lexi said softly. "A convergence. A culmination. Something greater than the sum of its parts."

Redington leaned back in his chair. "And what does that mean for us?"

Lexi looked down at the talisman. "It means the school is only the beginning. It's not about teaching the gifts. It's about awakening them— simultaneously. Harmonizing them. That's the next step. And… that step begins here. With us."

Kesia exhaled. "So, we're not just teaching a new generation."

Lexi nodded. "We're becoming the bridge."

For a moment, no one spoke. The air in the room thickened, alive with something unspoken.

Then Dorian stood.

"Then it's time we prepare. For what's to come."

Outside, the wind picked up again, stronger this time, rattling the ancient windows.

Lexi rose, her heart pounding—not from fear, but from something far older—a truth awakening.

The Nine Gifts had brought them here.

Faith would carry them forward.

And the sound they heard next—so soft, it could have been a dream—was not wind.

It was a song.

Not from a voice.

But from the talisman.

Chapter 83

Ahush had settled over the mountains the next morning as if the earth itself was listening.

Lexi stood at the edge of the monastery's western overlook, where ancient stone steps led down into the valley of mists. Below, pine trees rose like silent sentinels, guarding secrets older than any written scripture. The talisman hummed faintly against her chest as if preparing for something just beyond the horizon.

She wasn't alone.

The original circle had gathered—Redington, Isabella, Kesia, Sophea, Dorian—all standing at her back, their presence solid and unwavering. They had meditated together at sunrise, drawn by the same dream.

Each of them had seen the same image, a great wheel turning in the sky, its spokes glowing with the symbols of the Nine Gifts, and at the center—a radiant point of light pulsing with life, with song.

A doorway. A convergence.

"The school has done more than we expected," Isabella said quietly. "We planted seeds… and they've grown faster than we imagined."

"Some of them too fast," Kesia added. "A few students are already showing signs of gifts activating spontaneously—all at once."

"It's as if the separation between the gifts is dissolving," Redington said. "They're beginning to unify… without us even pushing for it."

Sophea nodded. "Because the veil is thinning. The time for fragmentation is ending. That's what Pistis Sophia meant. The age of isolated mastery is over."

Lexi turned back to face them. "Then we need to prepare the next chamber."

Dorian raised a brow. "The sacred vault beneath the inner hall? It hasn't been used in centuries."

"Exactly," Lexi said. "It was sealed for a reason. But it was never meant to remain closed forever. I believe it's where the final convergence must take place."

Redington's jaw tightened slightly. "You think this… convergence will be peaceful?"

Lexi met his gaze, steady and calm. "No. I think it will be a reckoning. One that tests the very essence of faith—not just ours, but everyone's. Because faith is not proven in comfort. It's forged in fire."

The words fell like a quiet prophecy between them.

As they descended the monastery steps toward the hidden chamber, students began to gather in silence, drawn by something unseen. They came without being called—intuitively, instinctively—like moths to a flame.

Some wore robes, others jeans, and boots. They came from different lands and different paths. But they moved as one.

Lexi paused before the great stone doors. The air thrummed with energy. The talisman pulsed against her heart.

She turned to face the crowd that had gathered.

"In every age," she said, her voice clear and unwavering, "There are those who are chosen—and those who choose themselves. You are both. Each of you carries a spark. A gift. But the next step... requires something more."

A hush swept over the crowd.

"We've learned the Nine Gifts. Studied them. Practiced them. But now we are being asked to transcend them—not to abandon them, but to let go of the illusion that they are separate. We are not called to master each one. We are called to become the space where they unite."

She turned back to the door.

"And that begins... here."

She placed her palm against the seal etched into the stone—an ancient symbol none of them had fully understood until now. The talisman, as if recognizing the moment, flared with golden light.

A soft rumble vibrated through the stone beneath their feet. Then—slowly—the great doors parted.

Warm light spilled out, not from torches or lanterns, but from within the chamber itself. The space glowed with a soft, pulsing energy. Symbols danced along the walls—Wisdom, Healing, Miracles, Knowledge, Faith, Tongues, Discernment, Prophecy, Interpretation—then twisted into spirals, merging into one another until no single glyph could be separated from the whole.

They had become One.

Lexi stepped through the threshold.

Behind her, the others followed.

There, at the center of the chamber, stood a crystal structure—a spire reaching toward the domed ceiling, its surface etched with languages from every corner of the world. At its base, there was a place for the talisman.

Lexi removed it from her neck and placed it into the cradle.

The chamber sang.

Not a song of sound—but of soul. Each person present felt it as a vibration in their chest, a resonance of who they truly were.

And then… silence.

Complete.

Still.

From the center of the spire, a radiant light expanded outward, sweeping through the crowd. And as it touched them, something miraculous happened.

Chapter 84

The light did not blind.

It enveloped.

Warm, expansive, infinite—it moved like breath, like memory. A golden shimmer passed over the crowd gathered within the ancient chamber, each individual standing still as the light found them, filled them…, and became them.

Lexi stood at the center, hands open, eyes wide—not in fear, but in awe.

As the radiant current swept over her skin, it didn't feel like energy. It felt like remembrance.

One by one, the students began to shine, not in dazzling spectacle, but in subtle, resonant truth. Their eyes closed. Some wept. Others knelt. A few simply stood, arms lifted as if greeting something they had long forgotten.

It was happening.

The convergence.

A young woman to Lexi's left began speaking in a language unknown to her lips—but understood by every heart in the chamber.

A monk behind her collapsed into sobs, hands glowing as he reached toward a fellow student and placed them gently over her heart. Her posture, once bent with grief, straightened. Peace returned to her eyes.

Whispers of wisdom danced through the air, phrases passed from one person to the next—guidance, knowing, truth. Not preached. Not taught. Given.

Lexi's breath caught as she watched Redington step forward, his palm touching the crystal spire. A soft pulse rippled outward. Instantly, clarity flooded the room—discernment, sharp and undeniable. The fear and doubt some students still held flickered and faded like mist in sunlight.

Isabella stood just beyond him, her hands over her heart, her lips moving in silent prophecy. Tears streaked her cheeks—not from sadness, but release. She saw everything now—not in fractured glimpses but as one unfolding story.

Kesia glowed with a soft golden hue, her presence becoming a balm. Wherever she stood, people found their center. Found themselves. Her touch no longer just healed pain—it revealed wholeness.

And Sophea… she stood perfectly still, eyes closed, her entire body vibrating with divine energy. The miracle she embodied was not of physical change but of awakening. A remembering of purpose. A restoration of inner light.

Lexi looked up.

The spire had begun to spin—not violently, but in a steady, sacred rhythm. Symbols lifted from its surface, floating through the air like ancient fireflies, weaving in and out of each other until they became a single word…

Faith.

Not just belief.

But surrender.

Trust.

Becoming.

From within the light, a voice echoed. Not aloud—but in every heart at once.

"You have remembered what was never lost. You have returned to what was never gone. You are not chosen. You are choosing. And in choosing, you awaken the world."

Lexi knew that voice.

Archangel Pistis Sophia.

A gentle wind swept through the chamber. The air shimmered. Time thinned.

The spire dimmed—but the people did not.

They now carried the light.

Lexi turned to face them, her voice steady but softer than ever.

"This is no longer about gifts," she said. "It is about embodiment. You are not here to master powers. You are here to live the truth. To be love. To walk faith. Not to lead others—but to be a mirror in which they may see themselves."

The silence that followed wasn't hollow.

It was sacred.

Behind her, Redington stepped beside her. He didn't speak. He didn't need to.

Isabella, Kesia, Sophea, Dorian—all gathered around her.

Their circle was whole again.

But this time, it wasn't exclusive.

The circle expanded. Spiraled. Merged with every soul in the room.

No more separation.

No more hierarchy.

Just unity.

Just faith.

Lexi looked out over the students—some just entering adulthood, others who had carried wounds for decades—and she saw not what they would become.

She saw what they already were.

The gates of the monastery swung open later that day.

Not with fanfare. Not with trumpets.

Just a quiet, steady rhythm of footsteps.

New faces. New souls.

Drawn by something they couldn't name.

Guided by something they hadn't yet seen.

And at the threshold stood Lexi.

No longer a seeker.

Now, a guide.

She knelt before a young woman at the head of the group, her voice soft with wonder.

"You already carry the light," she said, smiling. "Let's help you remember."

The young woman took her hand.

And together, they walked forward.

Into the school.

Into the light.

Into the becoming.

The seasons passed, but the light never faded.

The school—called Sophia's Path—rose not as a monument of stone and structure but as a living pulse upon the earth. It breathed with its people. The grounds bloomed year-round with herbs, fruit trees, and wildflowers, tended by hands guided more by intuition than skill. Students walked barefoot through labyrinths etched into the grass, their laughter echoing against the monastery walls.

No bell dictated their learning.

The curriculum was not fixed.

Each soul arrived with a key to their own unfolding—and found, in time, that the gates within were already unlocked.

Classes weren't merely lectures—they were experiences. One week, students might study healing by walking among the sick in nearby villages. Another, they might explore prophecy through sacred dreamwork, fasting beneath the stars. Some meditated in silence for days. Others practiced spiritual interpretation through music, or movement, or language no book had ever captured.

The nine spiritual gifts had become nine doors.

And every soul had a map inside them.

One evening, Lexi stood beneath the Bodhi tree near the outer courtyard. The talisman—its glow now faint, familiar—rested against her chest, worn like a compass. She often found herself here when she needed stillness.

Footsteps approached, soft against the stone.

Redington joined her without a word, his presence as grounding as ever.

"You always find me here," she said.

"I think you're the one always finding yourself," he replied with a gentle smirk.

She leaned into his warmth, letting the silence speak. After a moment, she said, "They're ready, you know. All of them."

He nodded, eyes fixed on the horizon. "Because you were."

Lexi smiled. "I wasn't, at first."

"No one ever is," he said. "That's why it's called faith."

Later that night, as the stars shimmered over the mountain peaks, Lexi dreamt.

But it was no ordinary dream.

She stood in the vast open sky, stars circling her like embers. In front of her was Pistis

Sophia—neither angel nor human, neither past nor future. Just light. Presence. Love.

"You have done what few dare," the archangel said.

Lexi's voice trembled. "What was that?"

"You remembered," Pistis Sophia said, her voice echoing like a bell in water. "Not only the gifts—but your divinity. And now, you teach others not how to follow but how to awaken."

Tears filled Lexi's eyes. "Is this the end?"

Pistis Sophia smiled, tilting her head.

"There are no ends, Lexi. Only thresholds."

And as the dream faded, the archangel's final words echoed through Lexi's heart,

"Walk with faith, for it will lead you home, not to a place—but to yourself.

Chapter 85

The sound of the waves was soft and rhythmic, a steady lullaby that carried through the warm afternoon air. The sun hung high above the horizon, its golden light softened by the shade of a large white umbrella. Somewhere between the hush of the tide and the warmth on her skin, the remnants of a dream lingered—a voice, clear and familiar, whispered once more, *"Meet me where the ocean and the earth speak as one."*

Lexi lay beneath the umbrella, stretched out on a soft beach towel, her wide-brimmed straw hat tilted low over her face. The sound of children laughing mingled with the cries of seagulls and the gentle crashing of waves against the shore. The ocean breeze rustled through the edges of her hat, cooling her sun-warmed skin.

Her lips parted slightly as she stirred, the sound of footsteps padding across the sand pulling her toward wakefulness. A shadow crossed over her face, and the soft clink of glass on the small wooden table beside her caused her brow to twitch.

She opened her eyes slowly, brushing the sleep from them as the brim of her hat tilted up. Her gaze adjusted to the sunlight, and then she saw him.

Redington.

He stood before her, his lean frame casting a long shadow across the sand. He wore dark swim trunks and a white linen shirt unbuttoned just enough to reveal tanned skin beneath. His hair was tousled from the ocean breeze, and he was holding a tall glass of something cold, condensation sliding down its sides.

"Figured you'd be thirsty," he said, setting the glass beside her with a small smile. His blue eyes were calm, but they held a trace of that quiet intensity she had always known in him.

Lexi pushed herself up on her elbows, the straw hat sliding slightly back on her head. "You always know what I need," she teased.

Redington's smile deepened as he sat down beside her on the sand, his arm brushing against hers. His gaze softened as he studied her face, the peacefulness etched there. "You were out cold," he said. "Must've been some dream."

Lexi rubbed at her eyes and gave a small laugh. "You have no idea."

He raised an eyebrow. "Care to share?"

Lexi leaned back on her elbows, tilting her head toward the sunlit sky. "It was… strange," she said slowly, trying to wrap her mind around the hazy remnants of it. "I was at a monastery, learning about faith and spiritual gifts. It felt… real. So real."

Redington smiled faintly. "Sounds intense."

She nodded. "I met a lady named Sophea—an old soul who seemed to guide me. And there were other students like me—Kesia, Isabella, even you." Her gaze turned toward him, her voice quiet. "We were connected. We all had these… gifts. Prophecy, healing, wisdom, faith. And there were trials. So many trials."

Redington's expression shifted, his brow furrowing slightly. "Sounds a little woo, woo."

Lexi's mouth twitched. "It was, but at the same time it wasn't. It was just about awakening the gifts inside of one's body. It was about… trust about believing in something even when you can't see it. I now understand what faith really is. Not control, not certainty—but trust."

Redington's hand brushed lightly over hers. "Sounds like a dream worth having."

Lexi smiled, her eyes growing distant as the images of the dream began to blur at the edges. "And then… there was this moment at the end. I stood at the gates of a school. The place we'd built together. The gifts were united, and there was peace." Her eyes sharpened. "But it wasn't the gifts that held it all together. It was faith."

Redington's thumb traced slow circles against the back of her hand. "And what happened next?"

Lexi's lips parted, but no words came. The dream was already fading—slipping through her fingers like grains of sand.

"I… don't remember." She shook her head, her mouth curling into a bemused smile. "I have faith that whatever the dream meant will stay forever in my soul."

Before Redington could respond, the sound of small, quick footsteps pounded across the sand.

"Mommy!"

Lexi turned just in time to see two small figures racing toward her across the sun-warmed beach—bare feet kicking up sand, laughter bubbling from their bright, sun-kissed faces.

The girl reached her first, her golden curls bouncing wildly as she threw her arms around Lexi's neck. "Mommy, come swim with us!"

Her younger brother arrived a second later, out of breath but grinning. His dark hair was a tangle of salt and wind, and his blue eyes were bright with excitement. "Come on, Mommy!" he urged. "The waves are perfect!"

Lexi's heart swelled. She wrapped her arms around them both, pressing kisses into their sun-warmed cheeks.

"I'll be right there," she promised, brushing a curl from her daughter's forehead. "Just give me a minute."

The children darted back toward the water, their laughter ringing out over the beach.

Lexi turned to Redington, a slow smile spreading across her face. "Well. This is all the realism I have ever dreamed of you and them."

Redington's gaze followed the children as they splashed into the surf, squealing as the waves chased their feet. Then, his gaze settled on his wife.

"You sure about that?" he laughed.

Lexi's smile faltered. For a moment, the sound of the ocean faded, replaced by the distant echo of voices—Kesia's gentle wisdom, Isabella's laughter, Sophea's calm strength. And the quiet hum of faith, steady and familiar beneath it all.

"Well," she laughed back. "Maybe let me go back to sleep, and I will tell you in a moment."

Redington's hand slid beneath hers, his fingers threading between hers. "Maybe we should just enjoy the day, and you can dream about it later."

Lexi's gaze met his, her heart swelling.

"We should," she said as her lips meet his.

"Mommy!"

She reached for her hat and stood, brushing sand from her legs. "Shall we?"

Redington stood beside her, taking her hand, his fingers intertwined with hers. "Lead the way."

Lexi smiled.

They walked toward the water. The sun shimmered across the horizon, casting golden light across the ocean. Their children splashed in the surf, their laughter bright and untamed.

And Lexi felt it—that quiet hum of faith, rising and falling with the waves.

Not certainty.

Not control.

Just faith.

She closed her eyes for a brief moment, taking in the last remnants of the dream, her heart opening to the unknown.

The sound of laughter and the waves rushing over her toes pulled her forward.

She opened her eyes and knew that she was exactly where she wanted to be, with Redington's hand in hers.

Lexi took a deep breath—and let the dream of the nine spiritual gifts slip away until she dreamt again.

Prayer to
Archangel Pistis Sophia

Divine Archangel Pistis Sophea, Keeper of
Wisdom and Faith,
Guide me with your eternal light.
  In moments of doubt, grant me clarity.
When fear arises, anchor me in courage.
Help me to see beyond the shadows,
And to trust in the strength within my soul.
  Teach me to walk the path of truth,
To honor the wisdom of my heart,
And to hold faith in the unity of love and light.
  May your presence illuminate my journey,
Balancing my spirit with your grace.
Let your voice echo in my mind,
A gentle reminder of the light I carry.
  Archangel Pistis Sophea,
Be my guide, my strength, and my teacher.
Fill me with unwavering faith,
And help me to bring light to the world.
  Amen.

Acknowledgments

This novel would not have been possible without the unwavering support, inspiration, and guidance of so many individuals who have shaped this journey.

To my readers: Your belief in these stories and the characters within them is the light that keeps this journey alive. Thank you for walking alongside me through every twist, trial, and triumph.

To the spiritual teachers and mentors who have shared their wisdom with me: Your insights into faith, energy, and the human spirit have deeply influenced this story. Your lessons resonate in every page and word.

To my family and friends: Your patience, encouragement, and endless support have been my foundation. Thank you for listening to ideas, sharing your perspectives, and reminding me of the beauty in persistence.

To my editor: Your sharp eye and dedication to refining this work have helped bring clarity and depth to the story. Thank you for being a partner in this creative endeavor.

To the unseen forces of inspiration: Whether in dreams, fleeting moments of clarity, or the quiet spaces of reflection, you have been my silent muse.

Lastly, to the characters who live within these pages: Thank you for allowing me to tell your story. Your courage, faith, and growth are a testament to the strength that lies within us all.

With deepest gratitude,

Dr. Constance

The **Nine Spiritual Gifts** from 1 Corinthians 12:8–10:

1. **Top Left (Open Book) –
Knowledge**
      - The open book symbolizes
divine knowledge and
spiritual truths.
2. **Top Center (Eye) – Discernment of
Spirits**

o   The eye represents the ability to see beyond the surface and discern the spiritual realm.

3. **Top Right (Curved Tongue) – Tongues**
    o   This curving symbol resembles a tongue, representing the Gift of Tongues.
4. **Middle Right (Raised Hand with Spiral) – Healing**
    o   A raised hand often symbolizes healing and the laying on of hands.
5. **Bottom Right (Hand with Twisting Motion) – Interpretation of Tongues** (paired with Tongues).
    o   Learnable but rarer than sign language.
6. **Bottom Center (Hand Open) – Miracles**
    o   A universal symbol for power and blessing—apt for working miracles.
7. **Bottom Left (Flame) – Prophecy**
    o   Fire or flame is often symbolic of divine inspiration, like the tongues of fire at Pentecost.

8. **Middle Left (Plant or Growth Symbol) – Wisdom**
    - Symbol of spiritual growth and rootedness, linked with divine wisdom.
9. **Center (Heart) – Faith**
    - Symbol of unwavering trust and inner light, the heart radiates the warmth of belief—anchoring the soul in divine assurance and the unseen path ahead.

Footnotes & Bibliography

Footnotes

1. The representation of **Archangel Pistis Sophea** as a figure of wisdom and faith draws inspiration from various spiritual and esoteric traditions, blending mythology, angelology, and personal interpretation to create a unique presence within this story.
2. Concepts of **faith and light overcoming darkness** are drawn from a variety of spiritual teachings, including principles found in Christianity, Buddhism, and metaphysical studies.
3. The description of **energy fields, talismans, and spiritual trials** incorporates elements from holistic healing practices, Reiki, and ancient wisdom traditions.
4. The **monastic setting and practices** were informed by research into both historical and contemporary monastic lifestyles, emphasizing themes of meditation, communal living, and spiritual growth.

Bibliography

Books and Spiritual Texts

- The Holy Bible: Spiritual inspiration for themes of faith, trust, and overcoming adversity.
- Campbell, Joseph. *The Hero with a Thousand Faces*. Princeton University Press. A cornerstone for understanding the archetypal hero's journey.
- Tolle, Eckhart. *The Power of Now*. New World Library. A guide to mindfulness and present-moment awareness.
- Gawain, Shakti. *Creative Visualization*. Bantam Books. Source of inspiration for understanding the power of imagination and energy.

Esoteric and Metaphysical Sources

- Steiner, Rudolf. *The Archangelic Hierarchy*. Anthroposophic Press. Insights into the nature and roles of angelic beings.
- Leadbeater, C.W. *The Hidden Side of Things*. Quest Books. A reference for understanding subtle energies and spiritual dimensions.

- Bailey, Alice A. *A Treatise on White Magic*. Lucis Publishing Company. Exploration of spiritual principles and their application to daily life.

Holistic Healing Practices

- Judith, Anodea. *Wheels of Life: A User's Guide to the Chakra System*. Llewellyn Publications. Reference for energy centers and their influence.
- Usui, Mikao. *The Original Reiki Handbook of Dr. Mikao Usui*. Lotus Light Publications. A foundational text for energy healing practices.

Cultural and Historical Research

- Thich Nhat Hanh. *Peace Is Every Step*. Bantam. A lens into monastic mindfulness and the practice of compassion.
- Paramahansa Yogananda. *Autobiography of a Yogi*. Self-Realization Fellowship. A spiritual autobiography highlighting the intersection of East and West.

Online Resources

- Angelic Lore Websites: Insights and interpretations on the roles of archangels in spiritual practice.
- Sacred-Texts.com: A comprehensive library of esoteric and spiritual texts from diverse traditions.

The Author

Dr. Constance Santego

Dr. Constance Santego is an esteemed author, educator, and holistic healer whose work spans across several disciplines including spiritual wellness, ancient mythologies, and personal development. With a doctoral degree in Natural Medicine, Constance has dedicated her life to exploring the intersections of spirituality, health, and human consciousness.

Born and raised in a small town steeped in folklore and surrounded by nature, Constance developed an early fascination with the stories and rituals that define different cultures. This curiosity blossomed into a lifelong pursuit of knowledge, leading her to travel extensively, in places as diverse as Greece, England, Mexico, and Spain.

Constance's academic journey is complemented by her practical experience in the healing arts. She is a certified Reiki Master, a practitioner of many modalities, and has conducted numerous workshops on meditation, energy healing, and mindfulness. Her holistic practice aims to integrate the body, mind, and spirit to foster well-being and spiritual growth.

Literary Contributions
Dr. Santego is the author of several books that explore spiritual themes through a blend of narrative fiction and insightful commentary. Her works often weave together elements of ancient myths with modern existential questions, creating a rich tapestry that resonates with readers seeking deeper understanding of themselves and the universe.

Faith of a Soul, her latest novel, continues this tradition by exploring the themes of balance, power, and transformation. It draws heavily from her scholarly research into mythological stories and her experiences in mystical practices. Through her narrative, she invites readers to contemplate the cosmic balance of light and darkness, and the individual's role within this eternal dance.

Also Available

Play the game Ikona and test
your Virtues and Sins
For additional information on
Constance Santego's wide range of
Motivational Products, Coaching Sessions,
Spiritual Retreats,
Live Events and Educational Programs
Go to
www.ConstanceSantego.ca

Follow me on:
Instagram - Constance_Santego &
Facebook - constancesantegoo
YouTube Channel - Constance Santego
Subscribe and receive free information &
Meditations

9 781990 062551